# THE
# CHILDREN
## OF THE
# WIND

# SEVEN CITADELS ◆ PART II

# THE CHILDREN OF THE WIND

## GERALDINE HARRIS

*GREENWILLOW BOOKS • NEW YORK*

J
c.1

Printed in the United States of America
First American Edition      10 9 8 7 6 5 4 3 2 1

Library of Congress Cataloging in Publication Data
Harris, Geraldine.      The children of the wind.
(Seven citadels ; pt. 2)
Summary: Kerish, prince of Galkis, travels through the deadly marshes of Lan-
Pin-Fria to obtain the key he needs to continue his search for his nation's savior.
[1. Fantasy] I. Title.
II. Harris, Geraldine.
Seven citadels ; pt. 2.
PZ7.H24143Ch      1982      [Fic]      82-12001
ISBN 0-688-01797-5

*To Jeff Tate and the missing sorcerer*

# THE HOUSE OF THE EMPERORS

†EMPEROR ZIN-LOKA
m. ZILLELA of Gannoth

†EMPEROR ZIN-LOKA and ZILLELA's children:

†PRINCESS MELDIKA
m. †ORALD of Morolk

IZELDON
*High Priest
of Zeldin*

EMPEROR KA-LITRAAN
m. (1) †MELFANEE of Jenoza
m. (2) RIMOKA of Chiraz
m. (3) †TAANA of Erandachu

PRINCE LI-KROCH
m. ZYRINDELLA of Tryfania

KOR-LI-ZYNAK

KA-METRANEE
*High Priestess
of Imarko*

PRINCE IM-LO-TORIM

PRINCE KERISH-LO-TAAN

PRINCE KA-RIM-LOKA
m. (1) KELINDA of Seld
m. (2) GANKALI of Forgin

PRINCESS KOLIGANI

*CHILDREN OF THE EMPEROR BY CONCUBINES*

1 By †VALDISSA

LORD JERENAC

2 By FOLLEA

LORD FOROLLKIN

3 By †MELZEEN (wife of the Governor of Tryfania)

ZYRINDELLA

# THE STORY SO FAR

The beginning of the story *Seven Citadels* is told in the book *Prince of the Godborn*. In the east of Zindar lies the great Galkian Empire, ruled from the golden city of Galkis. Here Zeldin, the Gentle God, and his human consort, the Lady Imarko, are worshipped. Galkis is under constant attack from the barbarian kingdoms along her borders and is weakened internally by intrigues and strife amongst the ruling family: the Godborn.

A fresh alliance of powerful enemies brings a new crisis and the wise High Priest Izeldon sees an ancient prophecy about an imprisoned Saviour as the only hope for Galkis. He asks the Emperor's third, and favourite, son, the seventeen year old Prince Kerish-lo-Taan, to go out into Zindar to search for the Saviour of Galkis. Kerish has no experience of the world outside the Galkian court and has never been trained to use the hereditary powers of the Godborn but he accepts the quest eagerly.

Izeldon reveals that the only way to free the Saviour is to win the seven keys to the gates of his prison, but each key is guarded by an immortal sorcerer. The first of these seven sorcerers is Elmandis, the tyrant of Ellerinnon, but no-one in Galkis knows for certain where the other six can be found. The Emperor insists that Kerish share his quest with his sensible half-brother, Lord Forollkin, and the two young men set out together.

On the sea voyage to Ellerinnon, Kerish's overconfidence leads to their ship being attacked by the cruel Brigands of Fangmere and Forollkin is wounded. When they arrive at Tir-Rinnon, the Citadel of Elmandis, Kerish has to swallow his pride and beg the Sorcerer to heal his brother. Elmandis proves to be a philosopher-king, ruling over a people dedicated to bringing peace and healing to Zindar. He looks on Kerish's arrival as a disaster, because any sorcerer who gives up his key loses his immortality. Kerish has to face a terrifying ordeal and use all his powers of argument to persuade noble Elmandis to surrender the first key.

The second sorcerer is Ellandellore, the younger brother of Elmandis, whose domain is Cheransee, the Isle of Illusions. Ellandellore is a crazed child who cannot be persuaded by reason to give up the key that has trapped him in eternal childhood. Kerish goes alone to Cheransee and plays a dangerous game with Ellandellore to trick him out of his key. As Kerish escapes from the island the angry sorcerer raises a storm and the prince is only saved from drowning by the power of Elmandis. Now that they have both lost their immortality, Elmandis hopes to help his brother to grow up at last. He tells the Galkians to seek the third sorcerer in the Ultimate Mountains, far to the north, and sends them on their way with a mysterious travelling companion, the ugly and insolent Gidjabolgo.

At the port of Pin-Fran, the prince and his companions leave their Galkian ship and buy a passage north on the boat of the Merchant Hunter Ibrogdiss. Kerish, Forollkin and Gidjabolgo face a dangerous journey through the grim marshes of Lan-Pin-Fria towards the Ultimate Mountains and the citadel of the third sorcerer. The story is now continued in *The Children of the Wind*.

# THE
# CHILDREN
## OF THE
# WIND

# Chapter 1

The Book of the Emperors: *Warnings*
*And the makers of dreams are blessed, when their songs are woven with the thread of life, and the web is strengthened.*
*And the makers of dreams are cursed, if their songs unravel the thread of life and the web is weakened.*

THE Frian marshes knew only a wet and a dry season. For three months of the year it rained. The land shuddered, the four great rivers and their tributaries flooded and fierce brown waters gushed into the settlements. The mud dwellings of the poor were swept away in their thousands and those who had found no shelter on higher ground were swept away with their homes. The same waters often roared under the houses of the rich on their strong stilts, but in a bad year even these would fall and whole villages drown.

Those who survived the flood were immured in their houses until the rains stopped and slowly the waters began to recede. The streets were left deep in mud and many died from diseases engendered in the river slime by the increasing heat. For five months the rivers were deep enough to be navigable and merchants sailed north in search of gauza and or-gar-gee skins, gir fruit and marsh cats. The poor built new huts from mud and reeds, gathered yulgor roots, and set traps for the birds and fish they were forbidden to shoot or spear. Then, in the rising heat, the smaller rivers vanished, the land was parched and men died of drought, until the rains came again to bring a quicker death to the old and the feeble, and life to the marshes.

In the month of Y-kor, when the rivers were swollen, the *Green Hunter* sailed north from Lan-Pin-Fria, bound for Lokrim. The current was against her, and often there was not enough wind to fill her sail. Then the crew of serfs was forced to row, while Ibrogdiss the Merchant Hunter paced the deck, beseeching his gods to let him reach the yalg groves before the best of the gauza had gone. On this trip, however, he was often forced to delay to accommodate the whims of his passengers.

Ibrogdiss did not complain, the Galkian lords were paying well; if they wanted to squander their gold on marsh weeds and birds they could have bought for the price of a gir fruit in any market, that was their affair. Everyone knew that the Emperor of Galkis was mad; and Ibrogdiss was pleasantly confirmed in his suspicion that all the Galkians shared his malady.

But on the seventh morning of the voyage it was not for the sake of her passengers that the *Green Hunter* remained moored in mid-river well after dawn. Ibrogdiss, his green hair loose on his shoulders and his face smeared with clay, tossed bitter herbs into a brazier and muttered an invocation to Log-ol-ben, Spirit of the Floodwaters. The crew crouched in a circle wailing prayers of appeasement. Hidden beneath his shabby cloak, the Galkians' servant slept on in the shadowy corner of the deck that he had made his own, but the noise disturbed his masters.

The flap of their tent was thrown open and a tall young man emerged, still fastening his tunic and irritably tossing back his long brown hair. He strode across the deck to Ibrogdiss.

"What in Zeldin's name is all this racket?"

"I have had evil dreams," whispered Ibrogdiss dramatically. "And it is a day of evil omen. A godjiic settled on the mast at sunrise, a leetor flew eastwards across our bows and a ko-lunga lies dead on the bank there without trace of a wound."

The Merchant Hunter fanned acrid smoke at the young Galkian.

"I will purify you, Lord Forollkin, and perhaps if you throw some jewel overboard and stay in your tent until nightfall the gods will not be too angry."

"But I will," snapped Forollkin. "If I stay in that tent a moment longer I shall suffocate."

"The omens," muttered Ibrogdiss. "I must make the Twelve Propitiations—"

10

"*You* are welcome to spend all morning propitiating a heap of feathers," said Forollkin. "*We* will take the boat and go out as planned. You mentioned some lilies . . ."

"No, no, the gods are angry. If you go, the marsh will take you and then who will pay me the rest of the gold you have promised? Lord Kerish, speak to your brother!" Ibrogdiss appealed to the second Galkian as he came out of the tent.

The crew of the *Green Hunter* wailed even louder.

"Tell me, Ibrogdiss," answered Kerish-lo-Taan, "why are your men afraid of me?"

"They say that you must be a spirit; Lord, they know nothing of the world and have never seen a foreigner who looked like you."

"But you know better, Ibrogdiss," murmured Kerish. "Haven't you told them that I am a man as they are?"

"I have told them, but they are serfs and cannot understand the world as we do."

"I see," said Kerish, noting that Ibrogdiss' hands were now clutching the motley collection of amulets that always hung round his neck.

"Well, we had better take the boat out before it gets really hot."

"Lord Kerish," wailed the Merchant Hunter, "I have told your brother, it is a day of evil omen, none of my men would go with you."

"Ibrogdiss, we are paying . . ." began Forollkin, but Kerish interrupted, "We are protected by a great spirit. The marshes will not harm us."

"No doubt your spirit has accepted your offerings and agreed to protect you," answered the Merchant Hunter, "but what does your spirit care for me or for my men? We have made him no offerings and we cannot speak his tongue."

"If I ask him, our spirit will protect you all," said Kerish calmly.

"Yes, tell them that," ordered Forollkin, "and let's be off."

"Ask them if anyone will go with us," murmured Kerish.

Ibrogdiss spoke in rapid Frian to his men. The wailing

11

gradually stopped and the Merchant Hunter picked out one of his men who spoke Zindaric.

"Dau will go with you."

Forollkin looked doubtfully at the serf and Kerish darted back into the tent. He emerged again, holding a piece from his zel set. He handed it to the startled serf and said slowly, "Carry this charm. It will protect you."

"Strong charm?" asked the Frian.

"Very strong," Kerish confirmed.

Dau stuffed the miniature gold and purple feather into his loincloth and darted to the ship's rail, to lower the reed boat. Forollkin toyed with kicking Gidjabolgo awake, but decided that the trip would be more peaceful without their servant's company.

Soon the crew of the *Green Hunter* could get back to the long and messy ritual of the Twelve Propitiations, while Dau paddled the reed boat along a backwater and out of sight of the ship. The mists that hovered over the rivers and pools dissolved in the mounting heat. Forollkin, who thought the Frian marshes ugly and desolate, slouched in the stern, scratching the insect bites and stings that were making him so irritable. Kerish, however, was constantly discovering fragments of beauty in the bleak landscape of mud and reeds and dank, tangled groves.

There were spectacular birds; tall birds that waded in the shallows, spearing fish with their beaks; small, brilliant birds that perched in the gir trees, preening and chattering; white birds that flew up from the reeds in great startled flocks; brown birds that floated lazily on the green waters amongst the dazzling marsh flowers.

As the backwater narrowed, Dau had to hack a channel through swathes of waterweed, while his passengers ducked to avoid the spiky gir branches. Kerish was haltingly warned not to trail his hand in the water, because of the snap-fish, snakes and leeches, and Forollkin took up the spare paddle.

The backwater ended in a stagnant pool covered with a kind of water-lily that Kerish had never seen before. With a quick movement that set the frail boat rocking, he leaned over to examine them. The flame-coloured petals were sticky for the golden heart of each lily exuded a white liquid, in which numerous insects were struggling.

"They eat insects," commented Kerish, wiping his hands on his damp blue robe.

"Just what I'd expect in a country like this," said Forollkin glumly.

"Flowers here eat birds," volunteered Dau. "Men too."

Forollkin snorted with disbelief and Kerish said sternly: "My spirit tells me you lie."

He instantly regretted it as the Frian's face contorted.

"Forgive, Lord? I have not seen, but I have heard it, truly, Lord."

"Forgiven," answered Kerish gently, wondering what kind of punishments the man was used to enduring.

"Now then," said Forollkin briskly, "we shall want three of these plants."

"You take them away, Lords? To grow again?"

"Yes," said Kerish. "In the Emperor's garden, far away in Galkis."

Dau continued to look puzzled but he had been taught never to argue. First he tried pulling up one of the plants, but after filling the boat with apparently endless lengths of white stalk and wet leaves, a sharp tug snapped it off before the roots. Dau saw that he would have to dive for the plants and loosen their roots from the mud and Forollkin promised him a special reward for this unpleasant task. With his knife between his teeth, Dau slid from the boat, kicked up his feet and went under.

After a minute or so the Frian broke through the green surface, gasping for breath and scraping the mud from his eyes. He held up the roots of one of the lily plants and Forollkin carefully gathered it into the boat, together with tiny silver fish, knots of water worms and a small snake. Kerish noticed the snake, wriggling an inch from Forollkin's hand, and without thinking, picked it up and tossed it back into the pond.

Treading water, Dau hissed in amazement: "Not bite?"

Kerish shook his head.

"Bad water-snake. One bite and you will die."

"Kerish, do you never think what you're doing?" demanded Forollkin angrily.

13

"My spirit protects me," said Kerish a little shakily.

"Well give him some assistance by just sitting still," snapped Forollkin.

Dau dived again and within a few minutes they had three intact plants piled in the boat. The Frian scrambled back into the boat and showed Forollkin the trick of getting rid of the leeches that now clung to his hands. He then horrified both the Galkians by eating the leeches he had just detached from his own skin.

"It is not good that they have my blood," he explained cheerfully. "I take it back."

Forollkin asked the Frian if he knew where more rare flowers might be found and Dau suggested a nearby lake.

"Charm strong, we will go safely, yes?"

Kerish smiled as the Frian drew the zel piece from his loincloth and kissed it.

"How far is this lake?" asked Forollkin, vainly trying to get further away from the wet, insect-ridden plants that half-filled the boat.

"Near, near," said Dau, and turning the boat he paddled down the backwater and into one of the channels that fed it.

They passed under the grotesque roots of a clump of gir trees, raising clouds of insects from the rotting vegetation that choked the rivulet. Forollkin flailed at them but Kerish sat motionless, and his pale, delicate skin did not seem to attract the bloodsuckers.

The water became very shallow. The Frian slipped out of the boat and waded, knee deep in mud, to push it through a wall of reeds. Forollkin would have helped him but Dau begged him to stay where he was, afraid that the Galkian would overturn the light craft. Instead, Forollkin crawled forward and hacked at the reeds impeding their path.

Soon they were in open water again and Dau climbed back on board.

Forollkin sat up straight to look at the broad green lake, with its floating islands of matted vegetation. It was very quiet and there was not a bird in sight.

Before either of the Galkians could comment Dau seized a paddle and propelled the boat back into the shelter of the reed thickets.

"What in Zeldin . . . ?" began Forollkin, but Dau pressed a

dirty finger to his lips and nodded towards the lake. Puzzled, Kerish and Forollkin peered through the reeds. The surface of the green waters was occasionally broken by ripples, but otherwise the lake seemed almost unnaturally placid.

Then, out of a grey sky, came a ko-lunga, a large fish-eating bird, the colour of storm clouds streaked with lightning. The ko-lunga swooped on a promising ripple and Kerish almost screamed with shock.

A huge head rose out of the water. It had only one eye in the centre of the horned forehead, but that eye had seen the ko-lunga. The great jaws opened, displaying a double row of jagged teeth. Too late, the frightened bird launched itself into the air. The jaws closed on the trailing legs and the head sank back beneath the surface, leaving only a circle of ripples and a few bloodstained feathers.

"Or-gar-gee," whispered the Frian as he slid out of the boat and began to push it back through the reeds, as quietly as he could.

When they reached the safety of the backwater, Dau broke into excited speech.

"Or-gar-gee. When it is hot, he sleeps, then Master kills. The Master will be pleased."

Ibrogdiss was indeed pleased. The bad omens were hastily forgotten and as soon as the lilies were stowed in tall jars in the hold, preparations for a hunt began.

The Merchant Hunter squeezed Forollkin's shoulder.

"You found the water-serpent, it is your right to throw the first spear."

Startled, Forollkin began to murmur something about conceding the right when a harsh voice spoke from behind him.

"My Master is still a tender youth, unused to such feats of strength and courage."

Gidjabolgo was awake at last. "It would not be right to tempt him to his own destruction. You understand, Lord Merchant, that it is a devoted servant's privilege to say what his master merely thinks."

"And to make stale jokes, without being whipped for it," said Kerish hastily. "My brother is a renowned hunter and

15

warrior but we are bound to complete the Emperor's mission . . ."

Even as he spoke, he knew from the set of his brother's mouth that he was wasting words.

"The Emperor will forgive me," said Forollkin. "I will gladly join your hunt."

"Good, good," murmured Ibrogdiss, who had been watching the sharp exchange between masters and servant with great interest.

"No doubt your spirit will protect you. I will lend you a spear and you must put on Frian clothes, or the eye of the or-gar-gee may see your scarlet among the reeds."

The Merchant Hunter hurried below to his small cabin and Forollkin smiled wryly at his half-brother.

"Have you a strong charm for me?"

"The water-serpents can't be as dangerous as they look," said Kerish hopefully. "After all, Ibrogdiss has led many hunts and lived to sport a double chin and grey in his green hair."

"Perhaps he always finds someone else to strike the first blow," remarked Gidjabolgo.

Forollkin turned on him angrily. "I'll thank you to hold your tongue."

"It will be the first thanks I've had from you for my services," said Gidjabolgo. "My Masters must forgive me if I do not play the servant's role convincingly. Should I crawl more, cringe more? Should I kiss the ground beneath your feet, or in this case the deck, or the river slime . . ."

"Just stay out of our way," growled Forollkin.

"Very well, Master, I will cease to serve your every need, cease to watch over your possessions when you leave them unguarded . . ."

He stopped as a Frian serf approached them carrying a moss-green kilt and cloak for Forollkin. The Galkians took them and retired to their tent.

"What was that last remark supposed to mean?" demanded Forollkin.

Kerish knelt among the cushions beside his travelling chest.

"It's been opened," he said.

16

"Is anything missing?" asked Forollkin as his half-brother rummaged through their clothes and jewels.

Kerish sat back on his heels. "Nothing. I suppose Gidjabolgo was only pretending to be asleep and saw someone enter our tent. Do you think Ibrogdiss doubts our story?"

"I can't say I'd blame him," answered Forollkin. "Well there's little in your chest to make him more suspicious."

"There are my zeloka jewels. He might know that only the Godborn can wear them."

Forollkin began to unfasten his tunic.

"If he knew that much, he'd know what the Godborn look like and your eyes will always betray you."

"Perhaps he does know," Kerish smiled wickedly. "You had better drop a hint that our mother received exalted visitors."

"Drop it yourself," growled Forollkin. "You're the better liar."

Kerish helped his brother to drape himself in the long Frian cloak and tie up his hair. When they came back into the fierce noonday sun, Ibrogdiss was crooning over his spears. He handed a long, bronze-shafted weapon to Forollkin, saying: "This is I-giya, my finest spear. She has killed nine or-gar-gee. You must make her your own, feed her with your blood."

Feeling very foolish, Forollkin scratched his hand and rubbed a few drops of his own blood into the smooth bronze. Next a bowl of river mud was brought to him and the Merchant Hunter insisted that Forollkin rub it into his face and body.

"Then the or-gar-gee will not smell you, and we shall come close enough to kill."

Very reluctantly, Forollkin allowed himself to be daubed with the evil-smelling mud, while Ibrogdiss stripped down to his kilt and a few favourite amulets.

Seeing the Merchant Hunter muffled in his green robes, the Galkians had thought him fat; now they saw that his oiled body was hard-muscled and strong. It seemed a stranger to his plump, unlined face.

The final preparation was the dipping of the hunters' spears in a bubbling pot of yellow liquid.

"This is poison, strong and quick," said Ibrogdiss.

17

"When you pierce the eye of the or-gar-gee, this will hasten its death throes. Remember you must aim for the eye. The rest of the hide is too thick, and do not scratch yourself with your spear again or you will die before your quarry. You are ready?"

Forollkin nodded but Kerish suddenly ran back to their tent and returned with something bright, half-hidden in his long hands.

"The High Priest's gift," he said in Galkian. "He promised it would never fail you."

Forollkin took the dagger and tucked it in the waist of his kilt.

Again the reed boat was lowered, with Dau chosen to paddle for the hunters. Kerish caused a delay by insisting on coming with them. After a short argument, conducted in rapid Galkian, Ibrogdiss intervened to suggest that Kerish should watch the fight from the safety of a nearby hillock. This was agreed and a serf was assigned to guide him there.

"And I will, of course, accompany my Master," said Gidjabolgo.

Kerish was still puzzling over the man's motive half an hour later as they reached a hillock crowned with gir trees. They had come by a circuitous and uncomfortable route through tall grasses that bit like blades into the unwary hand. The Frian gestured to Kerish and Gidjabolgo to climb up into one of the gnarled trees.

The young Galkian swung himself on to one of the broadest branches. Panting and complaining, Gidjabolgo, the Forgite, hauled his bulk on to a lower, spikier branch and the Frian serf crouched, out of sight and smell, under the roots.

The lake lay like a bronze mirror, dropped among the reeds. A few of the bolder birds had returned but there was an ominous stillness about the place. The gir trees grew on the only sizeable hillock for miles around. Kerish could see the ship still anchored in mid-river and a slight movement in the reeds betrayed the approach of the hunters.

Gidjabolgo was twisting about on his branch and muttering in Forgish. Why had he chosen to come? To see Forollkin die? If so, my brother's grave shall have a blood offering, vowed Kerish grimly.

18

"Can you see them, my far-sighted Master?" enquired Gidjabolgo sweetly.

"They are not through the reeds yet. Speak more quietly. We mustn't wake the or-gar-gee."

"I am not afraid," said Gidjabolgo. "Haven't you promised us the protection of the Gentle God? From all I hear he protected you most efficiently from the Brigands of Fangmere, though others were not so fortunate."

Kerish choked down his anger as the prow of Forollkin's boat clove the reeds.

"You are right," he said coldly. "I cannot swear that the Gentle God helps those who do not believe in gentleness."

"Or gods," answered Gidjabolgo lightly.

Crouching in the reed boat, Forollkin repeated Ibrogdiss' instructions to himself. The or-gar-gee was sleeping now but they must approach quietly for the creature's hearing was keen. Once awake, the protective lid would slide back from the great eye that saw in all directions at once. Then, if they were close enough, their spears could pass through the eye into the or-gar-gee's brain. If they missed their aim, the danger was considerable and even if they did pierce the eye the death throes of a water-serpent were long and terrible.

They had reached the edge of the lake. Signalling for absolute silence, Ibrogdiss parted the reeds. After a moment he beckoned to Forollkin, who edged forward. He saw something black projecting just above the surface: the nostrils of the or-gar-gee, its breath rippling the water. Ibrogdiss judged where the rest of the great body might be lying and how deep, and signed to Dau to skirt round the edge of the lake.

As they launched into open water, Forollkin felt a thrill of expectation. He was afraid, but pleasurably so. It would be a great feat to kill an or-gar-gee, something to boast of when they returned to Galkis.

Kerish and Gidjabolgo saw the boat glide towards the sleeping or-gar-gee. The Forgite was extraordinarily uncomfortable, and regretting the impulse that had brought him there. The branch on which he sat jabbed into him in several tender places, the leaves of the gir tree dripped water and slime on his head and a column of evil-looking insects was patiently crawling up the trunk towards him. Still, he had the consolation of watching Kerish-lo-Taan while the young Galkian was oblivious of him.

The Prince was sitting, straight-backed as ever, clutching the purple jewel he always wore. The hood of his tunic covered the black and silver hair and shadowed the fine-boned face but his eyes were more brilliant than ever. Gidjabolgo suddenly felt that their brilliance came from a light behind the eyes; its struggles to escape provoked explosions of colour, purple and gold and black . . .

With fierce concentration Kerish-lo-Taan framed prayer after prayer for his brother's safety. As always when he prayed, a part of him remained detached, almost mocking, and he used it to imagine his brother's progress. He remembered what it was like to sit in the shallow boat that rocked with every movement.

"Zeldin, hear me, protect my brother."

He remembered the smell of the river slime, the faint hum of insects everywhere, and the ominous ripples on the green surface.

"Imarko, Lady of Heaven, guard my brother."

He could almost feel the prickly cloth of Ibrogdiss' cloak, the drying mud caking on his cheeks, the shaft of the spear slipping in his damp hands.

"Zeldin, send him victory."

His sight blurred, the distant view of the lake melded with a wall of reeds, with the beads of sweat trickling down Ibrogdiss' back, with the glint of the dagger at his waist.

Forollkin began to feel remarkably confident. Dau was crouched over his paddle, mouthing a prayer. Ibrogdiss was taut as a bow-string, his chubby hands stroking the shaft of his spear. They were close now. The Merchant Hunter signalled to Forollkin to take up his position. The Galkian knelt on one knee, holding the spear in his right hand, and bracing himself against the boat with his left. Ibrogdiss crouched behind him, ready to throw the second spear. Dau barely dipped the paddle in the water as he propelled them forward. They could clearly see the snout of the or-gar-gee and the water around them eddied with the monster's breath. The boat glided to within a foot of the creature.

Ibrogdiss pointed to where the eye should be and shouted a sudden appeal to Thith-nek, the Spirit of Huntsmen. There were a few still, agonizing seconds, and then the lake became a whirlpool. The huge head rose out of the water. The jaws gaped in Forollkin's face. The scaly covering began to slide back from the vulnerable eye.

In panic Forollkin threw, too soon and too clumsily. The spear struck the creature's snout without even grazing its wrinkled skin. The or-gar-gee gave a roar of outrage, uncoiled its long body and lashed out at the reed boat.

As the boat overturned, Dau dived and swam for the reeds and Ibrogdiss threw his spear. It missed the eye and the Merchant Hunter sank beneath the slap of a wave. Forollkin was tossed into the air and landed, not in the water, but across the water-serpent's broad head.

He found himself lying beside the great eye that gleamed with a savage intelligence. His feet dangled inches from the snapping jaws. The or-gar-gee began to toss its head, trying to shake its burden off, so it could seize and crush him.

Forollkin knew it would only be a few moments before the water-serpent succeeded for he could not get a firm hold on the creature's slimy hide. He had forgotten the High Priest's dagger but Kerish had not. Suddenly his fingers were gripping the cirge hilt and Forollkin was sinking the blade deep into the monster's eye.

The or-gar-gee screamed and writhed, churning the lake. Forollkin was thrown clear and the sky whirled round him before he struck the muddied waves. After a few sips of foul lake water, he remembered to close his mouth and swim.

He struggled to the surface and someone grabbed him by the shoulders and pushed him against something buoyant. Forollkin opened his clogged eyes and found that he and both the Frians were clinging to the upturned boat.

In its death agonies, the or-gar-gee was rolling away from them, crushing the reeds that fringed the other shore of the lake. Forollkin watched it, numbly waiting for the lethal coils to reach towards him again, but gradually the

21

creature's struggles ceased and the lake began to settle. The or-gar-gee was dead.

Five minutes later, still dripping wet and pale with shock, Forollkin picked his way through the reeds to the gir tree hillock. He was greeted by the alarming sight of Gidjabolgo and the Frian serf kneeling beside his unconscious brother.

Forollkin pushed them aside.

"What happened?"

"He fainted from shock," said the Forgite, "just after you killed it."

Forollkin gave his brother an exasperated shake and Kerish opened his eyes and murmured: "I remembered, we . . . Forollkin, are you all right?"

"Oh, I'm all right, hardly a bruise, but I can't leave you for a minute, can I? Kerish, what's the matter? Is your head hurting? Did you hit it as you fell?"

"I suppose I must have done." Kerish slowly sat up. "I feel so tired. Forollkin . . ." He smiled suddenly. "I'm glad you killed it, even if you are dripping mud all over me."

For the rest of the day the crew of the *Green Hunter* worked feverishly, diving and fixing ropes to the or-gar-gee and dragging its huge carcass to the nearest firm land. There they hacked through the comparatively soft underbelly, peeled off the valuable skin and cut up the meat for smoking. At dusk there was a feast, and the usual fare of broiled fish and stringy marsh fowls was replaced by portions of roasted or-gar-gee, oozing with fat and smelling like river slime, and cup after fiery cup of girgan.

Lights were hung from the rigging and incense burners were lit to keep away the clouds of insects gathering round the huge corpse. For once, the Galkians ate on deck with Ibrogdiss and his men, sprawled among a pile of soft cushions.

Forollkin was wallowing in a sea of satisfaction. Fired by the girgan he magnified his achievement until it ranked with the deeds of ancient heroes. Doggedly chewing an almost indestructible piece of or-gar-gee blubber, Kerish watched his brother flourish the victorious dagger in front of Ibrogdiss for the third time.

"The gift of the High Priest of Galkis. He told me it would never fail to kill."

Ibrogdiss began to look mildly interested. The kill had been hardly more than a lucky accident and the Merchant Hunter was bored with the Galkian's boasting, but a magic weapon might be something worth having. He took the dagger and examined it closely.

"This High Priest is a powerful one? The dagger will always kill?"

"Only in my Master's hand." Gidjabolgo spoke from the shadows, where he crouched with his own platter of or-gar-gee and flagon of girgan. "A gift that one cannot give away is doubly generous."

Disappointed, Ibrogdiss returned the dagger. "I understand. It is the same with my spear. In my hands it holds the strength of Log-ol-ben, for I offered my fairest concubine to the shaman of the god, in return for his power."

"Your concubine?"

Ibrogdiss misinterpreted Forollkin's surprise and winked at him.

"Yes, a sacrifice indeed, for she was very fair, but she talked too much . . ."

Kerish rinsed away the rancid taste of the or-gar-gee with a mouthful of girgan and asked: "What kind of god is this Log-ol-ben?"

"A mighty spirit, the Hunter to whom the or-gar-gees are worms to crush beneath his heel."

"He is the greatest of your Frian gods?"

"Some would say that Ench-arkis the Thunderer is greater," answered Ibrogdiss as if he were discussing the relative merits of shipwrights or vineyards. "Or the Three Headed One, whose name should not be spoken; or Nar-Irk, the Master of Disease, the Slayer of the Weak; or Lig-a-loda, the Laughing One, the Lord of Gauza, but Log-ol-ben protects me on this journey."

"And if the journey proves unlucky?" asked Kerish.

Ibrogdiss shrugged: "Then I will make offerings to Lig-a-loda and spit on the shaman of Log-ol-ben."

The Merchant Hunter pressed his passengers to more meat but both refused. Ibrogdiss cut himself another slice, heedless of the grease dripping down his cloak, and said: "Tell me, young Lords, about the gods of your country. Are they many? Are they wild and difficult to please?"

"In Galkis we have only one god and his name is Zeldin the Gentle." It was Kerish who answered. "He was and is beyond Zindar, yet he walked in Galkis in the form of a man and loved the Lady Imarko, and grieved for her death. Their children were the Godborn, who ruled Galkis as the mirrors of the power and wisdom of Zeldin."

"Ruled? Are they not Lords of Galkis still?" asked Ibrogdiss.

Kerish looked down into his cup, stirring the girgan with his little finger before it could give him his reflection.

"The blood is weak, the power wanes and the wisdom is gone. Except in a few who still follow the paths of love."

"Love?" Ibrogdiss grinned. "This Zeldin is a god of lovers?"

Forollkin laughed. "Not as you mean it, Ibrogdiss. It is our goddess, Imarko, who blesses lovers."

"A goddess?" The Merchant Hunter was incredulous. "A god who is female? How can your Zeldin endure it? Why does he not strike her down? I see now why you call him gentle and do not fear him."

"You are mistaken," said Kerish soberly. "His gentleness is greatly feared."

There was a long silence and then Forollkin reached out to pour himself a fifth cup of girgan.

"Kerish, we've gone so quiet I can hear the mud forming; make us a song."

Gidjabolgo was dispatched to fetch the zildar from the Galkians' tent.

Kerish was soon seated, cross-legged, tuning the instrument. After a minute's thought, and when Ibrogdiss had ordered, and got, silence from all his serfs, Kerish strummed a lively tune and improvised a song of victory. The song was extravagant in its praise of Forollkin, and complimentary to the Merchant Hunter. It exaggerated the size of the monster and glossed over the clumsiness of the killing.

Forollkin was well satisfied, Kerish was not. He swept straight into *The Grief of Zeldin*, the ancient song that told of the Gentle God's agony as he watched his dying bride. The words were in High Galkian and Kerish's high, pure voice gave them little colour and yet the Frians understood their poignancy.

When the song ended Kerish was shocked to see tears on Ibrogdiss' smooth cheeks. He would have set down his zildar but the Merchant Hunter tugged at his sleeve.

"Play on, young Lord, sing to me of your own country, show me Galkis."

In Zindaric this time, Kerish-lo-Taan sang the *Lay of the Nine Cities*. He sang of Galkis itself with its three great walls and the fabled gardens of the Emperor; of Tryfis, ringed with cliffs of lapis; and Holy Hildimarn and its ninety temples. He sang of Montra-lakon, guarded by horses of stone; of Yxis where the silver wind-chimes rang through day and night; and Far Tryfarn on the easternmost edge of the Empire. He sang of Joze, the Dreaming City; Viroc, the mighty bastion of Jenoza; and copper-walled Ephaan, the greatest port on the purple Sea of Az.

Ibrogdiss listened, his mind drifting with Kerish's song from city to city. When the clear voice stopped the Merchant Hunter demanded more. Kerish played a chord but Gidjabolgo's voice broke the attentive silence.

"Pardon, worthy Merchant, but my young Master is surely tired. Let his humble servant play for you instead."

Ibrogdiss' face wrinkled into laughter.

"What, ugly one, can you sing? You look like a marsh-croaker and their voices are not sweet enough for me."

"You shall judge my sweetness, Masters all. Let me sing you a chant from the temples of Forgin. Will my Lord let my unworthy fingers touch the strings of his zildar?"

Kerish was too startled at the anger in Gidjabolgo's face to deny him.

The Forgite hunched over the fragile instrument and splayed his broad fingers across the strings. Stumbling a little at first, he began to play and then, to sing. Astonishingly, his voice was as sweet and flawless as Kerish's. That such a sound should issue from Gidjabolgo's face seemed almost blasphemous. It was several moments before Kerish could bring himself to attend to the words.

25

*Praised be the smiling God of the Strong who exulteth the cruel and murders the meek. Praised be the God who laughs at the slaughter of children and the prayers of the weak. Praised be the Wise who know that the world is fallen fruit of a crooked tree and men the maggots that crawl . . .*

"No!" Kerish tore his zildar from the Forgite's hands. "Liar, you defile all that you touch."

He was shaking with anger but Gidjabolgo answered calmly: "Prove me a liar."

Roused from his drowsy contentment Forollkin said hurriedly: "Well I've had enough music for one night. I am for bed."

"Tomorrow you shall sing again, young Lord," said Ibrogdiss. "But not you, ugly one; your voice is fair but your dreams are dark."

# Chapter 2

The Book of the Emperors: *Chronicles*
*And two of the Princes came to him from the temple after
prayer and fasting but the Third Prince had been drinking
and feasting in his own chambers. The two elder Princes
rebuked their brother but Jezreen-lo-Kaash said to them:
"From god or from wine cup all three of you sought comfort
and the mercy of forgetfulness. What did any of you offer in
return?" Then they were silent.*

THE next morning Forollkin had a monstrous headache. He refused all Kerish's offers of breakfast, cool
cloths for his forehead or general soothing and eventually
found the strength to throw a cushion at his over-solicitous
brother. Laughing, Kerish bound back his hair with a crimson fillet, put on a simple blue robe and left the sticky heat
of their tent for the comparative cool of the deck.

One of the crew brought him some unappetizing broth
and a flat Frian loaf with the taste and texture of well-baked
brick. Kerish thanked him in the few words of Frian he had
picked up on their voyage, but there was no response.

He watched the man return to his task of mending nets,
wondering what the life of a Frian serf could be like. Ibrogdiss seemed to treat his crew well but amid the danger of the
marshlands that might be more a matter of sense than feeling.

Ibrogdiss himself had gone to the nearest village to ar-
range with its headman for curing of the or-gar-gee hide
and the sale of most of its flesh. Gidjabolgo was nowhere to
be seen. Abandoning his breakfast after a few sips of broth,
Kerish decided he ought to pretend concern for the flowers
and birds stored in the hold. He went down through the
hatchway and groped past the rowers' benches as his eyes
adjusted to the semi-darkness.

In front of the stern cabins a space had been reserved for wooden cages and tall pottery jars for storing whatever the Galkians chose to collect. Over one of the jars stooped Gidjabolgo, stroking the flame-coloured lilies and murmuring softly.

Kerish felt immediately that he ought to leave before Gidjabolgo saw him. Instead he stepped noisily forward.

"Why, Gidjabolgo, I didn't know you were so fond of flowers."

The Forgite snatched his hand from the lilies as if they had bitten him but after a moment he said smoothly: "I am merely seeking information, the better to assist my Masters, since the Lord Forollkin does not appear to know an orchid from a stingweed, and the mad Emperor must have his garden."

"The Emperor of Galkis is not mad."

"No?" Gidjabolgo tested the bars of the wooden cages and did not look at Kerish as he spoke. "In Forgin they say he is crazed by the death of his Erandachi queen and sits in his garden howling over her corpse while the Empire rots. No doubt my Master knows the truth of it."

*"Do you want to see her?"*

*"No, please, no!"*

Kerish backed away from Gidjabolgo and from the memory of his father kneeling by a white sarcophagus.

"He is not mad," Kerish repeated tonelessly and Gidjabolgo smiled as he tugged at another bar until the frail wood snapped.

"My Master knows, and my Master would be wiser to conceal his knowledge better."

"You think Ibrogdiss is suspicious of us?" demanded Kerish.

"Of you. He fears you almost as much as his spineless serfs do and wonders why the older brother must always obey the younger."

"But he doesn't. I follow Forollkin's lead," protested Kerish, genuinely surprised.

"When it agrees with your purpose. You are too used to giving orders to notice that you never take them," answered Gidjabolgo. "I do not think Ibrogdiss would be too surprised if I told him that you were no petty lordling, if I

28

told him he had a Prince of the Godborn in his power, the Emperor's darling .... How high would you set your ransom?"

"But you will not tell him," said Prince Kerish-lo-Taan, "because if our voyage stops, so does yours. I don't know why you wish to reach the sorcerer of Tir-Zulmar and you do not know our purpose. Let us leave it at that and try to be courteous to each other until we have the pleasure of parting."

"Or the pleasure of a shared grave when Ibrogdiss cuts our throats," growled Gidjabolgo.

"If any harm comes to us, he will not get the other half of his payment from Engis' agent in Pin-Drouth."

"Yes, but is that payment equal to the treasures that you carry with you? Think about that, my Master, next time our merchant invites you to go hunting."

Gidjabolgo scuttled away into the darkness of the hold, satisfied by the look on Kerish's face that the blow had gone home.

Kerish thought carefully of his gold and irivanee jewels, the coins concealed in Forollkin's sword belt, his precious zel set, the purple gem and the emerald ring Ibrogdiss daily saw him wearing. Together they might well tempt the Merchant Hunter to treachery. He could only be grateful that Gidjabolgo's presence of mind had removed the High Priest's dagger from the list.

What could they do? In the middle of the Frian marshes there was nowhere to run to, and what Frian could they trust?

Distractedly Kerish moved among the jars and cages. As he bent over the lilies he noticed that they seemed to have acquired a scent that they had lacked the day before. A faint sickly smell permeated the hold but when Kerish held one of the lilies to his nose, the scent decreased.

Straightening, with a puzzled frown he wandered from jar to jar. None of them seemed to be the source of the powerful scent.

It was at its strongest around the door to Ibrogdiss' cabin. Curious, Kerish tried the handle but the door was locked. Dismissing the puzzle for the time being Kerish went back on deck to see if Forollkin was recovered enough for bad news.

During the next two days the *Green Hunter* rowed vigorously up-river and there was no opportunity for the Galkians to extend their collection. They spent a great deal of time in their sweltering tent, fruitlessly discussing Ibrogdiss' possible treachery. For the rest, Forollkin lost endless games of zel and paced round the deck, bored with the vistas of reeds and mud, while Kerish read from the Book of the Emperors, and Gidjabolgo appeared to sleep.

On the third day, the *Green Hunter* anchored in mid-river at noon and, when the worst of the heat was over, Kerish and Forollkin went out with Dau to explore a gir grove.

Scrambling on almost solid ground through the huge, fantastically contorted gir roots, they caught some green and scarlet lizards and gathered rare mosses. Dau named everything they saw and Forollkin asked him if he had been born in a marsh village. The Frian shook his shaven head and explained in his hesitant Zindaric that his mother came from the northern city of Lokrim.

"And your father?"

Dau looked at him blankly.

"The Master is of Pin-Drouth, but his house is in Lokrim too."

It was Kerish who understood what he meant.

"Ibrogdiss is your father?"

Dau nodded.

There was nothing to mark him out from any of the other serfs, except his Zindaric. He wore a simple linen kilt, his body was thin and the marks of former whippings were plain on his back.

"The son of a concubine," thought Forollkin numbly. "I should have thanked Imarko for my father's generous indifference."

"Is Ibrogdiss a good master to you?" Kerish was asking gently.

"He is . . ." Dau searched for the word, ". . . just, though if the dreams are bad . . ."

He stopped as if suddenly conscious that he had said too much.

30

"Dreams?"

"He is just, Lord," repeated Dau. "Do my Lords want birds? I will set traps."

Respecting the Frian's reticence, Forollkin helped him to fix a clap net between two gir roots and Kerish wandered deeper into the grove, thinking about the Merchant Hunter. His thoughts were gradually disturbed by a faint, insistent sound, perhaps made by an animal in fright or pain.

Kerish walked towards the sound and ducked under a root, to be confronted by a spiny tangle of bushes. The cries came from very close. Kerish began calling in a soft voice. For a moment the noise stopped and then continued more loudly to signal distress or anger. Kerish tried to push the branches aside but they were too strong for him. Reluctantly he knelt down and crawled under the bushes. Thorns caught in the fine cloth of his robe and pricked his shoulders, and tugged at his hair.

It was dark but Kerish saw at once the brilliant golden eyes of the small green creature crouching before him. Then the eyes saw Kerish and, with a mew of fright, the animal began to climb up into the thorn bushes. The Prince grabbed it and swore with a fluency that would have shocked Forollkin as the creature dug its claws and teeth into his hands.

Holding on tightly, he crawled back through the bushes. By the time he had got to his feet again, his robe was torn in a dozen places and covered with mud and his hands were beaded with blood, but Kerish was jubilant. He held up the spitting, scratching creature and called out: "Forollkin, come and look, I've found a marsh kitten!"

The cats of Galkis were descended from a pair brought in the first ship by Imarko herself. Rare and precious, they now lived only in her temple at Hildimarn, where Kerish had spent many happy hours coaxing them to notice him. Marsh cats were almost as rare, and sought after to be the beautiful companions and fierce guards of the noble and the rich. The creature Kerish held would grow to be four feet long, from the tip of its nose to the base of its tail. Its pale, fluffy fur would darken into a glossy green but its eyes would always be golden.

Kerish stroked the kitten's head and got another scratch.

Forollkin and Dau came squelching through the grove.

"Look, look, isn't she beautiful?"

Grinning, Forollkin put out a hand and withdrew it quickly as a slender paw lashed at him.

"They are fierce, Lord," said Dau, "for they are children of the Green One, the Lord of Animals, who hates men. You must beat her, then she is tame. I will fetch a cage."

"There will be no beating or caging," answered Kerish, and he wrapped the furious kitten in his cloak and carried her back to the ship.

Ibrogdiss congratulated him on his catch. "A fine strong kitten, Lord. The mother must be dead or she would have come at her mewings. Forty gold kekors a merchant of Forgin would give for such a kitten. Your Emperor will be pleased?"

"No doubt," murmured Kerish absently. "I shall call her Lilahnee, after the cat of the Poet Emperor."

"Yes, he will be most pleased," said Forollkin hastily, "so we shall raise your payment at the end of our voyage."

Ibrogdiss gave a bow of thanks and Forollkin could not see his face.

"Well, Kerish," he continued, "I'm afraid she must have a cage. She would tear her way out of our tent in no time."

After some argument, it was agreed that the kitten be allowed the run of the second stern cabin. When Kerish took her there, she immediately sprang from his arms up into the rafters and could not be coaxed down, even with a bowl of fresh meat. She sat there with her ears flat against her skull, pouring out feline abuse. She looked so thin that Kerish was tempted to force some food down her, but wisely decided to leave the kitten alone until morning.

Kerish and Forollkin were up at dawn on the next day to watch the crew drape a fine-meshed net over the *Green Hunter*, fixing it to the top of the mast and the ship's sides. It was like standing inside a large, dimly lit cage, but a cage to keep wild things out not in. The *Green Hunter* was due to sail through a yalg grove and to the yalg trees clung the gauza orchids, from whose pollen a powerful drug was made.

Where there were gauza orchids there were zzaga: brilliant black and green insects, each the size of a man's fist, and with a deadly sting. They built their mud nests in the yalg trees and made their pale sweet honey from the gauza pollen. Precious as that honey was, few merchants tried to obtain it, for the zzaga guarded their hives ferociously and often moved in great destructive swarms. Ibrogdiss had every inch of the net checked before he ordered the serfs to their oars.

When the ship came abreast of the shadowy yalg groves Ibrogdiss and four of his serfs wrapped themselves in thick strips of green cloth. Only their eyes and nostrils were left exposed and nets were draped over their heads for partial protection.

The Merchant Hunter had already enquired if his passengers cared to accompany him into the yalg groves. Kerish had almost said yes before Forollkin could refuse with a frosty comment which made Galkian disapproval of the Gauza trade plain.

Ibrogdiss had murmured a faint apology for offending them and tied on the last of his protective wrappings.

The Galkians then withdrew to their tent during the tense minute in which Ibrogdiss and his men slipped out from under the net, on to the riverbank.

"Do we disapprove of gauza?" asked Kerish. "I thought it was just used in sleeping potions."

Forollkin looked uncomfortable. "Well, that's one of its uses. Shall we go back on deck? It sounds as if they've gone now."

Peering through the net the Galkians could just see Ibrogdiss and his men moving slowly and clumsily among the dark trees. They could also hear a humming, louder and steadier than that of the usual marsh insects—the humming of the zzaga. It was like a suppressed murmur of anger, constantly threatening to rise into fury.

Kerish left Forollkin trying to talk to a group of nervous serfs and went down to the stern cabin. Some time during the night Lilahnee had eaten every scrap of her food but she was no more disposed to be friendly.

When Kerish came into the cabin she snarled and fluffed up her fur to make herself look bigger. The Prince choked an impulse to laugh, almost afraid that the animal would sense his mockery. He spoke to her in a low, gentle voice for a while and then replaced the empty bowl with a full one and locked the door behind him.

On deck Forollkin was still talking to the Frians but most of them hurried back to their tasks when Kerish-lo-Taan sat down beside his half-brother. Only Dau and one other serf remained squatting close to the Galkians' tent, as they plucked a brace of scrawny birds for Ibrogdiss' supper.

Forollkin had been asking Dau about the flood season but Kerish turned the conversation to the gods of Lan-Pin-Fria.

"Who is the Green One? Why are cats his children?"

Dau answered as he plucked. "The Green One was the last of the gods. They laugh at him for his . . . . I don't know the word, but he was green and he looked like that one."

Dau pointed to the Forgite, who sat close by in the shadow of the water kegs.

"Hideous," said the Forgite calmly.

"Hideous." Dau stored away the word and went on, "So the Green One made animals and they did not laugh at him but the other gods made men and they hurt the Green One's animals and sometimes killed them. So the Green One thought very hard and what he thought was a cat and the cat was like you, Lord."

This time the Frian pointed to Kerish.

"Men saw the cat and they wanted it to live with them but the cat did not care for the men. The more they gave, the less it took. The men were sad and the Green One laughed. Men kill animals but cats kill the hearts of men."

"That's very true," said Forollkin brightly. "Cats are ungrateful creatures."

"You are right, Dau," murmured Kerish, "they show us how greedy we are to want something back for everything we give."

"And which of your gods made women?" asked Gidjabolgo.

Dau would have answered but his words were drowned by the alarm cry. Everyone on deck froze, all chatter ceased and the Galkians realized that the air was throbbing with a noise like the distant roar of an angry crowd.

"The zzaga," said Dau.

The half-plucked fowl slid to the deck as he ran to the ship's rail. The Galkians and Gidjabolgo followed.

34

Through a blur of netting they saw five green figures running towards the ship as fast as their cumbersome wrappings would allow. Their arms were filled with something mauve and golden: the gauza orchids.

Kerish's head throbbed with the anger of the zzaga and before his eyes the darkness of the yalg grove fragmented into shadows, gashed with green, that swooped upon the Frians.

Ibrogdiss shielded his eyes with his free hand. The others copied him and they ran on, half-blind, towards the riverbank.

Inevitably one of them stumbled and fell. The orchids tumbled from his arms and the zzaga hovered over him. Then they began to land on his body and within seconds he was hidden by a mass of insects.

"Why don't they help him?" demanded Forollkin. "Why don't the others go back for him?"

"His death gives the others time," said Dau calmly. "Go to your tent, Lords. There is danger."

There was a thin scream as a zzaga found its way under the veil of the fallen serf. The man contracted in agony as stings were plunged into his eyes and lips. Forollkin grabbed his brother's arm and pulled him towards the tent, yelling to Gidjabolgo to follow them. Already some of the zzaga were rising from the dying Frian to pursue the others.

Ibrogdiss had reached the riverbank and was climbing the rope ladder towards the deck. He was slow because of the orchids bundled under one arm, and his remaining serfs crouched, moaning prayers, at the bottom of the ladder.

Above, the crew were cautiously unfastening a section of the net and lifting it just enough for Ibrogdiss to get through. The Galkians watched from their tent as the Merchant Hunter was hauled over the rail. He stumbled across the deck, put the precious orchids on a pile of sacking and turned to shout muffled orders. His Frians were preparing to fasten the net down again but Ibrogdiss counted the remaining orchids worth the risk and ordered it raised.

The first of the serfs crawled over the rail and then the second but as the third struggled up the ladder Ibrogdiss reversed his orders. Already there were zzaga clinging to the man's back and he could not protect his face and climb.

Obediently Ibrogdiss' serfs held down the net, even when the Frian on the ladder shouted to them and tried to claw his way upwards. Then he felt the first zzaga tickling his forehead, screamed, flung himself from the ladder and rolled into the river.

The Galkians saw none of this but they heard the cries of panic as a single zzaga that had got under the netting worked its way upwards.

Ibrogdiss rapped out orders which were ignored in a stampede for the hatchway. The Master had the protection of the cloth wrappings, the serfs did not.

With a buzz of fury the zzaga appeared over the rail, flew upwards and banged into the net again. Frustrated it swooped low over the deck.

Gidjabolgo dived under his Masters' bedclothes, clutching a pillow to protect his face. Forollkin would have pushed his brother further in and closed the tent flap but Kerish shouted: "Dau!"

The Frian serf, Kerish's zel piece clutched in his hand, was the last in the queue of men struggling to get down the hatchway. The zzaga hovered above his naked shoulders. Forollkin dashed forward and, ripping off his cloak, threw it at the zzaga, knocking it to the deck. Before the insect could struggle free, Forollkin's booted foot had crushed it.

"No, do not touch it, the sting can still kill you," Ibrogdiss said as Dau knelt to kiss the foot that had saved him. Much embarrassed, Forollkin pushed the Frian away.

Already some of the other serfs had returned to the rail but a cloud of zzaga beat against the net and there was no sign of movement from the river.

Ibrogdiss unwound the green cloth from his face.

"Two plants lost," he said, "but these three are good, eight flowers in all."

Forollkin stared at the Merchant Hunter, too sickened to speak and then strode over to his tent to drag out Gidjabolgo.

Ibrogdiss soon ordered his men to the oars and by nightfall they were clear of the yalg groves and the threat of zzaga. The Galkians ate supper in their tent and when

Ibrogdiss sent a message to Kerish asking him to sing, the Prince angrily refused.

After a restless night in the airless heat of their tent, Kerish woke at dawn. He dressed very quietly and left Forollkin sleeping. On the deck, he approached Dau and persuaded him to clean and chop for Lilahnee one of the fish intended for Ibrogdiss' breakfast.

Dau and all the other serfs that Kerish saw had painted green circles around their eyes and stained the palms of their hands. He asked if these were tokens of mourning but Dau did not know the word.

"Being sad for someone who is dead," explained Kerish.

"It is for the dead, yes," answered Dau as he deftly cut out the fish's backbone, "but not sad. The Marsh Gods care for those they kill."

The fish scales made glittering patterns on the Frian's hands. Kerish watched them as he spoke.

"Do they care for all? Serfs and masters."

"No." Dau looked Kerish fully in the eyes for the first time. "No, only for the serfs."

"And the masters?" asked the Prince.

"You are free, Lord," said Dau. "I may not speak of it, even to you," and he handed Kerish the bowl of fish.

When Kerish reached the hatchway, he found it closed and two serfs squatting beside it, as if on guard. He asked them to open it but they refused to understand his Zindaric and merely bowed their heads.

Impatiently Kerish stooped to throw back the trapdoor himself. One of the serfs burst into anxious Frian, the other attempted Zindaric.

"Lord, no. Master say."

"Your Master is paid to let me go where I wish."

The Prince stroked the purple jewel at his breast and stared directly at the Frians. They shrank back and let him pass without further protest.

As Kerish descended the ladder he began to cough and his first impression was that the hold was full of smoke. That was an illusion, but there was a smell, so sweet and sickly that he clung to the ladder, gasping for breath.

Scent seemed to engulf him in a great wave and then ebb

away. He knew it for the scent that had puzzled him before and now he recognized what it was: the scent of the gauza orchids. His first thought was for Lilahnee and he hurried across the hold to unlock the stern cabin.

Inside the scent was much fainter. Kerish held the door open for a moment too long and Lilahnee made a dash for freedom. He only just caught her and was badly scratched before he could close the door and put her down again.

Sucking his scratches Kerish tried to tempt Lilahnee with the fresh fish but she leapt back into the rafters and spat at him. The Prince sat down on the cabin floor frowning intensely at the angry kitten. How could he reach her?

Kerish thought of the chapter of the Book of the Emperors which told of the Poet Emperor and his cat. Tor-Koldin had understood his Lilahnee, people had even said that he could talk to her and she to him. Understanding... Kerish's thoughts jerked back to the day of the or-gar-gee hunt.

Several times he had been on the point of telling Forollkin what had really happened. He had held back, partly because he knew how angry he would be in Forollkin's place at such a violation of his privacy; partly so that he could comfort himself with the knowledge whenever Forollkin was irritating him.

The Power of the Godborn: the High Priest had praised the Emperor for forbidding his sons to be taught their ancient powers. Why? Because it was better to learn for oneself, or because of the harm such powers could do when used in anger or in spite? Kerish dismissed the second thought uncomfortably. After all, he had done nothing wrong, only helped Forollkin to save his own life. No, he would teach himself the limits of his own power and start with Lilahnee.

Kerish sat upright, in the traditional posture for zel meditation, closed his eyes and pictured Lilahnee, the slender body beneath the soft green fur, the lustrous golden eyes, the long sharply pointed ears and feathery whiskers . . . a proud animal, not be bullied into submission.

He tried to imagine how she would have felt when he found her, alone, motherless, her fur bedraggled with mud, crouched beneath the thorn bushes, with an unknown danger crawling noisily towards her. Then he pictured himself as a full grown marsh cat, coming to comfort her. With an effort of will he covered his pale skin in green fur and lengthened his nails into claws. He grew whiskers and a tail and tried to purr but he didn't know how to begin. His concentration was broken by the thud of Lilahnee dropping down from her rafter.

Patiently he built up the image again and then replaced it with a picture of his own hands reaching out to feed and stroke the marsh kitten.

"Friend," he murmured, and a surge of affection for the lost, lonely creature spilled over into an attentive silence.

Something cold touched Kerish's hand and his eyes flew open. Lilahnee was cautiously sniffing his fingers. Kerish longed to pick her up but sat quite still. Lilahnee gave his little finger a cursory chew and then fell on her food, ignoring him totally. Feeling that he had made some progress Kerish slipped out of the cabin.

He walked straight into the arms of Ibrogdiss. The captain's breath stank of the fetid sweetness of gauza and his face was dripping with sweat. Kerish tried to twist out of his grip but the Merchant Hunter was surprisingly strong.

"No-one must come here, no-one."

"I came down to feed the marsh kitten," said Kerish steadily.

His voice seemed to penetrate the Frian's stupor.

"Young Lord," Ibrogdiss' plump fingers reached up to trace the curve of the Prince's cheekbones and tug at his hair.

"Little Lord, singer of dreams."

"Ibrogdiss, let me go now."

"Never. When your brother is gone, I will keep you safe and you shall sing to me."

"I will sing to you whenever you want," answered Kerish cautiously, "but we must journey northwards to the mountains."

"All journeys begin and end in the marshes," murmured Ibrogdiss. "There is nothing beyond them, nothing. You have dreamed the land of Galkis. It is a good dream; mine were good once. Now they are bad and the marshes cover Zindar, there is no escape from them."

Kerish stopped struggling.

39

"Galkis is real, I promise you. Not all lands are as cruel as Lan-Pin-Fria."

Ibrogdiss did not seem to hear.

"The marshes will take me soon. They always take more than they give and the gods mock my offerings."

"Then make them a new kind of offering," suggested Kerish. "Free your serfs; feed the poor; protect the weak; offer the gods joy."

"You do not understand," said Ibrogdiss sadly, and he released the Prince. "The marshes grow in our minds, they choke us, drown us, darken our dreams."

Through the half-open doorway to Ibrogdiss' cabin Kerish could see the brazier in which the gauza had been burned. The fumes were making his own head swim and suddenly Ibrogdiss' face crumpled into the petals of a lily. Liquid oozed from his mouth and eyes, to trap Kerish, hold him struggling till he died.

Shaking, the Prince backed away as Ibrogdiss said: "When your brother and the ugly one are gone, you will sing for me and we will hide our dreams from the gods."

Kerish fled through the hold and up the ladder. Once on deck he was violently sick over the rail.

Within moments Forollkin's arms were round him and Gidjabolgo was an interested spectator. Both of them helped him back to the tent.

"Close the flap," murmured Kerish.

"No, you need air," exclaimed Forollkin. "Now just lie here."

"He needs privacy," said Gidjabolgo and closed off the tent.

Forollkin poured his brother a cup of tepid wine and Kerish washed away the bitter taste in his mouth.

There was scarcely room for the three of them inside the cramped tent but Kerish clearly wanted Gidjabolgo to stay.

"All right, but what is it?" asked Forollkin. "What's the matter?"

"Gauza."

The smell still clung to his hair and clothes, and Gidjabolgo nodded. "The whole ship stinks of it and Ibrogdiss worse than all."

"He takes it?" asked Forollkin. "But I thought it sapped

40

the strength and drove men mad, and Ibrogdiss seems strong and sane enough."

"Gauza gives health and strength," answered the Forgite. "It kills only when the taker stops, and they usually do. The dreams it gives are pleasant at first, but they change. In Forgin we call gauza the root of despair. I saw a man beheaded once for murdering his wife and children. Gauza dreams had driven him to it. He thought the world too bad for them."

"Yes, Ibrogdiss is like that," agreed Kerish, and he told them what the Merchant Hunter had said.

"I see," murmured Gidjabolgo, "the kindly King of Ellerinonn has arranged for us to be stranded in the middle of the Frian marshes on the ship of a prospective murderer."

"I don't believe that Ibrogdiss thinks of himself as a thief, or a murderer," said Kerish. "He would much rather lead you both into accidental deaths than murder you."

"Well we won't give him a chance," declared Forollkin. "No more trips into the marshes."

"But then he'll know we're suspicious and that will force him to move now," protested Kerish. "If we can delay him, the further north we get the better our chances. Even if we could steal the reed boat, we'd have little hope of surviving alone in the marshes, but if we were right at their edge, close to the northern foothills . . ."

"Yes, then we could go out with a couple of serfs, overpower them, take the boat and go north," said Forollkin.

"Having first unsuspiciously loaded food supplies, warm clothes and the Master's cat?" enquired Gidjabolgo.

"It may be the best we can do," snapped Forollkin. "The alternative is to overpower Ibrogdiss here on the ship. Now I'm well armed and the two of you might be of some help but everything depends on how many of his serfs would fight for him; there are eighteen of them."

"They should hate him," said Gidjabolgo, "but fear would make them fight for him, or where could they hide from the vengeance of all the other Merchant Hunters?"

"Kerish, what do you think?" asked Forollkin.

The Prince lay back among the cushions and rubbed his head as if it was aching. "I don't know. For some reason

Ibrogdiss' serfs do not resent his cruelty and something binds them together. I think they have a code of action but I doubt if even Dau will tell me what it is."

"Well, try. You're good at worming things out of people and in the meantime . . ."

"In the meantime, I think you look pale, Forollkin."

"What?" Forollkin stared at his brother.

"If you're stricken with a sudden fever, that will be a good excuse for not going ashore," said Kerish, "and if Ibrogdiss thinks you're going to die naturally, he won't move against us."

"But Kerish, he as good as told you he was going to murder us . . ."

"His head was full of gauza fumes," said Gidjabolgo contemptuously. "If you behave as normal he'll think he dreamed the conversation."

"Well, can't *you* pretend to be ill?" pleaded Forollkin. "You know I'm no actor."

"We'll feed you some rotten fish to produce the symptoms," suggested Gidjabolgo.

"No. Forollkin," said Kerish firmly, "it's not me that Ibrogdiss wants to dispose of. You'll have to do it."

That night Ibrogdiss again sent to Kerish, asking him to sing. This time the Prince agreed. He sang of the Grove of Imaald where the Ninth Emperor had lamented In-Kelda, his Queen, the Lady of the Rainbow; of the Sea of Az dyed purple by the hem of Zeldin's cloak trailing in the waters as he strode from Galkis to Ellerinonn; and of the White Strand of Hildimarn, where once a year the High Priestess searches for the footprints of Imarko.

Gidjabolgo went down into the hold where he could not hear but all the Frians listened intently and Dau whispered partial translations to his comrades. The evening ended with Forollkin stiffly claiming to feel unwell and Kerish anxiously taking him to their tent.

The next morning Kerish announced that Lord Forollkin had a slight fever and would stay in bed. Ibrogdiss was too busy to be much concerned since they were nearing another yalg grove. While the protective nets were put up again

Kerish left Gidjabolgo guarding the tent and climbed down into the hold to feed Lilahnee.

The marsh kitten leapt to the rafters as soon as he opened the cabin door, but she did not spit at him. Patiently Kerish set down the food and projected the same series of images. Then he sat quite still and watched Lilahnee come down and eat her food. When she had finished, the marsh kitten settled down, only a foot away from him, to wash herself.

Very pleased, Kerish got up quietly and went back to their stuffy tent.

During the day five gauza orchids were gathered and Ibrogdiss and his men all returned safely.

That night at supper, the Merchant Hunter was in an excellent humour and clapped in time to the sea-chants and marching songs that Kerish played for him. Yet when the Prince began a song of his own composition on the beauties of Ellerinonn, Ibrogdiss stopped him at once.

"No, no, young Lord, men say that land is ruled by a sorcerer, a wicked man."

"The King of Ellerinonn is not wicked, I assure you."

"All sorcerers are wicked," said Ibrogdiss. "They take their fate into their own hands and make the gods angry. Sing of something else."

The following morning Kerish told the Merchant Hunter that Forollkin was worse. Ibrogdiss said that it could be marsh fever, though that was rare at this time of the year.

Kerish asked what the symptoms were and was then able to agree that Forollkin had them.

Back inside their tent the Prince informed his brother that he was flushed, sweating heavily, had pains in the stomach and occasional spasms.

"Spasms of what?" demanded Forollkin.

"I'm not sure," said Kerish. "Oh, and you're to drink this, only I wouldn't if I were you, because I saw some of the ingredients."

For the next three days the *Green Hunter* rowed north. Each morning Dau asked with obvious concern how Forollkin was. Somewhat ashamed, Kerish answered him briefly but there never seemed to be an opportunity to question Dau about his feeling towards Ibrogdiss: the master of the *Green Hunter* was always hovering close by.

Kerish had to spend most of his time cooped up in their tent with Forollkin, while Gidjabolgo sat just outside, keeping up a cruelly observant commentary on the ship's crew.

Occasionally he allowed himself to escape to the stern cabin to sit with Lilahnee, and the marsh kitten was beginning to trust him. On the third morning she briefly allowed Kerish to stroke her, before cuffing away his hand. By the next day she was even taking food from his fingers.

As Kerish emerged from the hold with the empty dish in his hands he noticed that the morning was less hot than he had grown to expect. There was a slight breeze and he leaned over the rail for a moment to study the ways in which the landscape was changing.

The river was narrower, the bleak expanses of reeds were now broken by numerous gir mounds and in the far distance he thought he saw the shadow of the foothills of the northern mountains.

Suddenly Ibrogdiss' hands closed on his shoulders. Kerish winced at the smell of gauza but managed a look of polite enquiry.

"Young Lord, you are pale, you are tired. You have nursed your brother too long."

Ibrogdiss began to talk about marsh fever, explaining that its usual course was seven days. On the seventh night the climax came and the victim either died or began to recover.

"The fever is fierce then, very fierce; young Lord, you must rest. Two of my men will care for your brother. Rest in my cabin or you will be sick too."

Kerish thanked Ibrogdiss for his concern but firmly refused. Ibrogdiss smiled and bowed but Kerish sensed that the refusal angered him.

That night the half-brothers shared Kerish's supper, a tough stewed fowl and a cup of girgan. Afterwards Kerish suggested a game of zel. Gidjabolgo was sitting close to the tent and would warn them if Ibrogdiss, or any of his Frians, approached.

Forollkin agreed, without much enthusiasm, and while Kerish carefully set out the zel pieces, reciting the proper formula over each, he launched into a long complaint about

44

Lan-Pin-Fria. Having attacked the food, the climate and the landscape, Forollkin went on to the Frians themselves.

"And whatever they may say, they don't have a religion. Their so-called gods teach them nothing about how to behave to one another. They might as well worship a stick, or a pile of stones. I expect some of them do."

Kerish put down a crystal pyramidion murmuring: "*Behold the mountain where Zeldin spoke unto his son and showed him Galkis. May we be granted eyes to see all things new,*" then asked: "To teach us how to behave to each other: is that what gods are for?"

"Well that's the heart of it, isn't it?" said Forollkin. "Perhaps we should send some of our priests to the Frians. It's true their land is against them and they have to struggle to survive, but they blame everything on the marsh gods and do little to help each other. Zeldin, I hate this place. No wonder Ibrogdiss retreats into gauza dreams."

Kerish placed another piece. "*Behold the tear that Zeldin shed for Imarko and remember that even God grieves for us,*" and then looked up.

"Yes, and each of his retreats makes the defeat of Lan-Pin-Fria more certain. Perhaps Galkis has breathed the root of despair too."

"Our country sickens but it's not defeated yet," said Forollkin. "After all, here we are doing something to help, instead of wringing our hands before mere images."

"Are we really?" demanded Kerish. "Do we truly believe that there is something we can do, or are we just making this journey so that we don't have to sit still and watch the worst happen?"

"Kerish! You're the one who is supposed to understand our quest, not me. And would the King of Ellerinonn have given up his key and risked his kingdom if our journey was worthless?"

"I'm sorry, Forollkin. You know I just like to come at things from all sides at once. I don't really mean it."

"I should hope not," grumbled Forollkin. "Is the board ready?"

Kerish made the formal gesture of placing the invisible centre piece: "*Behold the emptiness at the heart of all things, which each man must fill.* Yes, ready."

After the standard period of silence Forollkin impetuously moved the Golden Star of Galkis towards the Double-edged Sword, muttering a few lines about the sacrifice of the One for the Many, memorized from a book of Zel meditations.

Kerish picked up the Winged Circle and, after brooding over it for a long while, placed it beside the Silver Stair. Outside they could hear Ibrogdiss calling orders to the nightwatch and the wailing prayers with which the Frians greeted darkness.

Kerish poured more oil into the lamp and they played on. Forollkin moved the Rainbow Bridge towards the Crimson Heart and misquoted a poem about Crossing the Gulf from Self to Other. Kerish intercepted him with the Wall of Desire: "*If you desire something of me, it you may have, but never me.*"

Snorting with irritation, Forollkin did not pause to think about this long. He used the Rainbow Bridge to pass over a Black Square: "*The Wise Man knows when to be afraid.*"

Kerish's hand hovered above the Mind Crystal and then over the Emperor Orchid. Even in the flickering lamplight Forollkin saw the change in his brother's face.

"You're thinking of him? Of Galkis?"

"The Emperor, our father," murmured Kerish. "I can never think of him as the link between us."

"Neither can I," answered Forollkin. "I can't think of myself as part of the Godborn at all. You fit. I don't. And as for my mother . . ."

Kerish looked down at the board but he could hear the pain in Forollkin's voice: "She'll know by now that I've gone off with you on some wild quest, instead of making a golden future for her in Ephaan. I sometimes think you're lucky, Kerish, to have lost your mother so young. At least you can weave dreams about her. It's easier to love the dead."

"Forollkin . . ."

Kerish stopped at the sudden sound of violent coughing. It was Gidjabolgo's signal. Forollkin hastily got under the sheets and Kerish knelt upright. There was a scrabbling at the tent flap and Dau crawled in, holding a finger to his lips.

"Dau, what is it?" whispered Kerish.

The Frian looked at the pile of bedclothes that hid Foroll-kin.

"The Lord is very sick?"

Kerish nodded.

"He will die?"

"No!" said Kerish. "The fever weakens him but it will not kill."

"Lord, he will die."

The Frian crawled forward till his knees touched Kerish and he spoke very quietly.

"My Master has said so."

Kerish heard Forollkin's breathing change but he didn't move.

"What has he said?"

"The Master is afraid you will catch the fever, Lord. He means to take you from your brother and keep you in the cabin with the marsh kitten. Then he will tell you that your brother has died of the fever and the ugly one, too, is sick."

"My brother is not dying," said Kerish.

"Lord, we are to nurse him and we will be lashed unless . . ."

Dau picked up one of the cushions and motioned as if to press it down over someone's face.

"You understand, Lord . . ."

Kerish nodded. Before he had only known the danger; now he felt it too. His stomach churned and he struggled to repress a desire to run out and find Ibrogdiss and scream at him: "Kill us, kill us all now. I can't bear to wait, knowing what you are."

Forollkin was shifting in the bed. He could not keep up the pretence of unconsciousness much longer.

"Dau," whispered Kerish, "will you help us against Ibrogdiss?"

The Frian shook his head.

"Lord, I must not harm my Master, or the curse of the gods will fall on me."

"We would not ask that of you," said Kerish cautiously, "but we need your help to escape. Remember, Lord Foroll-kin saved your life."

"I know it, Lord, and you have given me your god to guard me. I would die for you, and the gods could not be

47

angry," whispered Dau, "because you are free. If the Lord Forollkin were stronger perhaps . . ."

Forollkin threw back the sheets and Kerish gripped Dau's shoulders to check his startled movement.

"Lord Forollkin has recovered from his fever. We concealed it, thinking that Ibrogdiss would not harm a sick man . . ."

"But we were wrong," said Forollkin bitterly. "It seems your Master is bad enough for anything."

"The gods have made him," answered Dau, "and he must act as they have made him."

"Even against you, his son?"

"I am a serf," said Dau, with curious dignity. "The gods made us to be hurt and they will heal us."

Kerish was beginning to understand.

"But since we are free, we may struggle against Ibrogdiss, and surely you can help one master as long as you do not harm another."

"I think it is so," agreed Dau.

"We must plan," said Forollkin. "Is Ibrogdiss likely to leave the ship tomorrow?"

The Frian shook his head.

"Perhaps we should move tonight, then . . ."

"No!" Dau shook his head more violently. "At night the marshes are bad: the or-gar-gee hunt and south there are many or-gar-gee."

"But we are going north, to Lokrim and beyond," said Kerish.

They could see that Dau was very curious but serfs were trained not to question their masters.

"North then. I will take you to the house of my mother's kin, in Lokrim."

"But how are we to get away?" demanded Forollkin. "Will the rest of the crew help us?"

"Help, no, but they will not stop me." The Frian was rocking on his heels, frowning intently. "The Master trusts me in his cabin. Tomorrow I must take things from there to put in the other cabin, to make a prison for you, Lord. Time perhaps if . . . . Lords, do you have a firestick? The Master keeps his close."

48

"I have firestones," said Forollkin, who always carried a pair on journeys.

"Would your spirits let me use them? Could you teach me?"

"It's easy," said Forollkin a little scornfully. "There's no need for spirits."

Dau's half-smile suddenly gave him a look of Ibrogdiss.

"It is good then, but I must speak with my brothers. I will come again before dawn." And he wriggled noiselessly out of the tent.

"Can we trust him?" whispered Forollkin.

"Yes," answered the Prince with more confidence than he felt.

# *Chapter 3*

The Book of Emperors: *Wisdom*
*And he said to them: "Do you obey me?" His followers*
*answered, "Lord, in all things!" but he shook his head.*
*"That cannot be, for the first of my commands is this—never*
*obey without thought."*

As much to stop thought as anything else, Kerish moved quietly about the tent, packing the essentials for their journey north into one light carrying chest. Exactly what was essential provoked a long whispered argument. In the end Forollkin allowed Kerish his zildar and his copy of the Book of the Emperors, but forbade him to pack the heavy zel set.

"We'll leave it to pay Ibrogdiss' fee."

Occasionally they could hear the murmur of conversation but even Kerish's sharp ears could not make out what was being said. In the gloom of the false dawn, Dau slipped back into their tent.

"I have spoken to my brothers," he whispered. "It will be done, but you must help me, Lord."

He looked at Kerish who nodded. "Tell me what to do."

The Prince listened carefully to his instructions and repeated them once to make sure that he had understood.

"I must go now," murmured Dau. "The Master will be waking."

"Send Gidjabolgo to us," asked Kerish. "He must know what we're doing too."

Dau looked uneasy. "He will do as you say? It is not good that my brothers are punished for him; he is not a master."

"He will give no trouble. I'll answer for that," said Forollkin grimly.

Dau nodded and after Forollkin had shown him how to make sparks with the firestones, he left the brothers alone.

50

Kerish did not emerge from his tent to feed the marsh kitten as early as usual. He waited instead until he heard the crew haul up the nets they had set the night before, and re-fill the braziers with sea-coal and he could smell fish broiling.

Sweat was trickling down Forollkin's face as he lay, fully clothed, under the coverlet, his long sword at his side.

"Kerish, perhaps you should take my dagger . . ."

The Prince shook his head. "I've never worn one before so Ibrogdiss would notice."

Forollkin frowned.

"If anything goes wrong, yell and I'll come to you. Gidjabolgo has a knife now, and perhaps the two of us . . . ."

"Every Frian on board has a knife," said Kerish dreamily, "and some of them have bows. They would die to defend their Master, even from us. I'm going now."

"You've got the handkerchief?"

Kerish nodded and slipped out of the tent.

On deck Ibrogdiss sat amongst a group of serfs licking the grease of fresh cooked fish off his fingers.

"Good morning, young Lord. How is your brother?"

"He is much the same as yesterday," answered Kerish, "and surely that is good."

Ibrogdiss did not seem to have heard.

"You are tired, young Lord, pale cheeks, dark rings round your bright eyes . . . you must rest."

"I didn't sleep last night," said Kerish truthfully. "Ibrogdiss, will you come with me to feed Lilahnee? I thought last night that she seemed to be pining. Her coat is losing its lustre . . ."

"The marsh kitten? Ah, it is often so. They are stubborn creatures and will sometimes starve themselves to death, but we can force food down her."

He is pleased that I'm making things easy for him, thought Kerish and flinched as Ibrogdiss rose and gripped his arm.

"I will come with you, and Gül shall look at your kitten; he is wise in their ways."

The Merchant Hunter called to one of his serfs. Kerish could not think of a reason for refusing the man's advice, so the three of them went down to the hold together.

51

Ibrogdiss talked fluently of the difficulties of breaking a marsh cat's spirit until they reached the cabin door.

"Let me go first," said Kerish, "she's used to me by now. I'll call you in when I've got hold of her."

Ibrogdiss nodded and bent over one of the jars of lilies as Kerish slipped into the cabin, leaving the door slightly open. Lilahnee plopped down expectantly from the rafters and Kerish offered her the food he had brought. She did not attack it at once but stared at him, her whiskers twitching, as if she sensed his tension.

Kerish tried to project a calm he didn't feel. Then he heard a movement through the thin wall that separated the two cabins.

Kerish drew a handkerchief from the breast of his tunic just as Ibrogdiss called: "You have caught her, Lord?"

"Yes," answered Kerish, "but wait a moment longer while I—"

The door of the second cabin flew open and Kerish heard Dau rush out. He covered his mouth and nose with the handkerchief and kicked the door shut. For a moment there was pressure against it and muffled shouting. Then the sweet smell of gauza seeped into the cabin and the marsh kitten began sneezing. Kerish knelt down beside Lilahnee and tried to soothe her. For the first time the kitten let him hold her without struggling.

Then the door was pushed open. It was Dau who stood there beckoning, the lower part of his face wrapped in green cloth. Kerish smoothed Lilahnee's ruffled fur and stood up. Already he could hear laughter and when he came out into the hold he saw that the serf was doubled up, laughing hysterically, while Ibrogdiss cried without tears.

The smoking brazier that Dau had brought from his Master's cabin stood between them. Dau had burned a whole handful of gauza, worth a prince's ransom, and the effects were immediate. Even with the protection of the handkerchief, the fumes began to make Kerish light-headed.

The serf went on laughing, as if he had never laughed before, but Ibrogdiss stared at the Prince and his eyes were full of horrors.

"Young Lord, you are black inside like all the rest. Just

beneath the skin, darkness. I thought your voice sweet, but it sang me into a worse dream."

Kerish thought of his father, the lamp of his courage gone out, alone in the dark, but Ibrogdiss' son was tugging at his arm.

"We must go quickly."

Kerish nodded, but first he darted back into the cabin. Lilahnee had retreated to the furthest corner, her coat fluffed out in alarm. She spat feebly at Kerish as he picked her up. Her weight told him how fast she was growing. Unless she would come willingly, he'd have to release her over the side.

Supporting the kitten with one hand, and still keeping the handkerchief over his face, Kerish followed Dau through the hold. When they reached the ladder, Kerish said: "Surely someone will hear the laughter and come down . . .?"

"My brothers will not hear till I say their ears are open."

"They will be all right, Ibrogdiss and Gül? The gauza won't hurt them?"

"In an hour perhaps the dreams will be gone," said Dau.

"And what will Ibrogdiss do to your brothers?"

"They will say that he ordered them to let you take the boat, when the gauza was on him. He will not remember," promised Dau, "and he will not beat them hard for he will need every man to hunt us."

"And they will obey?"

"They will kill us," said Dau, "if the Master orders it."

On deck the serfs went about their tasks in silence, ignoring Kerish and Dau as completely as if they could not see them. Struggling to keep hold of Lilahnee, Kerish half-ran to the tent, to be met by Gidjabolgo's scowling face.

"It's done?"

Kerish nodded.

Gidjabolgo scuttled across the deck to help Dau lower the reed boat and Forollkin emerged from their tent with the carrying chest.

"Kerish! You're not taking her!"

Lilahnee had worked her way up Kerish's chest and was now digging her claws into his shoulders, her head beneath his chin.

"She won't be any trouble," pleaded the Prince. "Just sling my zildar on my back."

"We'll let her loose when we reach the bank," said Forollkin.

He fetched the Prince's zildar and then crossed the deck with drawn sword but no-one moved to stop them. In an eerie silence, broken only by the sound of muffled laughter from the hold, the four climbed down the rope ladder and into the reed boat.

Kerish was greatly hampered by the marsh kitten but he doggedly refused to let go and when they were all seated in the boat she made no attempt to escape.

Dau and Forollkin began paddling southwards. They didn't keep to the main river for long but turned up a backwater whose banks were covered with brilliant green moss.

"No-one walks here," explained Dau, "or they will sink down over their head and be gone."

"And the *Green Hunter* can't follow," said Forollkin, short-breathed from vigorous paddling.

"No, but the spare boats can," murmured Gidjabolgo.

They had all noticed the other two reed boats stored in the hold but Dau patted the knife tucked into his loincloth.

"I have slit them. They must work to mend them, hours perhaps."

"You inherit your father's slyness," said Gidjabolgo admiringly.

Forollkin handed the Forgite his paddle and tried to find a space to sit down. The small boat was now very crowded and low in the water. Everyone seemed to be sitting on a pile of netting and Kerish, as the lightest, was perched on the chest with the marsh kitten in his lap. Gidjabolgo was now kneeling next to him, with his own shapeless bundle of luggage squeezed in beside him. Forollkin had to share his meagre space with a flask and a pile of flat loaves. However he sat, his own sword or the bow slung across Dau's back seemed to dig into him.

Forollkin wondered how far it was to Lokrim and how long they might have to spend cramped together in the boat. Not long perhaps: the boat was too heavy to move fast and once Ibrogdiss had repaired his other craft . . .

"Dau, will Ibrogdiss guess the route we might take?"

"We are south now," answered Dau between strokes, "but soon we turn. We must hope he will think that we are going south. But the Master is wise, he may send men north too, and he will know the ways to take, the only ways."

"But surely Ibrogdiss hasn't men enough or boats to cover all the possible routes north and south?" asked Forollkin.

"There is a village just up-river from the *Green Hunter*. He will get men from there and pay for their boats."

Half an hour later they entered a stream that meandered north. The going was painfully slow since they could not hack away the reeds that impeded their path without leaving an obvious sign to any pursuers. They had to be quiet, too, in case they startled some large flock of birds and betrayed their presence.

Dau, Forollkin and Gidjabolgo took it in turns to paddle and soon only the Frian's hands were unblistered. It was oppressively hot, and the marsh kitten sat panting in Kerish's lap. To show her displeasure she occasionally bit his hand but she made no move to escape.

At noon they stopped briefly in the shade of a weeping tree to share one of the loaves. Dau scooped up some river water into a clay cup and mixed it with a little girgan. Kerish could barely swallow it without choking but Dau assured him that the cup had been expensively blessed by the shaman of Ix-lith and the water would not harm him.

Then they paddled on. The stream broadened out but was half-choked with gold and crimson lilies. At any other time Kerish would have found them beautiful; now they were simply an obstacle to speed.

In the distance rose a solitary yalg mound and in another half-hour they had reached it. Dau hitched the boat to the nearest branch and slipped over the side. Cautiously he clambered to the top of the mound, keeping behind a screen of trees.

In the boat Forollkin stretched his cramped legs and Gidjabolgo murmured, "And how far do we trust our Frian friend?"

"Completely," said Kerish indignantly.

"We can trust him then to kill his brother serfs if they attack us?"

"No-one would ask him to do that," protested Kerish.

"But if he won't fight on our side, will he let the Lord Forollkin spit his brothers on that magic dagger of his?"

"No-one must be killed," said Kerish. "If they catch up with us we shall have to try to persuade them to ..."

"Kerish." Forollkin spoke gently. "We'll try not to hurt anyone but we may have to. You, Ibrogdiss will probably spare, but we'll be fighting for our lives as well as our quest—"

He broke off at the sound of Dau slithering back down the slope.

"What did you see?" demanded Gidjabolgo.

The Frian ignored him and, stepping lightly back into the boat, spoke to the Galkians.

"Two boats follow, two village boats but perhaps some of my brothers are with them."

"How far behind?" asked Forollkin.

"Two hours, Lord. We must go on."

Kerish tore strips from his thin blue cloak to bind Forollkin's and Gidjabolgo's hands. He offered to take a turn at paddling, but Forollkin told him bluntly that he would do more harm than good. Dau untied the boat and they moved forward at a faster pace. After an hour's paddling they reached a fork in the stream. Dau lifted his paddle from the stream and stared ahead frowning.

"What is it?" asked Forollkin, grateful for the brief rest.

"One stream is narrow, full of choke weed, very slow; the other is broad, deep, we can go fast, but perhaps it is too late in the day."

"Too late for what?"

"Or-gar-gee," answered Dau. "At noon they sleep, at dusk they hunt. We must be past the pools before they wake."

"Or-gar-gee like the one Forollkin killed?" asked Kerish.

"No, small, not so big, but still bad," said Dau.

Forollkin's hand moved to the dagger at his waist.

"We'll risk the or-gar-gee."

Dau nodded. "We must be quiet, soft, no noise, no talk." Kerish tried to make himself comfortable on the hard chest. The constant spray of water from Gidjabolgo's paddle was welcome in the fierce heat.

Surely it wasn't cool enough yet for an or-gar-gee to wake and hunt?

The stream was bounded now by tall feathery grasses and the surface was a glass green, free from water-weeds or flowers. Within half an hour they had reached the point where the stream bulged into a small lake.

Silently, Dau handed his paddle to Forollkin and knelt in the prow, shading his eyes against the sun. After a few seconds he gave the signal and Forollkin and Gidjabolgo began to paddle as fast and evenly as they could.

Nervously Kerish stroked Lilahnee's head over and over again and she began to purr. The noise seemed appallingly loud but no-one else seemed to notice and the boat sped safely across the lake, disturbing nothing worse than a cloud of amber butterflies.

Once in a narrower channel again, they rested for a while but the sight of a swathe of crushed reeds, where an or-gar-gee had passed, spurred them on.

When they reached the next sizeable pool, the Forgite took up his paddle and whispered to Kerish: "If we rouse an or-gar-gee you can always toss the cat to it."

They were in open water before the Prince could reply.

Dau's keen eyes searched the surface of the pool. Suddenly he raised his hand and Forollkin and Gidjabolgo snatched their paddles out of the water. Dau pointed towards the edge of the pool.

Only Forollkin knew what to look for and he saw at once the dark nostrils of an or-gar-gee and the green glint of its snout. The ripples of its breath spread out towards them.

Forollkin tried to guess how large the creature was and where the bulk of its body might be lying. Dau took Forollkin's paddle. They were beginning to drift away from the centre of the stream towards the sleeping or-gar-gee.

Barely dipping his paddle in the water, Dau steered the boat, letting it glide forward under its own impetus for as long as possible.

Kerish's hands communicated his tension to the marsh kitten. She twisted round in his lap to stare up at him. Kerish closed his eyes and concentrated on imagining himself on dry land feeding fish to Lilahnee. The marsh kitten flexed her claws contentedly. Kerish grimaced at the pain but made no attempt to unfasten her from his knees. As he opened his eyes again he saw Forollkin draw the High Priest's dagger, ready to lunge for the or-gar-gee's eye if the creature woke.

They were no more than five feet from the submerged head when the shriek of a marsh bird jarred them all. The boat rocked slightly but the pattern of ripples did not alter. Slowly and carefully they moved across the pool and into the next narrow channel. After a few minutes Dau thought it safe to pause.

Forollkin re-fastened the cloak he had discarded earlier in the day. The sun no longer beat down on them and the Galkians had been in the marshes long enough to know that the days cooled quickly as dusk approached.

"How many more pools?" asked Forollkin.

"One," answered Dau. "The longest."

"Is it still hot enough to cross? Should we wait till tomorrow?"

The Frian shook his head. "It is not good here. At night the or-gar-gee move through these reeds. We must go on."

For the next half-hour they paddled the overladen skiff as fast as it would go. It was still light when they reached the third pool, but no longer hot. The evening breeze was rising, tugging at the reed boat so that Dau's skill in steering with the paddle was constantly needed.

At the edge of the pool the Frian paused, letting the boat glide. The stretch of open water was so long they could only just see the gap in the reeds on the far side.

"Lord," Dau twisted his head to look at Kerish, "your spirit will protect us? You have asked him?"

Kerish nodded. "Yes, and you wear his charm."

Dau plucked the zel piece from his loincloth, spat on it for luck and kept it clenched in his hand as he steered the boat forward. Gidjabolgo took the second paddle and Forollkin knelt with drawn dagger.

They were halfway across before Dau spotted the or-gar-gee. He was forced to turn sharply for the creature lay in the centre of the pool. The ripples of its breath were enough to rock the skiff; the pool must be filled with its coils.

Kerish closed his eyes as Dau steered towards the edge of the pool, in the hope of creeping round the or-gar-gee. He concentrated on calm images; on sitting in the Emperor's garden with Lilahnee on his lap, just as the Poet Emperor had once sat with his kitten, refusing to disturb her even for a council of state. All the great Lords and Ministers had been forced to squat on the grass before the Emperor and the wind blew away their words. Kerish smiled as he thought of it and his own Lilahnee purred. Then, just as he had stopped expecting it, the boat caught on something.

After a moment's frantic paddling it was free but the gentle ripples turned to waves as the or-gar-gee stirred. They had struck one of its coils. Bubbles of foul gas broke on the surface as the mud in the depths of the pool was churned.

"Zeldin and Imarko aid us," whispered Kerish, and Lilahnee gave a mew of fright as a huge green coil surfaced just beside the boat, knocking the paddle from Gidjabolgo's hands.

Water slapped over the bows as the coil submerged again. Forollkin leant over and grabbed the floating paddle just in time. Dau hissed a frantic order and they thrust the boat forward.

Kerish turned, expecting to see the great head rise from the waters, the single eye open ... but the or-gar-gee twitched once more, violently rocking the skiff, and slept on.

For three long, agonizing minutes they paddled steadily across the slowly settling pool, while Gidjabolgo used the Frian's cup to bale out the skiff. Even when they reached the channel Dau would not let them stop until they had rounded a curve and were out of sight and smell of the pool.

Lilahnee was complaining bitterly over her drenched fur, clawing at Kerish's knee. He hardly noticed her.

"Or-gar-gee do not wake quickly," said Dau with a smile, "drowsy, stupid, big and stupid."

"How much further before we can stop?" asked Gidjabolgo.

There was blood on his bandaged hands.

"Not far," said Dau, taking up his paddle again, but it was another hour before they reached a large gir mound and the Frian let them tie up the boat.

They clambered stiffly out, ducking under a tangle of

roots and branches. Near the top of the mound there was enough space for the four of them to lie side by side but it was muddy. Forollkin sacrificed his cloak for them all to sit on and Dau divided another loaf.

There was nothing for Lilahnee and the marsh kitten struggled in Kerish's arms. Reluctantly he put her down. Lilahnee sniffed at the bread and then darted off the cloak and into the trees.

Forollkin grabbed his brother's arm. "No, Kerish, you're not moving from this spot. It's nearly dark and you'd never catch her."

For a few minutes the Prince stood where he was, calling softly to the marsh kitten while the others ate. Finally Forollkin persuaded him to sit down and take his share of the bread.

"I'm sorry, Kerish, but perhaps she'll be happier free. She is wild after all."

He turned to Dau. "Should we set a watch? How far will those two boats be behind us?"

"Four hours now, or five," answered Dau. "They will not enter the or-gar-gee pools and be caught there at dusk."

When Kerish lay down beside his brother on the cold, damp ground, he was sure he would never be able to sleep, but exhaustion rapidly overcame discomfort. Disturbed once in the night by the sound of an or-gar-gee crashing through the reeds, he merely rolled closer to his brother and slept again.

Just after dawn he was woken by something cold and sticky falling against his cheek. He sat up quickly to find that the marsh kitten had returned, bringing him a present of a mangled frog.

Forollkin woke to see his brother hugging Lilahnee, and was rather less impressed by her hunting prowess.

Gidjabolgo stretched and yawned. "Encourage her, we may yet be grateful for her leavings."

Dau had been checking the boat and he returned with another damp indigestible loaf. When they had eaten and warmed themselves with sips of girgan, Forollkin bundled up his filthy cloak and they scrambled down the mound to the boat.

Throughout the long day Kerish sat on the hard chest,

constantly shifting to try and ease the ache in his back and wishing there was something he could do to speed their journey. His only occupation was noticing the different species of birds and flowers and the dark head of an occasional animal, swimming for its burrow.

For part of the day they were passing through gir groves and were forced to take a tortuous route to avoid the many roots snaking across the stream.

When they emerged into the open marshes Forollkin took the second paddle again. His arms were aching with the strain and his hands were a mass of blisters.

Gidjabolgo was in a worse state.

"How long will Ibrogdiss keep up the chase?" asked Forollkin.

Dau shrugged. "Three days perhaps, or four, not longer. There is gauza to be gathered."

"And do you think we can keep ahead that long, even with our present advantage?"

"I do not know, Lord; our boat is heavy and we are slow for . . ."

"Gidjabolgo and I are not used to paddling," finished Forollkin. "Well if the worst comes, we'd better stop in a defensible place. You have a bow . . ."

"Lord," said Dau quickly, "I have thought. There is a way we can take, where the others will not follow."

"What way?"

Dau pointed to the shadowy groves a mile or so to their west.

"Yalg," he said, "but at night the zzaga sleep, all but the hive guards and if the moon is good . . ."

Forollkin glanced at his brother.

"All right then, the yalg groves."

At dusk Dau found a patch of stable land and they all got out of the boat. The Frian cut two long stout reeds and over these he draped the net they had been sitting on. All but one section of it he fastened to small wooden hooks that stretched along the boat just above the water line. Once they were back inside, the net was loosened just enough for the two paddles to go down into the water.

Lilahnee disliked the cage of fine meshed net and struggled in Kerish's arms.

"If she tears the net with those fledgling claws . . ." began Gidjabolgo, his hand on the dagger at his waist.

"I'll keep her still," promised Kerish.

It was dark now and they shared another loaf, waiting for the moon to rise.

Dau murmured prayers while the others ate, till Gidjabolgo said abruptly: "If you wanted the gods to save you, you should have stayed with Ibrogdiss. The gods save those who never place themselves in danger."

It was too dark to see the Forgite's face and Dau was clearly puzzled.

"You think I am bad to have run from my Master?"

"I think you are bad to have ever served him," murmured Gidjabolgo. "Tell me, if the zzaga kill us all, what happens to you after?"

"I cannot speak of it before my Lords," whispered Dau.

"You mean you don't like to tell them that they have no hope, though the gods have a fine new life waiting for obedient serfs?"

"What Masters have is here— " began Dau carefully.

"What *you* have is here!" snapped Gidjabolgo. "You and your brothers throw away your lives for a dream. A dream like gauza, bringing sweetness in despair."

"No, the gods . . ."

"Your gods are the Merchant Hunters—"

"Gidjabolgo, stop it!"

The Forgite turned to Kerish.

"Your pardon, Master. I did not know you honoured the gods of Lan-Pin-Fria. I was only trying to pass a weary time with pleasant chatter . . ."

"The moon's rising," said Forollkin.

They took up their positions and for about fifteen minutes paddled through open country towards the yalg groves. Dau peered anxiously ahead. If any obstacle blocked the channel they would have to turn back, if there was space to do it.

Lilahnee seemed to be asleep. Kerish was perched on the chest and his hair brushed the netting. At the first sound of a zzaga he would have to crouch down with his head in his lap or it might sting him even through the net.

His eyes were adjusting and he could see the yalg trees

shadowing the pallid moonlight. Above the soft splash of the paddles and the sound of his own breathing, Kerish heard a faint humming. The noise was not as threatening as when he had last heard it, but it brought back the shrieks of the dying Frian.

They were under the trees now and it seemed very dark. The stream was narrow but deep, and branches arching over it constantly blocked out the light. Dau took the lead paddle from Forollkin and steered them round a floating log. The scent of gauza was faint but pervasive.

Glancing up, Kerish saw one of the orchids nestled in the fork of a tree. Its garish colours were bleached by the moonlight but the marks on its petals were like bloody fingerprints. How many had died for such flowers over the centuries?

For ten minutes the boat glided forward. Once they thought that a branch stooped over the stream was too low to let them pass. Very cautiously Forollkin loosened the reeds that held up the net, lowered it a little and they were through.

The soft humming grew louder as the stream led them close to the hive itself. Kerish was afraid to look for it among the trees, as if even a glance might alert the zzaga to their presence.

They were near to the edge of the grove when all of them heard a change in the even humming. It was closer, louder, more urgent.

Dau stopped paddling and let the boat drift and Kerish glimpsed a flash of green amongst the trees. It was a lone zzaga flying in circles. At first it did not seem to have felt their presence, then the skiff bumped against one bank. Dau pushed them off again for they were dangerously close to a spiny tangle of bushes that might tear the net.

The zzaga narrowed its circle and flew over the stream, over the boat. Kerish ducked, pressing his face against Lilahnee's fur. The humming changed to a fierce staccato. Kerish knew they had been heard and expected at any moment to feel the creature beating against the net, but the noise was already receding.

"It has gone for the warriors of the hive," whispered Dau. "We must go fast."

63

The skiff jolted as Dau and Gidjabolgo plunged their paddles in the water. They had perhaps a minute before the humming surged again and a dozen zzaga with the broad green stripes of the killer insects hurled themselves through the trees and on to the boat.

Lilahnee growled in protest as Kerish pressed down on her, shrinking from the net as the angry insects struck against it. Gidjabolgo had stopped paddling but Dau hissed an order and the boat moved forward again. The zzaga followed. Forollkin knelt, holding the reeds quite steady.

They can't get at us, thought Kerish, not unless a branch tears the net. But if we stick on something, by day there'll be hundreds of them. We could never get out to free ourselves. We'd starve till we chose to die by their stings . . .

Dau and Gidjabolgo were paddling steadily forwards but with fascinated horror Kerish saw three zzaga hook their feet into the net, inches from his face. They swarmed over it, buzzing furiously, searching for a weak place.

"Keep your head down, Kerish," Forollkin was saying, "and mind Lilahnee's tail."

The marsh kitten was snarling at the zzaga. She batted at the net with her paw just once before Kerish grabbed her tight. The humming drilled into his head.

Forollkin was drawing the High Priest's dagger. Slowly and carefully, never getting his hand too close to the net, Forollkin prodded the nearest insect with the tip of the dagger. It clung still but the humming changed and Kerish knew it was hurt.

The skiff bumped against the bank again. Dau could hardly see to steer for the insects crawling in front of him. Forollkin reached over and patiently waited his chance to stab each one of them. Then he called to Kerish.

"Can you take the dagger and hold Lilahnee?"

Gidjabolgo took one hand from his paddle to pass back the dagger. Kerish straightened just a little and slowly moved the dagger towards the nearest zzaga. He was terrified of cutting the net, but it was strong and almost a quarter of the sharp blade would pass through the mesh. He felt it pierce the soft belly of the insect, felt the zzaga writhe, hurting itself irrevocably as it twisted on the dagger.

This is the first live thing I've killed, thought Kerish. His hands were shaking as he tried to withdraw the point and scrape off the zzaga.

Several of those Forollkin had injured had now fallen dead from the net. The humming was still fierce but at night the hive slept and the guards were few. Kerish spitted a second insect and a third. He could see them quite clearly and suddenly he realized what that meant. They were out of the grove.

Four or five zzaga still clung to the net, with a few more wounded. In spite of the increasing pain in his bent back, Kerish waited calmly for each insect to crawl within his reach as they feverishly searched the net. It was almost a pleasure now to feel the point going home.

They were paddling through reed thickets and Kerish wondered how far the insects would follow them.

Dau seemed to answer his thought. "We must kill them all, or they will cling for ever."

It took another hour to be certain. Even then they didn't dare take down the net and camp on dry land. Desperately uncomfortable they huddled together in the boat for what remained of the night.

At first light Dau paddled them to a gir mound and they got out of the skiff. The Frian wrapped his hands in cloth before disentangling the last of the dead insects and folding up the net.

Kerish stood rubbing his back. It hurt him to stand straight and he was cold and hungry and tired but he smiled when Dau said: "They will not catch us now."

# Chapter 4

The Book of the Emperors: *Secrets*
*And Kal-Vairn built a great wall, not to make a division
between the two peoples but to show the gulf that was
already between them and the peril of crossing it.*

B Y their third day in Lokrim, Dau had found two
Frians willing to guide the travellers north. Forollkin
went out with Dau to help in the protracted negotiations
and to buy new cloaks and boots for hill walking.

Kerish and Gidjabolgo were left behind in the house of a
leather worker who was Dau's uncle. There were only two
rooms and the whole house stank of the hides curing in the
yard.

The travellers were occupying the women's quarters, a
pile of cushions behind a tattered screen. Dau's mother had
been born where they now sat and sold into serfdom after
a bad year's trade. It was a usual fate for artisans' daughters
and Dau did not appear to resent it.

After the discomforts of their journey, the tanner's house
had seemed a haven. Now they were bored and anxious to
be moving again.

Dau and Forollkin returned in time for the dismal evening meal of dry bread and stewed yalgor roots. Forollkin
flopped down on the dusty cushions.

"Well, we've hired a couple of boats and two Frians to
paddle them, Aüg and Lal."

"Lul," amended Dau, "they are brothers."

"Yes, Lul. They don't speak much Zindaric but they
know the route north. They'll take us as far as a place where
the Pin-Fran runs underground: the Forbidden Hill."

"Why forbidden?" asked Kerish.

Dau looked uneasy. "Frians do not go beyond the Hill.
The marsh gods forbid it. The brother of my mother says

66

that those who climb the Hill do not come back. Lords, there is nothing north but rivers and grass and the great hills. Do not go. I will find a ship to take you south, back to your own country."

Forollkin smiled. "Don't worry. We've no intention of dragging you beyond this Forbidden Hill. We'll give you enough gold to start a new life anywhere in Fria."

"We will be safe," Kerish assured the anxious Frian. "Our spirit sends us beyond this hill, and you know that it is strong."

Dau delved in his loincloth and brought out the zel piece. "But you will need your charm."

Kerish smiled at him. "No, keep it to protect you always."

"I will not need it for what I must do," said Dau, "but I will keep it." He stared at the gold and purple feather in his palm. "Lords, may I speak?"

"Say what you like, and we'll be grateful for the advice," promised Forollkin, "but we must go north."

"Lords, you should not take the ugly one," began Dau. "He speaks against the gods and will bring you bad luck."

"All my life I have brought bad luck," said Gidjabolgo calmly. "I don't deny it."

Forollkin sighed. "We are bound by an oath to take Gidjabolgo, and in any case we couldn't abandon him in the heart of Fria."

Dau bowed his head. "I have said."

Kerish broke the awkward silence. "When do we leave?"

"Tomorrow," said Forollkin, "early."

They were woken by the street noises not long after dawn, but Dau had already gone. At first they thought he was out buying more provisions. He had left a message for the travellers with his uncle but it was several minutes before Forollkin understood it.

Gidjabolgo was bundling up his luggage and Kerish was soothing the marsh kitten when Forollkin strode back behind the screen. Kerish stared at his brother's grim face.

"What's happened?"

"Dau has gone back to Ibrogdiss."

"I don't understand," said Kerish blankly.

"He took the reed boat," Forollkin sounded as if he

couldn't yet believe it, "and is paddling back downstream to find his Master."

"But surely Ibrogdiss will never forgive him."

"Our host tells me that the usual penalty for such disobedience is the loss of the left hand," said Forollkin, "or the nose and ears."

"He deserves it," muttered Gidjabolgo, with curious vehemence. "They all do."

"Couldn't we go after him?" pleaded Kerish. "Try to catch him up."

"He has two hours' start," answered Forollkin, "and his uncle wouldn't help us. He seems to think that Dau is right to go back. The only thing our host will do is take us to the landing stage and see us north."

The rest of their preparations were made in silence and it was a sombre group that set off for the landing stage. Two Frians were waiting for them there on long, black boats, each hollowed from a single tree-trunk. Aüg and Lul complained in fractured Zindaric about the presence of Lilahnee. Forollkin told them she would give no trouble and sweetened his words with an extra gold piece. Dau had sworn that these dour, silent northerners were trustworthy. Forollkin prayed it was true.

Gidjabolgo got into one boat with most of the luggage, and Kerish, Forollkin and Lilahnee into the other. Dau's uncle hurried off, clearly glad to be rid of his visitors.

The boats moved away from the island of Lokrim and northwards across the lake. Kerish wrapped his new green cloak around him and tried not to think of Dau.

It was a dreary journey. From dawn to noon each day the Frians paddled the narrow dug-outs, helped, and sometimes relieved, by Forollkin and Gidjabolgo. After a brief rest and a meal of bread and dried meat they would go on until dusk. When they had found a dry place to make camp, Aüg usually shot a bird for supper and roasted it over a fire of gir branches gathered by Lul.

The days were warm but the nights were increasingly cold. The Frians smeared themselves with or-gar-gee grease and did not seem to mind the chill winds and Lilahnee was thriving. She slept for most of each day, curled up in the bottom of one of the boats, and hunted each night. There were very few mornings when Kerish did not wake to find the bloody remains of her kill laid at his feet.

In the spring, when the snows melted and the rains came, the river was a swollen torrent, and a voyage up-stream would have been impossible, but now the waters were low and sluggish.

During the first week of their journey the reed thickets gave way to expanses of treacherous suck-grass and moss, studded with gir mounds. By the second week, the brilliant green of the bog plants had blended into the soft grey of flat grasslands, stretching into the distance, to the shores of the ocean itself.

They had reached the edge of the vast plains of Erandachu and Kerish realized that, for the first time, he was seeing the country where his mother had been born.

Within a few more days the last of the gir mounds had disappeared and they had to carry enough wood to stiffen fires of moss and grasses. There were still plenty of birds for Aüg to shoot but Lilahnee had poorer hunting.

One morning, as the mists cleared, the travellers had their first sight of the Forbidden Hill. Over the next week the shadow on the horizon grew and occasionally they glimpsed beyond it the foothills of the Ultimate Mountains.

Several times Kerish tried to get the Frians to talk about the Forbidden Hill and what they believed to lie beyond it. Both Aüg and Lul muttered a few words about danger and relapsed into an inability to understand Zindaric.

On the day they reached the Hill it was almost dusk and its upper slopes were hidden by mist. As Dau had warned them, the river itself vanished into a cleft and ran on underground.

The travellers camped in a hollow, sheltered by a single wind-bowed tree. After a long cold wait, Lul managed to get a fire alight and cook a brace of small birds. As usual, they were burnt on the surface and half raw inside but the travellers ate them gratefully.

Forollkin spread out one cloak to shield them from the damp grass and another to serve as a coverlet. He and Kerish shared a pillow of a rolled up tunic and Gidjabolgo curled up close by. For once, however, the marsh kitten stayed beside Kerish and the Frians sat by the fire as if they had no intention of sleeping.

Kerish was never sure if it was the Frians' voices or Lilahnee's soft growling that woke him in the middle of the night. He reached out a hand to stroke the marsh kitten and felt the fur prickling along her spine. Kerish opened his eyes and was blinded by a sudden light.

The dark slopes above them were ringed with a blue glow. For a few seconds it burned fiercely and then vanished. Kerish was suddenly reminded of the lights he had seen coming from the rocks of Lind, the lights of Lind that drove men mad, and the brilliant blue seemed imprinted on his eyes, following him into the darkness when he closed them.

Kerish sat up suddenly and for the first time the Frians noticed that he was awake. Their backs were to the Hill.

"A light . . ." began Kerish.

"Not look," hissed Aüg. "Sleep."

Kerish felt Lilahnee's warm, rough tongue licking his hand and the light in his mind faded. It was a dark night and cold. Kerish huddled closer to his brother and went back to sleep.

At dawn, before the mists had cleared, the two Frians returned to their boats. Once only, Aüg asked the Galkians to return with him to Lokrim. Forollkin refused and the Frians handed over the remaining provisions, a pouch of dried meat and a sack of hard, dry bread. They would support themselves by hunting on the voyage home.

Forollkin was now equipped with a bow, but the Frians could not tell him how plentiful the game might be beyond the Forbidden Hill. Gidjabolgo watched the Frians paddle downstream while Forollkin divided the baggage.

Kerish had wandered a little way up the slope, with Lilahnee at his side, and was staring at the Hill. Near its summit was a row of black pillars, or were they statues? They would soon know if they were to cross the Hill and rejoin the river.

Forollkin strode up to his brother carrying a heavy bundle tied in a cloak.

"Here, this is your load."

The Prince of the Godborn stared at him blankly.

70

"I'll strap it to your shoulders," continued his brother cheerfully, "so your arms will be free for climbing. Hold it for a moment."

Kerish staggered under the weight.

"Forollkin, have you slipped your senses? I have my zildar to carry. Give this to Gidjabolgo."

"He already has more than enough to carry and so have I. Bear your own burdens or leave them behind."

As Forollkin walked off, Kerish's anger got the better of his amazement.

"Forollkin, come back, come back!"

The young captain ignored his brother.

"Gidjabolgo, are you ready?"

The Forgite nodded and looked curiously towards Kerish.

"Is our Prince swallowing his pride or choking on it?"

Forollkin slung his bow where the load at his back wouldn't bump against it and set off up the hill. Gidjabolgo followed, chuckling. When Kerish realized that they were really leaving him behind, he struggled after them with Lilahnee padding at his heels, sniffing the damp grass.

By the time he caught up with his brother he had thought of several unanswerable arguments but they were driven from his head by Forollkin's sudden exclamation of disgust.

Gidjabolgo had stopped but Kerish ran the last few feet to join his brother by the lowest of the circle of black pillars.

"What is it, what's the matter?"

"There's something inside, trapped inside. No, Kerish, don't look!"

But Kerish was staring at the pillar already. A shaft of light penetrated the dark stone and it was just possible to see a faint shape; long hands, an eyeless skull, a mouth distorted in a silent scream.

"A trick of the light," snapped Gidjabolgo and pushed the Prince past the black pillar.

For a moment he felt as if he were falling and the step he had just taken could never be retraced.

Beside him Gidjabolgo was an odd colour. Forollkin hesitated on the other side of the pillar and Lilahnee was growling. Kerish called to her but she didn't seem to hear.

71

The marsh kitten backed away from the pillar, her ears flattened to her skull.

"Pick her up, Forollkin, we'll have to carry her for a little way."

Forollkin obeyed and the marsh kitten's scratches seemed to restore his confidence. He strode past the black pillar and dumped her down at his brother's feet.

"She's getting too big to carry. Come on, let's see the view from the top."

By the time they reached the summit there were sharp pains in Kerish's chest and Gidjabolgo was gasping for breath, but such minor discomforts were forgotten in the wonder of what they saw.

The Ultimate Mountains, still half-veiled in mist and unimaginably huge: the northern boundary of the world.

"Well," said Forollkin, "it's going to be cold."

They walked slowly down the northern slope of the Forbidden Hill, to the narrow valley through which the river flowed before disappearing under ground. Scrambling down a steep bank they chose a stony path beside the sleek, tumbling waters.

"Well, the King of Ellerinonn told us to follow the river to the feet of the mountains," said Kerish. "That should be easy enough."

"And those are all the instructions you have?" asked Gidjabolgo, incredulous.

"That's all," said Forollkin, trying to gauge the distance to the nearest mountain and the citadel of Tir-Zulmar.

"The days are long. I'll need some light for hunting but we might manage nine or ten hours walking a day."

"Ten hours!" exclaimed Kerish.

"With one rest at noon," said Forollkin briskly. "You and Gidjabolgo both need hardening if we're to reach the mountains."

All that day they walked. Forollkin chivvied his companions on, striding ahead, clambering over rocks, finding the easiest paths. As the light was dimming, he shot a scrawny bird that Gidjabolgo plucked and roasted over a fire of twigs and dead grass. The meat tasted bitter. Lilahnee refused to touch it and went off to forage on her own.

Kerish unstrapped the load from his aching shoulders and

bathed his blistered feet in the river. Only resentment had sustained him throughout the long day. Forollkin gave him the best portions of meat and gently bound up his feet. "I'll make a warrior of you yet," he said.

The next morning Kerish woke in agony, his muscles rebelling at the slightest movement. Gidjabolgo was little better and muttered dark Forgite curses as he shouldered his load again.

Forollkin eventually forced his companions to walk for most of the day. As soon as they stopped Kerish fell asleep and the Forgite curled into a ball and refused to move.

Wearily, Forollkin gathered enough wood for a fire, soaked the hard bread to make it palatable and divided up the remains of the cold meat. He woke Kerish and Gidjabolgo to make them eat and spread out the ashes of the fire for them to sleep on.

Forollkin would have preferred to keep a watch but the others were obviously too tired to take their turns. He lay down beside his brother, with his hand on his sword hilt, the marsh kitten between them.

Kerish woke long before dawn. The wind had dropped and the night was almost unnaturally still, but in the distance there was music. At least, that was his first thought. As he sat up fully awake, it sounded more like the howling of an animal in pain or anguish. Could an animal feel anguish? Now he listened carefully he didn't know why he had thought the noise sad either. The complex, broken rhythms seemed to pull each nerve in his body taut. Every few seconds there was silence and the silence seemed more potent than the sound, but he could not work out the pattern, though his fingers moved to it.

Abruptly he knew that he hated the noise but he had to find out what made it. Kerish began to slide from beneath the cloak he shared with Forollkin but it was Gidjabolgo who first stumbled to his feet and walked dazedly towards the sound.

That jolted Kerish to his senses. He sprang up and shook the Forgite by his shoulders.

"No, Gidjabolgo!"

He stared blankly at the Prince.

"I must go closer."

The Forgite's body moved to the pattern of the distant voice.

Kerish snatched up his zildar and his cold fingers stumbled into the tune of a Galkian hymn. He played as loudly as he could, staring down at the gilded wood, forcing his hands not to stray into the weird rhythm that haunted him still.

Forollkin sat up, blinking the sleep from his eyes.

"Idaala's Breasts, Kerish, what are you doing? If you don't care about squandering your own rest you might have a thought for mine."

Kerish stopped playing. "Don't you hear it? It's faint now but—"

"A wild beast, howling its hatred of men," broke in Gidjabolgo and sat down beside them. "My Master has frightened it off with his music."

"You're both sleep-sodden," said Forollkin and rolled over with his back towards Kerish.

The Prince looked for a moment at the Forgite and then moved nearer to his brother, burying his head under his cloak.

At sunrise Forollkin got up and bathed in the icy river. He woke his companions and they began their day's march. They were passing through a desolate land of bleak hills, wind-tortured trees and countless streams. In spite of the thin sunlight it seemed to be growing colder every hour.

Forollkin still thought it preferable to the marshes and whistled Jenozan marching songs as he strode along the rocky paths. Kerish and Gidjabolgo were both very quiet. Lilahnee bounded ahead; she was growing fast and her coat was changing to a sleek, glossy green.

At noon they paused in a sheltered hollow to eat the meagre ration of dried meat that Forollkin allowed them. Afterwards, while the others rested, Forollkin strayed from the path a little and climbed a nearby hill.

"Kerish, Gidjabolgo," his voice floated back towards them. "Come and look."

They came slowly, complaining at the climb, and then stared in silence where Forollkin pointed.

At the far end of a deep valley lay a vast stone city. Its buildings coiled and writhed in shapes that men could never

74

have inhabited. The city was ringed with black pillars and statues crouched between them. Kerish was glad that he could not see them more clearly.

"Is there anything moving there?" asked Forollkin. "Kerish, you've keener eyes than me."

"Only shadows. It's a dead city, long dead, I would guess. Look—there are rents in the ground and most of the buildings seem to be broken; perhaps there was an earthquake or a flood."

"Those pillars seem the same as the ones on the Forbidden Hill," said Forollkin.

"Sentinels," murmured Gidjabolgo, "with no-one left to guard."

"I hope so." Kerish shivered. "Let's get down, out of the wind."

As the day drew on, Forollkin began to find the silence of his companions oppressive.

"Kerish, can you spare the breath for a song or a story?"

The Prince shook his head.

Determinedly cheerful, Forollkin tried again.

"Gidjabolgo, then, if you can sing a civil song. We know you can play."

"My Masters must excuse me, I was not trained to be civil."

"And what were you trained for then in Forgin?" asked Forollkin.

"Laughing at my fellow men, picking out other's faults for my Master's pleasure."

"Not a job well paid in thanks or money I would guess."

"On the contrary, my Masters always paid handsomely to watch their friends discomforted."

"And the friends?"

"Thought envy natural to such a miserable creature as myself and smiled at my offences," said Gidjabolgo.

They went on in silence. Kerish hardly noticed his chafed shoulders and blistered feet any more. He felt curiously detached from his surroundings, almost as if he were floating, allowing himself to be carried along by some unseen current. Part of him knew that this was dangerous, but he was too tired to struggle.

The river abruptly curved round and out of sight. The

path narrowed, following the bend of the cliff with a twenty-foot drop on one side. Forollkin went first to test the way over the slippery rocks. The others followed, close behind. The young captain was edging cautiously along, hands flat against the rock, when Lilahnee gave a piercing yowl and fled back along the path, nearly knocking Gidjabolgo into the river.

Forollkin clutched at his brother to make sure he was safe and found that Kerish was trembling violently.

"Kerish, you can't fall. I'm holding you."

"I can't see, Forollkin; it's too dark!"

Fighting a surge of panic Forollkin answered calmly: "Here's my hand, let's get down off this path. Then we'll . . ."

"No." Kerish wrenched his hands away and staggered back to be caught by Gidjabolgo.

"Keep still, Kerish. That's an order."

Forollkin took his brother's hands again.

"Close your eyes and take one step forwards."

"It's forbidden."

"Just one step," repeated Forollkin and this time his brother obeyed.

Inch by inch Forollkin led Kerish along the narrow path and down to the river.

When they had reached flat ground again Kerish opened his eyes.

"Are you better now?" asked Forollkin. "It's a long time since you did that to me."

"The night of Kor-li-Zynak's presentation." The Prince spoke quietly. "Yes, I'm better. Look behind you."

A dark hole gaped in the bank. Before it stood two black pillars and between them lay a body.

Reluctantly Forollkin came closer. He saw the corpse was that of a Frian and not long dead, for there were no signs of decay. In one still hand the man clutched some kind of metal ornament, bright with jewels.

Gidjabolgo came down the path and stood beside Forollkin as the Galkian knelt and gently turned the body over.

The wind moaned in the tunnel and Kerish almost shrieked aloud. The Frian's lips were drawn tightly back in the grin of death and between his eyes was a terrible wound.

76

"There's blood on the ornament and his hand," said Gidjabolgo.

"He couldn't have done that himself," protested Forollkin.

"Do you think that tunnel leads to the city we saw?" asked the Forgite. "Will my Masters order their servant to bury him, or shall we go on?"

Forollkin hesitated for a moment.

"Go on," he said. "Quickly."

He turned the Frian back on to his face.

"Lilahnee . . ." murmured Kerish.

"She must follow in her own time. Come on."

The pace Forollkin set was cruelly fast but neither of his companions complained.

By nightfall they were five miles from the valley of the city. They stopped in a hollow only a few feet from the rushing waters. It was too dark to gather wood for a fire and they huddled together chewing scraps of dried meat and crumbled bread.

Tired as they were, sleep would not come easily and Forollkin broke the tense silence.

"Kerish, you know more history than I do. Did the priests ever teach you anything about this country?"

"Nothing, but I have been wondering about the Western Wall."

Gidjabolgo obviously could not sleep either.

"What wall is that?" he asked.

"It runs down the western boundary of the Empire," answered Kerish, "past Morolk and Tryfania from the mountains of the North to Fangmere. It was built by the grandson of Mikeld-lo-Taan, the first of the Emperors. None of our other borders are so guarded but in all our history what enemy ever came from the far Northwest? Perhaps the Book of Secrets gives a reason for the wall, but I do not know it."

"And who can read this Book of Secrets?" enquired Gidjabolgo.

"The reigning Emperor, High Priest and Priestess; no-one else."

"You think the wall might have been built to keep out whatever lived in the city?" pursued Forollkin. "Well, it may be so but I wish the Emperor had built his wall in Jenoza to keep the Five Kingdoms out."

"The strangest thing of all," said Kerish drowsily, "is that Galkis was empty when the first ships came, and where did the ships sail from? Where did we come from?"

"From some other part of Zindar, I suppose," said Forollkin, "though even the priests don't seem to know."

"You didn't come from Forgin," murmured Gidjabolgo. "Our legend is much the same as yours, though without a god to welcome us ashore. A long voyage and an empty land."

Forollkin yawned. "We must ask the Sorcerer of Tir-Zulmar for an answer to the riddle."

"If you can pay the price for knowledge," said Gidjabolgo. "Do you have mysteries to trade? I think not, though the Prince perhaps . . ."

"I'm sure you've enough for the three of us," interposed Forollkin. "For Zeldin's sake, let's get some rest."

They did sleep in the end, so soundly that it was an hour after dawn when Gidjabolgo woke with a shout as Lilahnee leapt down into the hollow and padded across the others to lick Kerish's face.

Forollkin sat up swearing and rubbing his stomach for the marsh cat was no light weight now. Kerish hugged her and Lilahnee backed off spitting, but her claws were sheathed and she had brought them a plump skon fowl, so they made a good breakfast.

For the rest of the day they followed the path closely and never climbed the banks to see if there were other ruined cities.

Kerish felt happier when the river dipped down and the banks rose until they were walking in a gorge. They were out of the wind at last but after two days Forollkin began to fear that the path might disappear and that their food supplies could not last.

There proved to be a narrow space always running between the river and the cliff that looked as if it could have been the remains of some ancient road, but nothing grew in the gorge except moss and ferns too damp to burn. Nor was there anything to shoot, and they were forced to live on the dwindling sack of hard bread and dried meat.

Lilahnee hunted small, slimy river creatures and devoured them, growling with disgust. Once Forollkin and Gidjabolgo caught some tiny fish in a pool and ate them raw. Haughtily denying his hunger, Kerish refused to touch them.

On their seventh day in the gorge they heard a distant rumble that increased to a thunderous roar as they walked. By noon they stood below a great waterfall and were forced to climb the steep and slippery path that ran beside it. It took them an hour to reach the top of the cliff and suddenly they were in the wind again.

Kerish and Gidjabolgo were exhausted. It was Forollkin who made them change into dry clothes, who gathered twigs and handfuls of grass and struggled against the wind to get a fire alight. Muttering a brief prayer to Imarko, he unslung his bow to hunt for game. He was lucky almost at once and shot a small plump animal that seemed to be too stupid to run away. He skinned it quickly and roasted it on a stick. When it was done he woke the others and gave them the best share. They burned their fingers tearing at the hot meat and sucked the bones bare. Too tired to travel further in search of shelter, they slept on the windswept hill.

Kerish woke when Lilahnee returned from her hunting, before it was light. He lay looking up at the sky, forgetting the cold by trying to name each star. There was one he was not sure of. It could be Keshnarmeynee, the Star of Morning, for it was very bright, but surely too low in the sky.

He thought of the same stars shining on Galkis. It would be late autumn in his father's gardens, the time of the Hair Festival, when the lock of Imarko's own hair kept in her temple at Hildimarn was shown to the people and every black-haired lady in the land cut off a matching lock to scatter on the fields. He had heard that in the country the women were chased and put up mock fights before letting the young men of the village cut their hair. Nothing so lively had ever happened in the Palace. Kerish's thoughts drifted through the Inner City as he watched the sudden Northern sunrise.

The light woke Forollkin. He got up and surveyed the country ahead. On bleak grey hills mile upon mile of gaunt trees stood sentinel against the snowline.

They had rations left for three or four days.

"I wish to Zeldin we knew how long it will take us to reach Tir-Zulmar," Forollkin said aloud.

"Elmandis only said 'follow the river'," answered Kerish; "that *must* be all we have to do."

So they followed the river as it dwindled into a mountain stream.

Kerish never remembered much about that journey except the inescapable cold. No cloak could keep out the icy wind. When they did find enough wood for a fire it never gave enough heat to drive the aching coldness from their hands and feet. There was little for Forollkin to shoot. Once Gidjabolgo found some berries but he crammed them in his mouth before the others saw them. Lilahnee's ribs were showing through her fur. She growled when the Prince tried to stroke her but she would not leave them.

On the fourth day they finished the last of their provisions and the next evening they reached the snowline. Forollkin knew they must turn back, but perhaps it was already too late. Kerish looked like a walking ghost.

"We can't go on," Forollkin shouted against the wind. "We must go back down among the trees, or we'll freeze."

"No, Forollkin, we *must* go on. The river is still there beneath the snow. We're nearly at the end. I know we are."

Kerish began to struggle uphill, though the snow was knee-deep in places. Lilahnee followed, sniffing suspiciously at the strange new whiteness.

"Kerish, come back! It's nearly dark and you can see there's a storm rising."

Forollkin stopped shouting and started in pursuit. Gidjabolgo slumped down on the edge of the snow. It had begun to snow heavily and the wind caught the thick flakes and threw them in the travellers' faces.

Half-blinded, Forollkin lost sight of Kerish and the shriek of the rising storm drowned his shouting. He blundered into a deep drift and as he struggled out again his sodden clothes froze to his body.

Further up the slope Kerish forced himself on until his knees suddenly gave way and he collapsed into the snow. Exhausted as he was, the Prince continued to crawl upwards. His hands were so cold he could no longer feel them.

He wanted to lie down and rest but he knew that that would be fatal. His eyelashes were freezing together but he still looked up into the driving snow.

A little way above him a silver light was shining through the blizzard. He had an odd conviction that it was shining for him, to guide him to the source of the river. Once he reached it, he knew he would be safe, but he couldn't do it. He was too cold, too tired.

"Zeldin, Imarko, help me. I must do it. I must."

Kerish's breath frosted as he spoke but he crawled on and the light was nearer. As the snow swirled away from him for a few seconds he saw that the light came from a silver door in the mountainside.

I must be dead, thought Kerish calmly.

Just before he lost consciousness the Prince stretched out his hands and the tips of his fingers touched the silver gate.

# Chapter 5

The Book of the Emperors: *Sorrows*
*Though you may build your house in the furthest desert or
the highest mountain, the sorrows of the world will always
be with you. Nor can true peace be found in solitude, for it
must be shared to reach completion.*

Lapped in warmth, the Prince of the Godborn slept, high above the plains of Erandachu. When he finally stirred and opened his eyes what he saw confirmed his opinion that he was dead. Kerish lay on a low bed in a circular chamber carved from ice. The walls were translucent, glowing with changing colours as the morning sunlight filtered through. Intricate patterns were etched on the ceiling and set with ice crystals.

Kerish shivered at the room's cold beauty and sat up. Forollkin and Gidjabolgo were sleeping on either side of him, beneath coverlets of fur, and Lilahnee was sprawled across his feet.

Kerish slid out of bed. Someone had replaced his ragged travelling clothes with a soft robe of glimmering blue silk sewn with seed pearls. The floor sparkled with frost but Kerish's bare feet felt no cold. He paced across the room and found an archway hung with a jewelled curtain. Beyond lay another chamber, furnished with three chairs and a long table spread with steaming dishes of enticing food and flagons of wine. Kerish went back through the archway and shook his brother awake.

"Kerish, curse you, come back—" Forollkin stopped and stared about him. "Where in Zeldin's name are we?"

"I don't know. I've only just woken myself, but there's food in the next room."

"I remember a snowstorm," Forollkin was saying bemusedly, "and falling into a deep drift and ..."

"Waking up here," finished Kerish, "dressed like a Loshite."

Forollkin realized that he was wearing a clinging robe of amber silk.

"Blood of Idaala! If you think I'm going to wear this cobweb . . ."

"It's either that or go naked. There's no sign of our luggage."

The Prince crossed to the third bed and jabbed the snoring Gidjabolgo in the ribs. He woke, gabbling in Forgish, and then stared mutely at the icy beauty of the room. Forollkin had climbed out of bed and was pacing the frosted floor.

"I can't understand why I'm so warm—and look at Lilahnee. How she's grown! As for you, Kerish, you were thin as an arrow and now you look strong and well."

Kerish laughed. "I'm certainly plumper than I was." He ran his hands down his body but stopped with a jerk at his waist. "Forollkin, the keys, they're gone!" The brothers searched both rooms but the golden chain and its keys had vanished. Gidjabolgo watched them with interest.

"What are these keys that cause my Masters such concern?"

"The keys to a prison," answered Kerish curtly.

"Perhaps our host, whoever he is, took them with our clothes, meaning no harm," suggested Forollkin.

"Perhaps, but he left me the Jewel of Zeldin," said Kerish. "And if our host is the sorcerer of Tir-Zulmar he would have every reason to steal the keys."

"Well, we'll think better on a full stomach," proposed Forollkin. "You did say there was food."

The food had no smell but it tasted ordinary enough and the travellers ate in greedy silence for a while. Then Gidjabolgo asked, "What is this prison with many doors?"

Kerish didn't answer but Forollkin said, "Since you're to travel with us, you might as well know. Kerish and I were sent by the Emperor of Galkis to seek seven keys. Each of the keys is guarded by a sorcerer but our scriptures say that they unlock the gates to a prison where the Saviour of Galkis is kept. Once he is free, he will help our Empire in its darkest hour."

"Where is this prison?" asked the Forgite.

Forollkin looked down at his plate, "We don't know."

"Well who imprisons this saviour," persisted Gidjabolgo, "and why?"

"I don't know," said Forollkin wearily. "I don't even know if there is a Saviour or a prison, but we're going to obey the Emperor's orders."

"Obey a madman? Then you are greater fools than I took you for." Gidjabolgo's voice was harsh with contempt. "A saviour! Mere babble to lull fools into keeping quiet while their throats are cut."

Forollkin stared at him and said quietly, "What do you worship, Gidjabolgo?"

"Myself," rasped the Forgite. "Like any wise man."

"Well you don't seem to have grown rich on the offerings . . ."

Suddenly Kerish put down his cup and got up from the table. He paced round the room, searching for a way out. "Forollkin, we must find the keys!"

He struck angrily at the ice and the colours faded from the wall. The ice became wholly transparent and then melted away. A long passage was revealed, shaped in green ice like an avenue of weeping trees.

"A sorcerer's citadel if ever I saw one," growled Gidjabolgo, but his eyes were round with wonder. Kerish hurried back to the other room and woke Lilahnee. Her large fierce presence was comforting as they came out into the passage. They walked slowly and cautiously and only their footfalls disturbed the silence.

They rounded a corner and were suddenly confronted with a huge window of clear ice. Kerish gasped at what it showed. Through drifting clouds they glimpsed the mountainside dropping sheerly down to the shadowy foothills three thousand feet below. Behind the window, filling a vast cavern, was a great crystal globe—the lamp of Tir-Zulmar that Kerish had mistaken for the Morning Star.

They stood for a long time between the lamp and the window before continuing their search. The travellers wandered through dozens of rooms cut from ice and rock; all beautiful, silent and empty. The Prince began to feel that each chamber had only just been vacated. They walked more quickly, dissolving fragile walls with the touch of a hand and once Kerish thought he saw through the thin ice a shadow moving away from them. Finally they came to a spiral staircase of black ice.

"Shall we go up?" asked Forollkin.

"One slip and we'll break our necks," muttered Gidjabolgo, but Kerish had already started to climb with Lilahnee at his heels. The others followed; neither of them wanted to be left alone with the eerie beauty of Tir-Zulmar.

They climbed for almost half an hour to reach a silver door studded with black gems. Lilahnee flattened her ears and gave a chilling howl.

"Do we go back?" panted Gidjabolgo.

"No." Kerish sounded strangely excited. "We're close now."

"I say we go back," declared Forollkin. "Look at Lilahnee!"

The marsh cat crouched at the top of the stairs, the fur stiff along her spine and her eyes wide and dark, but Kerish had already opened the black door.

He walked through it into a thick mist. After a few paces he stopped and turned. "Forollkin? Gidjabolgo?" They answered, but Kerish could not see them. He knew that they were close, but so was something else, the presence that he had sensed moving away from them. Now it was motionless; waiting. Impulsively, Kerish shouted: "Sorcerer of Tir-Zulmar, by the Seven Keys and the Seven Gates, I conjure you to appear!"

Each of the travellers saw a patch of mist coalesce into a pale shape. Its skin was transparent and the bones gleamed through. Its face was a mask of ice with jewels for eyes. Its voice was cold and cruel and from the sorcerer's crown hung gems like crystallized eyes, still human and desperate.

"Death is the only fate for those who pass the silver door into the Hall of Mists. The flesh shall be frozen from you; your bones shall be clothed with ice; your eyes shall be jewels in my crown."

The creature of bone and ice moved towards Gidjabolgo and the Forgite fled down the black stairs. Then it turned on Forollkin.

"Kerish, run!" The Prince dreamily shook his head. Forollkin wavered for a moment and then ran after Gidjabolgo. At every step he heard behind him the snap of bone on ice.

In the Hall of Mists the sorcerer approached Kerish. "Such eyes are fit even for Tir-Zulmar's crown!"

Long fingers reached out to tear them from the Prince's face. Kerish was repeating over and over again the lesson of Tir-Racneth. "Illusion, illusion, this is illusion. It cannot hurt me."

He forced himself to stand still. "I have true sight, my father's gift; let me see the true shape of the sorcerer of Tir-Zulmar!"

In a swirl of mist the terrible figure vanished. In its place stood a woman with frozen teardrops shining on her pale cheek. For a second they stared at each other and then, with a sweep of her glittering cloak, the woman turned and the mists closed about her.

The Prince tried to follow but he could hear no footsteps to guide him. For a long time he stumbled through the mist without reaching the edge of the hall. Kerish jumped as something touched his leg, but the sound of purring told him it was Lilahnee. Gradually the mist began to melt away, leaving him in a huge, empty hall. Its walls were richly carved with pageants and triumphs but every relief was marred by patches of cloudy gems that seemed to spread like mildew across the ice.

At the far end of the hall Kerish found a second silver door and beyond it a stairway of milky ice. With the marsh cat padding behind he climbed the second stairs and then paused for a moment before rapping on the third door. It swung open at his touch and he walked into a circular room hewn from black rock. Seven windows were set in the rock but they were shuttered and barred with silver. On a throne in the centre of the room sat the sorceress of Tir-Zulmar and in her right hand was a golden chain with two gold keys.

Kerish had never seen a lady so beautiful, nor one who looked so sad. Her silver hair was woven with ice flowers. No traces of age marked her snowy skin but her green eyes seemed immeasurably deep. Clothed in white and silver, she was taller than the Prince and very slender. Her voice was as cool and beautiful as the snows of her mountain citadel.

"Prince of the Godborn, Sendaaka of Tir-Zulmar welcomes you and gives you back what is worthily yours."

Kerish knelt to take the golden chain and fasten it around his waist. "Lady Sendaaka, if I am worthy to wear two keys, might I not be worthy to wear three?"

"You have courage and clear sight," said Sendaaka gently, "but do you have enough strength to carry all the world's hopes and sorrows? Prince, I have lived for generations and many have called me wise. This is my advice. Return the keys and go back to Galkis and to your father, before it is too late."

"My father needs me?"

Sendaaka's green eyes seemed to look through the Prince and far beyond him. "Each day he walks alone in his garden; each night he kneels by a white sarcophagus, praying for his son. It is rumoured in the Inner City that the Third Prince is dead; drowned in the marshes of Lan-Pin-Fria. The Emperor knows that he would have felt his son die, but he is afraid for you."

"The High Priest will comfort him," said Kerish unsteadily.

"Lord Izeldon is angry with his Emperor," answered the sorceress. "Your sister Zyrindella begs to be reunited with her son and she has appealed to the Galkian law that forbids a mother to be separated from her child."

"That is the law," agreed Kerish, "but the High Priest wanted to keep Kor-li-Zynak safe in the temple, where Zyrindella couldn't use him to plot against the throne. He thinks she means to make her son Emperor . . ."

"Your father knows that she does," said Sendaaka calmly and Kerish shivered. "Yet he has upheld the justice of the Godborn. Even as we speak," murmured the sorceress, "Kor-li-Zynak is travelling north to meet his mother and since Li-Kroch refuses to be parted from the child, Zyrindella will have her husband back too."

Kerish remembered Li-Kroch cowering before his wife's anger in the temple of Zeldin, drugged with zigul and threatened with the rope.

"So each day," continued Sendaaka, "the Emperor walks in his gardens brooding on what he has done."

"Do you know what will happen now in Galkis?"

Sendaaka studied the Prince's anxious face. "I cannot see far into that darkness, but it is far enough for me to say to you—go home."

Kerish knelt with bowed head and did not answer.

"It is my custom," she went on, "to help all those who reach my gate. I took you from the snow and healed you. I have surrounded you with warmth so you do not feel the eternal cold of my citadel. Now I will give you all the provisions you need for the journey south."

"But it is winter," began Kerish.

"You have slept for longer than you think. The wind-flowers are blooming on the plains of Erandachu; it is spring. For the third time I say—go home."

Kerish stood up. "Lady Sendaaka, I am grateful for all your kindness. Tell me, why did you appear to us in such an ugly shape?"

"It is three hundred years since any man saw my face," answered the sorceress. "I swore that none should do so until they had outstared horror."

"Your vow robs the world of much beauty," murmured Kerish.

Sendaaka rose from her chair and paced away from the Prince. When she spoke again her face was towards one of the shuttered windows. "Though I have lived alone for so long, I have not forgotten how little men's flattery means. Go to your friends; you will leave tomorrow. Do not set foot on the white stairs again, or I will freeze you to them."

"No, Sendaaka."

The sorceress stiffened but Kerish hurried on. "I will not go until you tell me why spring never comes to Tir-Zulmar, and who you weep for."

"I weep for no man." She turned her proud face towards him. "I am no longer human. My tears would freeze before they fell."

"Yet this citadel is built of frozen tears," said Kerish. "I see its beauty, but I feel its sadness. Lady . . . can I not help you?"

Sendaaka heard the earnestness in his voice and Kerish did not flinch from her searching gaze. "I will tell you why Tir-Zulmar weeps, then you will understand that you cannot help me and go home. Sit for a while and listen; you too, furred one."

Lilahnee had been crouched in the doorway, ready to spring to the Prince's defence. Now she padded into the room and curled up at the sorceress' feet.

"Many centuries ago, I was born on the island of Gannoth; the only daughter of its Prince. My father was an ardent scholar and he taught me well. I spent all my waking hours studying ancient wisdoms until there were few in Zindar as learned as I was, and none who knew as much of star-lore. But then . . ."

Sendaaka's long fingers tugged at a strand of her silver hair. "Then a young nobleman of Seld came to my father's court, seeking knowledge. His name was Saroc. When we first met I asked him something about his writings, but he stared at me and did not answer. Then he asked me to forgive him and said that he had expected wisdom but not so much beauty."

The sorceress bent to stroke Lilahnee. "We were married that autumn and he took me to Seld, to his castle near the White Hills. After two years a daughter was born to us and we were very happy. Both of us continued our studies, sometimes together but often apart. Both of us searched for the Keys of Power and endured the Seven Ordeals . . . Prince, there is a great deal that I cannot tell you, but when our daughter was fifteen, both of us won the right to a key.

"Now my husband is a proud man and when he understood that I was his equal in this as in everything, he was not pleased. Then we learned that if both of us took a key, we should have to part for ever. If only one of us accepted a key then we could live together in one citadel for ever."

Bitter memories darkened Sendaaka's voice. "I would have given up my key unasked. I had opened my lips to speak when Saroc demanded that I renounce my power. Such was my anger, I told him that I cared only for the key and immortality. I departed for my new realm, taking our daughter with me. We travelled slowly north, for I thought he would come after us, but I have not seen Saroc since that day."

Kerish watched tears spill from Sendaaka's eyes and freeze on her cheeks like frosty jewels. "So I came to the mountains and in the first glory of my power I built Tir-Zulmar. It was fire amongst the ice, high summer amongst eternal winter. My daughter lived with me, my joy and comfort; immortal too as long as she kept within my citadel. Then Saroc sent messengers, asking that she might come and live with him for a time. I had no right to refuse. I surrounded her with protective spells and sent her to her father, but his care did not equal mine. Our daughter died beyond his citadel . . . I cannot speak of it."

Kerish took Sendaaka's cold hands. "Lady, your husband *has* wronged you, but surely after centuries of loneliness he will be more than ready to acknowledge you his equal. If you renounced your key to show him . . ."

"Never!" The sorceress dashed the tears from her cheek and they shattered on the floor. "I will never crawl to Saroc and beg to be his wife again; if he is sorry, let him come to me."

Kerish thought for a moment and then said carefully, "I am sure Saroc longs to come, but is afraid to seek your forgiveness, afraid to be refused."

"What do you know of Saroc?"

"I know what a man's pride is, and the harm it can cause," said Kerish ruefully. "Lady Sendaaka, prove yourself the greater by showing him the way."

"I would renounce my key," murmured the sorceress, "if he surrendered his. If he still loves me let him prove that he would rather die with me than endure immortality alone."

"Give me your key and I will go to Seld and speak to Saroc," promised Kerish. "I won't tell him that I have the key, only that you are lonely. I will send him to fetch you home from Tir-Zulmar. If he does not come, I swear that I will return your key and abandon my quest."

"The Citadel of Saroc is guarded by terror." There was a tremor in Sendaaka's cool voice. "You would never reach him."

"I cannot go back to Galkis until we have tried," said Kerish firmly.

"And what if you are killed on the journey?" asked Sendaaka. "And my key is lost?"

90

"Would age and death be so terrible to you?" demanded Kerish.

The sorceress did not answer.

"Would it, Lady?"

"Prince, I must study the stars."

Sendaaka seemed restored to icy calm. "Return when it is day again and bring your brother."

Kerish bowed. Lilahnee still seemed to be asleep beside the sorceress' chair.

"Lady Sendaaka, I'm not sure if I can find my way back."

"Go to the foot of the white stairs. Set your hands against the wall and close your eyes."

The sorceress walked towards one of the barred windows. "Go quickly!"

At the foot of the stairs the Prince braced himself against the ice. The moment he closed his eyes, Kerish had the sensation of falling very fast; like the sudden drop he had sometimes experienced on the edge of sleep. He could no longer feel ice against his palms. He imagined wildly that he was alone with utter nothingness and that the world would be recreated when he opened his eyes. But he was not alone; someone was calling his name.

"Kerish, is it really you?"

Forollkin gripped his brother's arm. "Get away from the wall. I can see it through the ice!"

Shocked by the fear in his brother's face, Kerish closed Forollkin's eyes with his fingertips. "No, there's nothing there. It's only an illusion."

"I saw it," muttered Gidjabolgo, "coming to tear out my eyes!"

"Believe me, there is nothing evil in Tir-Zulmar, nothing to hurt us."

The prince's calm voice reached the two men and suddenly Forollkin couldn't remember why he had been so afraid or how he had got back to their chamber.

"An illusion?"

Kerish smiled at his brother. "An illusion sent by the sorceress of Tir-Zulmar to test our resolution."

"What sorceress?" Forollkin still sounded dazed.

"Lady Sendaaka, mistress of Tir-Zulmar," answered

91

Kerish. "You are to meet her at daybreak and I think she will give me her key."

"What about the other two?"

"I'm wearing the chain again. Can't you see?"

"I don't have your eyes, thank Zeldin," said Forollkin.

"Hark at our brave Captain." Gidjabolgo had also recovered. "Obviously it's easier to snap at a Prince than to find the courage to face a sorceress."

Forollkin turned and struck Gidjabolgo a blow that drove the Forgite's lips against his teeth and left them bruised and bleeding. Kerish darted between them.

"Forollkin, stop it!"

Forollkin shook his brother off and stalked into the sleeping chamber. Kerish dipped a napkin in a cup of wine and bathed Gidjabolgo's mouth. "You brought that on yourself."

"I am not complaining," mumbled the Forgite. "And were my words worse than the thoughts behind your smile?"

Kerish let the napkin drop and walked into the other room. Moonlight flooded through the walls, silvering the ice. Forollkin lay on his bed, one arm across his face. "Do you know it's spring outside?" said Kerish.

"It can't be." Forollkin's voice was muffled.

Kerish sat down on the end of the bed and said carelessly, "Well, perhaps you will believe it from the Lady Sendaaka. Remember, brother, you will need your courtly manners."

Forollkin snorted and turned over and Kerish relaxed.

At dawn, the Prince was woken by golden light filtering through the walls. He sat up, blinking at the mounting brightness and woke Forollkin. In the next room they found Gidjabolgo slumped over the table. Anxious to be rid of their obligation, they shook him awake.

"The sorceress did not summon you," said Kerish, "but I think you should come with us."

Gidjabolgo bowed, the bruises dark against his sallow skin. "I thank my Masters for keeping their word."

The apology Forollkin was about to make stuck in his throat and Kerish stepped up to the wall, hoping that he knew how to reach the sorceress. "Close your eyes and take hold of my arms."

He pictured the silver door that led to the white stairway and closed his own eyes. Again there was a violent jolt and Kerish felt as if his body had spread out like a net and the world was passing through him. Then a finger of mist chilled his forehead.

"We're here now. You can both let go."

Kerish ordered the Forgite to wait at the head of the stairs and Gidjabolgo squatted down on the top step. He knocked on the silver door and it swung open. The black room had changed; it was lit now by hundreds of stars glowing on the dark ceiling. Forollkin forgot his nervousness at the sight of a lovely woman seated on a throne of ice, with a green marsh cat curled at her feet.

Kerish bowed. "Lady Sendaaka, may I present my brother, the Lord Forollkin."

"Welcome," murmured Sendaaka.

Awkward in his silken robe, Forollkin also bowed and haltingly thanked the sorceress for her kindness. While he spoke Kerish's eyes were fixed on a small golden casket, which now stood in front of one of the barred windows. Shaken by Sendaaka's cool gaze, Forollkin was floundering, "We never expected such help ... not that we had heard any evil of you ..."

"Lady," interposed Kerish. "Have you considered my offer?"

"I have watched the stars dance," answered Sendaaka. "The light of hope is very faint but it still shines. Its reflection glimmers in your faces. I will lend you my key. Before you thank me, hear the conditions.

"You must journey to Tir-Tonar, the citadel of Saroc. If you reach the sorcerer, ask him to renounce his key and come north to Tir-Zulmar." She laid her finger like a breath of frost on Kerish's lips. "Saroc must not know that you have my key. Speak one word of it and your tongue will freeze in your mouth. If Saroc will not give up his key, you must return mine to Tir-Zulmar or die in the attempt. You will be worse than dead if you try to break your word."

"I will keep my word for its own sake, not in fear of your threats," said Kerish.

The sorceress almost smiled. "Your anger is the warmest thing in my citadel. Open the casket!" Kerish turned the second key in the golden lock and took out a third key set with a clear white gem. Then he knelt to kiss Sendaaka's hand.

"We will send you the spring."

She turned to Forollkin. "Sit beside me now; unless you are still afraid of the sorceress of Tir-Zulmar."

"Who could fear such beauty?" said Forollkin, with clumsy gallantry.

"What is more dangerous than beauty?" asked Sendaaka. "But do not be ashamed of your fear. The Prince has the gift of true sight, the heritage of the Godborn. You have a different kind of sight and a different kind of courage. Both will be needed to penetrate Tir-Tonar. For my sake, I must speed you on your way. Tomorrow your possessions shall be returned to you, together with provisions for a long journey and horses to carry them."

"Horses!" exclaimed Forollkin. "But surely the way is too steep . . ."

"My citadel has many gates," said Sendaaka. "One of them opens on to the plains. You must cross Western Erandachu and travel through the Gap of Lamoth into Seld. Ask there for directions to Tir-Tonar."

"How long will this journey take?" asked Forollkin.

Sendaaka reached down to stroke the marsh cat and her silver hair half-hid her face. "That will depend on who you meet. The plains are not empty and it would be strange if you escaped the vigilance of the Children of the Wind."

"Would these plainsmen harm us?" persisted Forollkin.

"Most tribes kill every stranger they meet," answered Sendaaka. "But they will not harm you, Kerish-lo-Taan."

The Prince did not ask her why, but the sorceress went on, "Centuries ago, I pitied the darkness in which the Erandachi lived so I walked among the tribes, appearing to certain women to teach them a more gentle wisdom. I turned their hair as silver as mine as a sign that they were truly inspired. The descendants of those women are still priestesses of their tribes and the consorts of chieftains. From time to time, men are born with silver in their hair and they are honoured as prophets of the Mountain Goddess. Even now, when the tribes are turning to the old ways again, they will honour your silver hairs."

"My mother had silver hair," said Kerish softly.

Sendaaka answered his unspoken question. "I watched her grow into beauty and courage. Taana was worthy of her fate."

"She was a slave and died young," protested Kerish.

"She was a queen and died loved," said Sendaaka. "Remember that. But now, there is a third traveller waiting at my door. Fetch him in, Forollkin."

The sorceress showed neither surprise or distaste at Gidjabolgo's appearance and greeted him courteously. "Welcome, Gidjabolgo of Forgin; I am glad that you find my citadel beautiful. What is it that you desire of me?"

The Forgite made a clumsy bow and rose with scowling face.

"Ah, perhaps you do not care to speak in front of the others," suggested Sendaaka. "It cannot be a very fierce desire."

"I will slave for you or kill for you. Name your fee," growled Gidjabolgo. "You know what I want."

"Yes, I do," agreed the sorceress placidly. "My fee is small; simply unbar that window."

She pointed to a window, opposite the silver door and set deep into the rock. Gidjabolgo almost ran to it, but before his plump fingers touched the bars Sendaaka said, "Understand me, if you open that window you will see what no human has ever seen before. You alone will know what lies beyond the Ultimate Mountains; beyond the world's end. What will you see? Strange stars? A new world? The dark pit of infinity? Open the window if you dare and learn how frail a thing our Zindar is!"

Gidjabolgo fumbled at the bars; he had only to push the shutters back to gain his heart's desire. Forollkin looked away as the Forgite raised one shaking hand.

"Come," whispered Sendaaka. "Open the window!"

Still Gidjabolgo did not move the shutter.

"Do you hesitate?" demanded the sorceress. "Then you shall never have your wish from me."

"No, I will open it," shouted Gidjabolgo but in a movement quicker than sight Sendaaka stood between the Forgite and the window.

"You shall never have it from me; ask again of Saroc. Go

now, all of you, but when my lamp is lit I shall summon you to a feast and we shall drink the cup of parting."

When she was alone the Lady of Tir-Zulmar opened the silver shutters and gazed out for a while. Then she knelt and, burying her face in Lilahnee's soft fur, wept her frozen tears.

The two Galkians walked quickly down the spiral stairway. Gidjabolgo followed with dragging steps. Kerish stopped for a moment to study a pattern of ice crystals and was suddenly struck from behind by the Forgite's full weight. He fell headlong but Forollkin was only a few steps below. He caught Kerish and stumbled back to sit down abruptly with his brother in his lap and the breath knocked out of him.

When Forollkin could speak again, he yelled at Gidjabolgo, "What in Zeldin's name do you think you're doing?"

"In Zeldin's name—nothing," said Gidjabolgo sulkily. "My foot slipped."

Trembling with shock, but quite unharmed, Kerish soothed his brother and they found their way back to their rooms.

The rest of the day was spent in listening to Forollkin's plans for the journey. Kerish was bored and Gidjabolgo sat watching them both, saying nothing. At nightfall the ice turned black but gradually the walls were pierced by points of starlight. Moonrise dissolved the last of the blackness and the travellers suddenly found themselves standing in a vast cavern that seemed to be formed of glittering snowflakes. Kerish marvelled at the intricate patterns while the others noticed a dais and four white thrones.

On one of the thrones sat Sendaaka, dressed in the pale, pleated robes of a Princess of Gannoth. "Welcome again. Sit down and I will try to entertain you as you deserve."

When the travellers were seated, Lilahnee slid out from under the table and affectionately dug her claws into Kerish's calf. The table was spread with jewelled goblets and gold and silver dishes, but all of them were empty.

"Want bloats a belly more than having," muttered Gidjabolgo.

"When men are hungry, they think only of food," said

the sorceress, "and imagine their favourite dishes spread before them. Look again, Gidjabolgo."

Sendaaka waved her hand and in front of the Forgite was a dish of tender, young thawgs, the tastiest fish in the Dirian Sea, served in a cream and wine sauce.

"And for you, Forollkin?" asked the sorceress, but before he could answer he was staring at a plump dorf, stuffed and roasted and awash with rich sauces. While his brother was still blinking in astonishment, Kerish thought up a dish of Ellerinionn fruit and a cup of nectar.

Sendaaka herself only drank water from a crystal goblet as she watched her guests eat. As Kerish picked up a glossy maroon fruit he remembered the question Forollkin had intended to ask their next sorcerer.

"Lady Sendaaka, who built the city beyond the Forbidden Hill?"

"Zindar is old and mankind is young," said the sorceress, setting down her crystal cup and staring into the clear liquid as if she could see an answer there. "There were five such cities once; now three are desolate. If you reach Gannoth, my own country, ask its Prince where the first ships sailed from and what they found in Zindar."

"But the men who built these cities . . ." began Forollkin.

"They were not men," said Sendaaka, "but creatures far more ancient and rich in power and knowledge. Yet they must have lacked wisdom, for they destroyed each other. Grief and hatred overshadow the ruins of their cities and the ancient guardians of their useless treasures keep their deadly trust."

"So that poor wretch we found must have tried to steal the treasure and was killed by its guardians," murmured Forollkin, "while the city keeps its secrets."

"Alas, it does not."

Kerish flinched at the pain in Sendaaka's voice.

"The Guardians were defeated once," said the sorceress, "by one who holds the Power of the Key: the Sorcerer King of Roac. Everything between the Forbidden Hill and the Ultimate Mountains lies within my territory, so Shubeyash came to me and humbly asked if he might study the ruined city from a safe distance. I should have listened to Elmandis' warnings but, foolishly, I believed that I could see into the King of Roac's heart. I let him wander freely in my lands.

"Shubeyash entered the city, discovered the worst of its secrets and then tried to make himself the greatest of the seven sorcerers. He failed; his body was destroyed and his Kingdom devastated." Sendaaka shuddered. "Yet because his key still lies in its casket in dark Tir-Roac, the spirit of Shubeyash is still chained to Zindar."

"Must we go to Roac?" asked Forollkin.

The sorceress nodded, white jewels glinting in her silver hair. "The key of Saroc unlocks the casket of Shubeyash; but we should not talk about your task tonight. This must be a joyful feast."

Sendaaka clapped her hands and in the same instant created a different illusion for each of her guests. Kerish's favourite stories of the Poet Emperor were acted out before him, Forollkin watched the whirling sword-dancers of Viroc and Gidjabolgo smiled at his private vision. Sendaaka could not enchant her own eyes so she stared at ice and emptiness for as long as she could bear them. Then she clapped her hands again and the illusory performers vanished.

"Tomorrow you begin your journey. The horses I will lend you know their path across the plains. Look back each night towards the mountains, and you will see my lantern shining to remind you of Tir-Zulmar."

Kerish would have knelt to kiss her hand, but with a melancholy smile and a shimmer of frost, Sendaaka faded from their sight. The snowy walls crumbled and they were back in their own rooms. As they lay down to sleep, Kerish wondered where they would wake.

Forollkin was roused by the clatter of hooves on ice. He sat up and shook Kerish and Gidjabolgo. They lay on the floor of a small cave beside a pile of luggage that included sacks of food and new clothes made from grey fur and brightly dyed leather.

When they had dressed, the travellers explored a short tunnel that led to a second, much larger, cave. Three sturdy dappled ponies and two white horses, with silver bells jangling on their purple harness, were galloping to and fro, their hot breath clouding the frosty air. Kerish smiled rapturous-

98

ly at the beautiful creatures, while Forollkin wondered how they were ever going to catch their mounts.

The Prince held out his hands and the stallions came to him, completely docile. They did not even flinch when the marsh cat paced around them, sniffing suspiciously at their legs. The ponies surrounded Gidjabolgo, almost knocking him down with their friendly nudges. He protested vigorously against mounting one of them until Forollkin enquired if the Forgite wanted to walk the length of Erandachu.

Their luggage was strapped to the broad backs of the remaining ponies and Kerish and Forollkin each chose a stallion. They trotted towards a tunnel of translucent ice that led southwards out of the cave. Gidjabolgo dug his fingers into the pony's mane, closed his eyes and kicked.

After an hour, ice turned to rock and the tunnel was lit by torches that burned with steady blue-green flames. After three hours riding they came to a silver door that opened before them and swung shut behind them. Blinking in the sunlight and buffeted by the north wind, they looked out on a vast expanse of grass and nodding flowers. Their journey across the plains of Erandachu had begun.

# Chapter 6

The Book of the Emperors: *Sorrows*
*Much may be learned from the contact of two peoples, and
more may be unlearned.*

THE great plains of Erandachu were white with windflowers. The limpid skies were darkened only by
hovering birds, solitary hunters in the vastness of the grasslands. The three riders struggled against the west wind and
a growing consciousness of solitude.

For the hundredth time that morning, Forollkin brushed
back the brown hair that whipped across his face and pointed to something. "Kerish, can you make out what that is?"

The second rider stood in his stirrups for a moment. "Just
a mound, I think, crowned with a stone."

"We'll make for it then," said Forollkin. "We should get
a good view from the top."

"What of?" snorted the third rider. "Windflowers?"

"Why, Gidjabolgo," murmured Kerish, "don't tell me
that you actually want to see other people again. I thought
you despised us all."

"So I do," answered the Forgite calmly, "but I'm bored
with your voices; I'd welcome something new to hate."

Kerish was learning to laugh at such remarks and did so
now. "Well, I fear you may find it a change for the worse.
The Erandachi have unpleasant ways of dealing with sharp-
tongued travellers."

"What Erandachi?" demanded Gidjabolgo. "If they
exist, where are they?"

"Just beyond every horizon," said Kerish.

It was over a month since they had left the Mountain gate
and in all that time they had met no-one. Once, they had
come to a place where the grass was cropped as if it had been
grazed by some huge herd. Once Kerish thought he saw a

100

rider on a horned beast, far in the distance. They had met no other signs of men's existence.

After a gentle canter they reached the mound. Harried by Lilahnee, the pack ponies trotted after them. Forollkin and Kerish dismounted; Gidjabolgo stayed hunched warily in the saddle. Someone had kept the mound free from grass, tearing it out by the roots, leaving the red earth bare. Forollkin knelt to examine the soil.

"Look, Kerish, men have been here, and recently too."

The Prince had run up the mound to study the rock at its summit. A long time ago, to judge from the weathering, someone had scratched the crude images of a man with a spear catching hold of a woman with stars in her hair.

"What's this, an Erandachi temple?" asked Forollkin, striding up to join his half-brother.

"A holy place, certainly," answered Kerish.

"But with no priests and no worshippers," said Forollkin; "perhaps Gidjabolgo is right - the Erandachi don't exist."

"If they don't, then neither should I," murmured the Prince.

"Kerish, if you wanted to pause and search for your mother's people . . ."

"No."

Kerish didn't look into his brother's worried grey eyes. He gestured at the pack ponies. "Shall we stay here to eat, or are we not allowed a noonday meal any more?"

Their supplies would soon be finished and they would have to rely on what Forollkin could shoot.

"Not after today, unless we care to eat Lilahnee's leavings."

At the sound of her name, the marsh cat licked Forollkin's hand with her barbed tongue.

"Ouch, demon cat, you'll take my skin off!"

He pushed her away, so Lilahnee entwined herself round Kerish's legs until he knelt to stroke her soft green fur.

Forollkin shouted to Gidjabolgo to unload the last bundle of food. He left the horses cropping the lush grass, knowing they would not stray far.

Gidjabolgo doled out three meagre portions of dried fruit and unhooked a flask of wine from his saddle-bag. The travellers sat down at the base of the mound, grateful for a partial shelter from the wind.

Forollkin took a sip of wine, swilling it round his mouth to get rid of the cloying after-taste of the fruit.

"What I wouldn't give for a well-roasted garpin!" he declared, with a sigh that was only half-mock.

"Are you regretting you came, brother?"

"No," answered Forollkin seriously. "I have travelled a long way from Galkis and from what I was there. Elmandis and Sendaaka have taught me that the world is wider than I thought, and full of terrors. I'm not as sure of anything as I was but I'm beginning to see wonders as well as terrors. Perhaps by the time we get back to Galkis I'll feel more like one of the Godborn."

"And I less," answered Kerish, but he was smiling in pure delight. "You may make a warrior of me yet."

"I'll pledge that," said Forollkin, but as he raised the flask, Lilahnee streaked down the slope, the hair stiff along her spine.

"What is it . . . danger?"

They all knew it would be rash to ignore the marsh cat's warning. Gidjabolgo moved towards the horses but Kerish raced up the mound and stood, silhouetted incautiously, against the skyline. He saw at once that it was too late for escape.

Barely a quarter of a mile away was a hunting party of some twenty Erandachi warriors, riding long-horned, russet-furred Irollga. Their hoof-beats were muffled by the thick grasses but they were making straight for the mound.

Forollkin joined his brother and immediately reached for his bow.

Kerish shook his head. "We must show that we are peaceful—and Sendaaka promised that the Erandachi would respect the silver in my hair."

"She also told us that they kill strangers," said Forollkin grimly, but he stood motionless.

Gidjabolgo looked up at them, bewildered.

The Erandachi wore sleeveless tunics of green and cloaks of dazzling scarlet. Their braided hair jangled with ornaments of carved bone and each man had a short spear in one hand and a whip coiled round the other. They had obviously seen the travellers for the leading rider shouted something and the spears were raised.

Gidjabolgo stumbled up the slope to join the Galkians.

The Erandachi circled the mound. At a single command the Irollga stood with their horned heads lowered and the first rider dismounted and walked to the edge of the grass.

Kerish guessed him to be about forty years old, since there were strands of grey in the chestnut braids and his pale golden skin was deeply scored.

Forollkin, noting the breadth of the man's shoulders and the obvious strength of his arms and thighs, guessed he would still be a hard opponent in a wrestling bout.

Both the serenely arrogant bearing and the bronze weapons and ornaments marked him out as a chieftain.

He assessed Forollkin and Gidjabolgo with a brief glance but looked long and hard at Kerish before he spoke.

"Stranger, why do you tread on soil sacred to the Mountain Goddess, where only her Torgi may walk?"

The accent was strange, but the man was speaking Zindaric and Kerish understood him.

"Because I bear the mark of the Goddess," he answered, "and we are under Her protection."

This reply seemed to satisfy the Chieftain. He nodded to his men to lower their spears, and spoke again.

"What is your tribe, stranger? Why have you left your circle?"

"My father is a Lord of Galkis, far in the East," said Kerish hesitantly, "but my mother came from Erandachu; her name was Taana, she . . ."

There was a murmur of surprise from the Erandachi and the Chieftain paced forward.

"When did your mother come to the land of the Galkis? How many winters?"

Kerish thought for a moment. "Twenty-two."

"And she is dead?"

"Yes."

"Come to me."

Kerish obeyed and the Chieftain touched the silver streak in Kerish's dark hair.

"Such eyes," he said. "The eyes are strange but you are hers and I take you into our circle, the circle of Tayeb."

103

He cupped his hands over Kerish's heart and the Erandachi shouted in salute or welcome.

"But who are these?" asked Tayeb. "It is our law to kill strangers who see our holy places."

Kerish beckoned to Forollkin.

"This is the son of my father."

"Then he is of our circle too."

Tayeb held his hands over Forollkin's heart for a moment.

"And the ugly one?"

"Gidjabolgo, our travelling companion."

"He is not of your kin?" asked Tayeb.

The Prince shook his head.

"Then he is not ours and he has defiled the Holy Place."

Tayeb summoned one of his men, who slid off his Irollga and calmly raised a spear to plunge it into Gidjabolgo.

"No!" Kerish stepped into the path of the barbed spear as it thrust forward. With an oath Tayeb pushed the man aside. The spear flew crookedly from his hand and thudded into the ground an inch from the Prince's foot.

Forollkin saw the anger in Tayeb's face, but before he could move the Chieftain had seized Kerish by the wrists and slapped him hard across the cheek.

The Prince gasped and nearly fell. "I have a right to defend my companion!"

"To speak in his defence, yes," answered Tayeb, loosening his painful grip, "but not risk your life! You belong now to the tribe. We have only two Torgi and your life is precious. If you will not guard your body from foolish risks, you will be punished until you learn."

"You must not hurt Gidjabolgo," said Kerish stubbornly, "he is my servant, he belongs to me. You should respect that."

One of the tribesmen spoke quietly to the Chieftain. "There is a use the ugly one could be put to at the Great Gathering."

Tayeb frowned. "The Council shall decide; until then he shall be a slave of our circle. You, kinsman . . ." he turned to Forollkin. "You have no scarlet cloak and your hair is not braided, and yet you carry weapons. Do you claim the status of a warrior?"

"Yes, among my own people I am judged a warrior," answered Forollkin firmly.

Tayeb nodded but the small, red-haired tribesman who had spoken about Gidjabolgo looked Forollkin insolently up and down and said: "His weapons are strange; let him sleep in the tents of the women or the old men."

"He shall be tested, Enecko," promised Tayeb, "his skills will be judged by all the tribe."

Enecko smiled, as if he had won a point in some long-standing competition, and bowed to his Chieftain.

"Mount your beasts," ordered Tayeb. "We shall return to our tents and—" The Chieftain spun round as every Irollga bucked and brayed.

Lilahnee, who had been sitting quietly in the long grass, had suddenly left her hiding place. She bounded across to Kerish, who hastily put his arms round her to protect the marsh cat from raised spears.

Tayeb had drawn his bronze knife, but now he rammed it back into its sheath.

"This creature is yours?"

"She travels with us," said Kerish.

Tayeb knelt beside Lilahnee.

"She is like the great white hunting cats that kill young Irollga, but she is smaller and I have never seen fur of such a colour."

"She comes from the marsh lands," explained Kerish, "and her name is Lilahnee."

Tayeb smiled suddenly. "She is beautiful."

He stroked her head and after a moment Lilahnee's growl softened into a purr.

Then Tayeb got swiftly to his feet and ordered his men to bring round the horses. Kerish glanced at his brother who shook his head, very slightly. For the moment there was nothing they could do but submit to the Chieftain.

When everyone was mounted, Tayeb called to the Prince to ride beside him. Kerish was fascinated by the Chieftain's sturdy, long-furred Irollga and the ornaments dangling from its leather collar and painted horns.

Tayeb was no less interested in the horses.

"I have seen a horse once before, though that was black.

The Chieftain of the Bokeela rode one to the Great Gathering. I know that he traded many Irollga skins for it and that it came from the East, perhaps from your Galkis. Our Torga was right to say that everything about you would be strange."

"Your Torga . . .?"

"She dreamed that we should find a Torgu in the Holy Place, sent by the Goddess in answer to my prayers."

"So you came to meet us?"

"Yes, though many did not believe, and even I doubted."

Kerish tried to take in the implications of what Tayeb was saying. "Why did you doubt your Torga? Has she never had a true dream before?"

"Only rarely, like all Torgi in these times; besides," Tayeb's voice softened, "she is my daughter. It is hard to believe that your own child can be touched by the Goddess."

"I understand. But why did the others not believe?"

Tayeb scowled. "You will find that not all our tribe revere the Goddess, or worship the Hunter of Souls in the new ways. Some murmur that the Goddess has left us and will never come down from the High Places again. They will show you little respect if my dagger is not near, but that shall soon be changed. Kinsman, what name have your father's people given you?"

"Kerish, Kerish-lo-Taan. My brother is Forollkin."

Tayeb repeated the names slowly.

"The name of Taana's first son should be Talvek. Your brother must have a tribe name too, but that can be chosen after the Testing."

Kerish began to ask about the Testing but they were abruptly challenged by three mounted warriors.

"Who comes to the tents of the Sheyasa?"

"The Chieftain of the Sheyasa," called Tayeb.

Staring at the strangers, the three sentries lowered their spears.

It was the first of many challenges, and a mile further on, just over a slight rise, Kerish saw the vast herd that the sentries were guarding. The gentle females, kept for their milk, were grazing freely, but the fierce Irollga bulls were tethered, and the geldings, soon to be broken for riding, were kept in makeshift pens. Beyond the herd were pitched circle upon circle of brightly dyed leather tents. The Erandachi dismounted and, in spite of the Galkians' protests, the horses were taken away to graze with the Irollga.

Tayeb led the travellers up one of the muddy avenues that went deep into the Sheyasa encampment. Women, old men and children peered from their tents, or left their cooking fires to stare at the strangers or exclaim over the marsh cat.

Tayeb pointed at Forollkin. "Take him to the tents of the warriors and prepare him for the Testing."

"No, I will stay with my brother," said Forollkin.

"You will see him before evening," answered the Chieftain and gestured to his men.

Two of them grabbed Forollkin's shoulders and pushed him through the entrance of a large scarlet tent. Kerish heard his brother arguing angrily as Tayeb hurried them on.

Finally they stopped in what seemed to be the centre of the encampment; a circle of beaten earth, surrounded by squat blue tents patterned with many-coloured felts and hung with strips of carved bone.

"Kinsman, we will drink together in my tent," said Tayeb. "Take the slave to his place."

Gidjabolgo was seized and tethered by a leather thong about his ankle to a pole standing outside one of the tents.

"He may enter your tent if you need him," said Tayeb, "but he cannot stray far."

Gidjabolgo yelled abuse and tugged at the thong but Kerish was too worried about Forollkin to protest for long.

He found himself pushed through the flap of a large tent, divided into several rooms by embroidered hangings. There was no furniture, only pelts on the hide-covered floor and hanging lamps that burned Irollga fat and gave out an unpleasant smell and a wavering light.

Kerish copied Tayeb and sat down cross-legged on one of the thick furs. Almost immediately a woman entered, carrying two bronze cups, filled with fermented Irollga milk flavoured with herbs. She knelt gracefully, her braided hair brushing the ground, and set down the cups.

She was not young and had never been beautiful but her

calm grey eyes and the smile twitching at her lips attracted Kerish.

"Here is the Torgu of Gwerath's dream," Tayeb was saying. "Kerish-lo-Taan, this is Eamey, the first woman of my tent."

Eamey bowed, and made the sign of a circle with her hands. After a moment, Kerish did the same.

"Welcome, tribesman." Her voice was low and resonant.

"It is as a kinsman of my circle that you should welcome him," said Tayeb. "Taana lived long enough after her circle was broken to bear a son."

"She is dead?" asked Eamey. "I have often prayed that the spear of the Hunter brought her a swift death."

"My mother died loved and honoured," said Kerish. "You knew her?"

Tayeb spoke first to Eamey, "Fetch my daughter," and then to Kerish: "Taana was my only sister."

"Your sister!"

Tayeb smiled and lifted his cup. "Gwerath dreamed well and I praise the Goddess for sending home my sister-son. Our circle is complete again."

He drank and the Prince also swallowed a mouthful of the sour liquid.

"Uncle ..." Kerish savoured the word, "Uncle, my brother must not be harmed."

"He looks strong," said Tayeb, "he will be accepted, never fear."

"Accepted by whom?"

"By the warriors of our tribe. Is it different in your father's tribe?"

"Tayeb, everything is different in my father's circle. I know nothing of your tribe or its customs."

"Nothing?" Tayeb put down his cup. "Then my daughter must teach you. Knowledge does not matter as long as the power is present and no-one could deny that you belong to the Goddess. Did She send a dream to guide you home?"

"No. Uncle, you must understand, we didn't mean to come here and we cannot stay here long ..."

Tayeb smiled. "You will stay and learn to understand

Her will for you. The circle cannot be broken. The Hunter of Souls has lowered his spear."

Before Kerish could ask who the Hunter was, Tayeb had risen to greet a young girl who threw her arms about his neck.

"Do you doubt my dreams now, father?"

Her grave face and the proud tilt of her chin were belied by the glee in her voice.

Tayeb pushed her gently away. "Your dream did not tell us the best news; that we should be welcoming your cousin."

"Cousin!" She turned and stared, unabashed, at Kerish.

He stared back and judged that Gwerath was a little younger than himself. She was dressed like a boy and wore a bone dagger at her waist; but her hair, a tangled mass of purest silver, fell unchecked to the small of her back.

Kerish had barely time to take in the honey-coloured skin, the large grey eyes and the short nose, slightly crooked where it had once been broken, before Gwerath was kneeling before him and placing her hands in a circle over her heart.

"Welcome, kinsman," she said. "You look just like you did my dream. I told you about the eyes, didn't I, father? Purple and gold and black!"

"You also told me of two gold and purple birds fighting over a silver feather drifting on the wind, and where are they?"

The bubbling spring of Gwerath's laughter suddenly ran dry and Kerish was sorry for her.

"No doubt it was the symbol of some great truth, cousin."

"You are skilled at interpreting dreams? That is good," said Tayeb. "Gwerath, take your cousin to his tent and see that he has the proper robes. I will fetch you to the Testing when it is time."

"Oh cousin, what a beautiful creature, and the gold of its eyes!" Fearlessly, Gwerath knelt to caress the marsh cat.

Lilahnee's tail thwacked impatiently but she let herself be petted.

"Daughter!"

"Oh yes, come, cousin . . . I don't know your name . . ."

"Kerish."

They left the Chieftain's quarters and Gwerath led Kerish to a blue tent lavishly equipped with cushions and furs. The Prince's luggage was piled in one corner and some strange clothes and ornaments had been laid across a straw pallet.

"See, I have prepared everything. I knew you would come," announced Gwerath. "The Goddess doesn't send me many dreams but I was sure about this one. You have brought some wonderful things with you. Are they really from Galkis? Is it true that a great Chieftain lives there in a city all made of gold?"

Kerish was amused but tried not to show it.

"Well, the walls of the Inner City are covered with sheets of gold, so men call it Golden Galkis."

"You've seen it, you've really been there?"

"I have lived there all my life," Kerish assured her, "until we began this journey."

"Oh cousin, there is so much I want to ask you, but there's no time now. Here are the clothes you must wear."

She picked up a soft white and blue robe, a leather tabard and a fillet sewn with horn beads. "Shall I knot your hair for you? I can never do mine without help."

Kerish gently refused.

"Then I'll help you dress," offered Gwerath.

"No, I thank you, no."

Gwerath still showed no sign of leaving, so Kerish asked: "Do you not have to robe for the Testing?"

"Oh yes, I suppose I must, or I will be late and my father will be angry. My tent is opposite yours, cousin, if you need me."

When she had gone Kerish struggled to tie the fillet round his unruly hair, stripped off his travelling clothes and put on the robes of a Torgu of the Sheyasa.

Weapons were offered to Forollkin but he preferred to keep his own sword, knife and bow. He resisted attempts to braid his hair, drank a bowl of Irollga milk, wished he hadn't and sat worrying about Kerish until three warriors were sent to fetch him.

Forollkin was taken to the edge of the camp where the fiercest young bulls were penned, bellowing and stamping

110

and rolling their small yellow eyes at the noisy crowd. Round the pens were gathered almost all of the tribe; scarlet-cloaked warriors leaning on their spears, black-robed elders, women with young children tugging at their broad skirts, collared slaves.

Above them all hung the banner of the Sheyasa, embroidered with the symbols of the tribe, a spear impaling a windflower, and suspended between two poles of precious wood from distant Seld.

The Chieftain of the Sheyasa was seated on the only stool in the whole encampment and surrounded by the Council of warriors and elders.

Among them Forollkin noted a girl with a mass of braided silver hair that pulled back her shapely head and seemed too heavy a weight for her slender neck. A girl robed in blue with a kind of restless energy about her, rare in a woman.

Beside her was Kerish.

Returning the stranger's gaze, Gwerath saw a young man who was taller than any warrior in the tribe, whose brown skin was only a shade lighter than his long loose hair, and whose eyes darkened suddenly from grey to violet.

Nothing of the tension Forollkin felt showed in his strong hands or calm face, except in a slight throbbing of the white scar on his cheek.

Tayeb, who had been talking to a group of elders, suddenly rose, took Kerish's arm and led him forward. The crowd jostled to get a better view of the strangers, and children were lifted to their parents' shoulders. The Chieftain signed for quiet.

"Tribesmen, here is Talvek-Kerish, my sister-son. Here is a new Torgu for the Sheyasa. Give him a welcome!"

There were some shouts of welcome, mainly from the women, but also murmurs of doubt and here and there the harsh sound of open hostility.

Enecko stepped forward.

"We welcome your kinsman, Tribe-leader, but how may we know that he is indeed a Torgu?"

"Have you changed eyes with your Irollga, tribesman? Can you not see the mark of the Goddess?"

"I see it, Tribe-leader, but surely he should not be

111

acknowledged as a Torgu until he has been tested. Is that not the old way, Torgu of the Hunter?"

He spoke to the frailest of the elders, an old man bowed by the weight of his black and scarlet robes and leaning on two spears.

"The old ways are dead, kinsman," muttered the Torgu, "but if the tribe will not acknowledge him he should be tested."

"What does the Torga of the Goddess say?" asked Tayeb.

"Let him be tested at the festival of the Spring Calving," answered Gwerath calmly. "Do you agree, kinsman?"

"Yes," said Kerish helplessly, unaware of what the argument was about but sensing Tayeb's anger.

"Now bring forward the other," ordered Tayeb. "Kinsman, do you still wish to claim the status of a warrior of the tribe?"

"I do," answered Forollkin steadily.

"First you must be accepted by the Bull of the Herd. Then you must show us your skill with a spear and in combat with a warrior of the Torgu's choice. You will be taken to the pen. You must kneel to Igeshu, and it is forbidden to draw weapons against him. Good fortune, kinsman, and remember," said Tayeb, much more softly, "keep very still."

The warriors led Forollkin into an empty pen and secured the gate behind him. He knelt with head bowed, concentrating on a brief, formal prayer to Imarko.

The Sheyasa crowded up to the hide ropes, silent now with expectation.

Forollkin heard the gate at the far end of the pen open and the sudden whisper of reverence and fear. Moving only his eyes Forollkin looked up.

The massive Irollga bull stood some twenty feet away, sniffing suspiciously. Its weak eyes saw Forollkin only dimly but it smelled him strongly. The bull pawed irritably at the ground and lowered its great head.

Forollkin shut his eyes, realizing that the important thing was to control the physical signs of fear that might provoke an attack. He heard the heavy tread of the animal as it moved towards him and sweat trickled down the hollow of his back.

112

It was worse not to know how close death might be.

Forollkin opened his eyes and through lowered lashes saw the huge head of the bull only a few feet away. Close enough to see the flaking paint overlaid with darker stains on the long, cruel horns; close enough to count the flowers in the incongruous garland around the creature's neck; close enough, after another moment, to feel the bull's hot breath on his face.

Forollkin closed his eyes again and tried vainly to relax the angles of his tensed body. Ponderously the creature circled him; once the thick fur brushed against Forollkin's shoulder but he did not move. Once the bull nudged him, almost gently, and the tip of one horn dug into his back. After a moment the pressure was released.

Forollkin clenched his hands, trying to stop them trembling and then Tayeb was calling to him. He looked up. The bull had wandered away and stood in a corner of the pen, ignoring him. The gate seemed a very long way off and it was not easy to turn his back on the bull and walk calmly towards it.

Forollkin fumbled with the latch, then the gate was open and he was through.

Tayeb smiled at him. "You are honoured, kinsman. Igeshu accepts you as his own."

Forollkin tried to catch his brother's eye and share his relief, but Kerish's face was impassive.

For a moment Forollkin was gripped by the absurd idea that he was looking at an empty shell, that there was nothing behind the glittering eyes. He tried to shake off the sensation and attend to what Tayeb was saying. ". . . You must strike the target between the lips."

The crowd had drawn back and the Chieftain was pointing to a hide shield fastened to a distant post and painted with a grotesque face.

Tayeb took a bone spear from the Torgu of the Hunter, who muttered a brief blessing over it.

"You have only one cast," he said and offered it to Forollkin.

The young Galkian remembered the last time he had needed to throw a spear accurately. It had nearly cost him his life.

"Tayeb, I am clumsy with the spear . . ."

"Clumsy! What is a warrior without his spears? You cannot kill a wild Irollga with a knife, unless it is already wounded . . ."

"I would kill it with this," said Forollkin loudly. He unslung his bow and drew out one of his precious store of arrows.

"You could strike the target from here with this weapon?" demanded the Chieftain.

"From twice the distance," declared Forollkin rashly.

Enecko's voice rose over the murmur of astonishment.

"This weapon is strange to our tribe and to the way of the Hunter; he should not use it."

"That is for the Council to decide," snapped Tayeb.

Elders and warriors surrounded the Chieftain, talking rapidly while the crowd grew restive and Forollkin nervously plucked at his bow-string.

"It is agreed," said Tayeb finally, "you may use your feathered sticks, from twice the distance, as you boasted."

Forollkin walked back to the edge of the pens, and turned to face the target. His bow was light and small, with a range of some hundred yards and even the best of arrows might not fly true.

As Forollkin fitted an arrow to the string Kerish's body tensed with the bow, his whole mind willing Forollkin to succeed. With graceful strength the Galkian drew back the bow and loosed a well-judged shot. The arrow sank deep into the target, between the grinning lips.

Within seconds he had put another arrow beside it and scarlet-cloaked warriors were crowding round the shield.

"Your weapon is good," said Tayeb. "Could you teach us how to use it, how to make such weapons?"

"Why yes," agreed Forollkin, "if you have the wood."

Tayeb laughed and clapped Forollkin on the shoulder.

"Do you hear, tribesmen? The Goddess has sent us a gift and Gift-bringer shall be your name, Tribesman."

"He must fight before he is proved a man."

It was the dry voice of the Torgu of the Hunter.

Tayeb nodded. "Kinsman, if you are victorious in this combat you shall sleep in the tents of the warriors and receive the warrior's portion. If you die, you shall have a warrior's funeral. Torgu of the Hunter, name his opponent."

There was an eager movement at the Torgu's side and the old man murmured: "Enecko."

"Kinsman," said Tayeb, "you may fight with spear, with dagger or with your hands: the choice is yours."

"With my hands," answered Forollkin immediately.

"You have chosen bravely," rasped the Torgu; "Enecko is the best wrestler of the tribe."

With my stars he would be, thought Forollkin and began stripping off his tunic.

# Chapter 7

The Book of the Emperors: *Promises*
*You have been taught always to think of your fellows and to*
*help them and this is good; yet I tell you that we must not*
*weave the lives of others, saying "This pattern is better than*
*another". Each man must weave his own pattern from the*
*threads that are offered him and in each man there is a place*
*where Zeldin himself does not enter unbidden.*

FOROLLKIN and Enecko laid their weapons in a heap at
Tayeb's feet. The Torgu of the Hunter briefly touched
both men with the spear in his right hand.

"Offer to the Hunter of Souls his own gifts of strength
and courage."

Enecko bowed to the Torgu and to the banner of the tribe
and Forollkin copied him.

"What are the rules of this combat?" he asked.

"Defeat your opponent," answered Tayeb grimly.
"Begin."

Forollkin had the advantage of height but, now they were
both stripped to boots and breeches, he saw that Enecko
was thickly built, with hands that looked as if they could
crush stone.

"Begin," repeated Tayeb and the Erandachi warrior
attacked, kicking Forollkin on the shin with one booted
foot.

Swearing as he hopped back, Forollkin finally realized
that this was no stately contest played to royal rules. To win
he would have to forget about courtesy. He had just time
to wish that Kerish wasn't watching before Enecko
attacked again.

Forollkin tried to back-heel his opponent, but Enecko
snatched at the Galkian's hair and pulled him off balance for
a second, while trying to knee him in the groin. Forollkin

twisted round, caught the blow on his thigh and grunted as his arms locked around Enecko's ribs. The Erandachi didn't try to remove the squeezing hands. Gasping for breath he concentrated on trying to kick Forollkin off balance again but the Galkian was in command now and with one swift, unexpected move, he dragged his opponent off his feet.

They fell together, with Forollkin on top, maintaining his cruel embrace. Then Enecko's thumb almost gouged out the Galkian's eye. Gasping from a simultaneous kick in the stomach, Forollkin turned his head and bit Enecko's hand but his grip was broken.

Enecko's muscles convulsed for a new attack and the watchers saw the two men roll over and over, struggling to do as much damage as possible to each other's close-pressed bodies.

It soon seemed that Forollkin's strength and will were failing. For a long moment he lay trapped beneath Enecko, his knuckles white with effort as he pushed vainly upwards. Then Enecko grabbed at the Galkian's hair again to jerk up his head and strike it against the ground.

With a surge of strength Forollkin arched his body, thrust upwards and wrenched himself away from Enecko's hold. He had somersaulted backwards out of reach and sprung to his feet before the Erandachi could rise.

Forollkin leapt on him, slamming his opponent into the ground with the whole weight of his body and fastening his hands around Enecko's throat.

Pinned down by Forollkin, Enecko could only wriggle like a speared fish and dig his nails into the Galkian's hands. Within a few seconds he realized that such defences were useless. Forollkin was inexorably forcing his opponent's head towards his chest, knowing that the pressure would break the man's neck.

Frantically Enecko beat his hands on the ground and Tayeb stepped forward.

"Kinsman, he asks for mercy!"

The look of fierce concentration on Forollkin's face did not alter and at any moment Tayeb expected the sickening snap of bone.

"Kinsman!"

117

Abruptly Forollkin drew back his hands, though he still knelt over his opponent.

"In the name of the tribe I desire you to yield," said Tayeb, "and preserve for us your life."

"I yield," whispered Enecko.

Forollkin sat back on his haunches, looking dazed. Enecko got unsteadily to his feet, rubbing his bruised throat.

"Tribesman, you will take your place behind the new warrior in hunt and in battle," said Tayeb, his face impassive, but it was a long moment before Enecko bowed to his Chieftain.

"Gift-bringer," Tayeb touched Forollkin's shoulder and the Galkian scrambled up to face him.

"Gift-bringer, you are welcome as a warrior, to the Sheyasa."

The Torgu of the Hunter nodded to one of his attendants who brought forward a scarlet cloak and wrapped it round Forollkin's shoulders. A second attendant lifted a scarlet fillet but the silver-haired girl suddenly snatched it from him.

"I will crown him," she declared; "he is a warrior for the Goddess."

Forollkin had to stoop for her to tie the fillet round his head.

"Welcome, kinsman," she whispered and stepped back.

"Warriors," called Tayeb, "welcome your brother."

Forollkin found himself embraced by every warrior of the Sheyasa, and last of all by Enecko: "Welcome, Tribesman."

"Now your brother warriors will escort you to your tent," said Tayeb, "and at moonrise we shall feast you."

"Thank you, but first I must speak to my brother."

Kerish was standing very quiet and still, not looking at Forollkin.

"Later, kinsman," answered Tayeb, smiling but implacable and Forollkin was led away to the scarlet tents of the warriors.

It soon became clear that by defeating Enecko he had gained as many friends as enemies. Forollkin downed another bowl of Irollga milk, explained the working of his bow several times, exchanged boasts and eventually persuaded one of the warriors to take him to the tent of the new Torgu.

Kerish was lying on his back with his arm around Lilahnee. The Prince languidly turned his head as Forollkin entered the tent. His eyes were dark with weariness and seemed larger than ever in his pale, taut face.

"Welcome, warrior," he said softly.

Forollkin laughed. "Don't you start!"

He glanced round the bare tent. "Not a chair in the whole camp! I'm sick of squatting on the floor and as for those bowls of stinking milk they keep giving me, I've a headache already, without the pleasure of feeling drunk first. Well, what did Tayeb say to you, and what, by Imarko, is a Torgu?"

"A kind of priest, an interpreter of dreams I think . . . Tayeb said . . . Tayeb is my uncle."

"Your uncle!" Forollkin sat down on the pallet beside his brother. "I'm glad for you then, Kerish."

"Glad?"

"Surely you must be happy to have found him; he can tell you so much about your mother."

"Yes. He has a daughter, Gwerath, my cousin. The girl who crowned you. She is the Torga of the Mountain Goddess. You know who the Goddess is?"

"Sendaaka," said Forollkin uneasily. "Perhaps we shouldn't say anything about her."

"Gwerath believes that the Goddess sent her a dream about us. They would never have found us without it." Kerish sat up. "Yet why would Sendaaka do that? Every day we stay here delays our quest, stops us reaching Saroc and sending him to fetch her home!"

Forollkin frowned: "If she sent the dream, well, she must have thought it was important that we meet the Sheyasa."

"And tell them that their Goddess is false?"

"She must have wanted you to find your family," went on Forollkin. "A brief delay won't hurt our quest and Sendaaka has waited centuries."

"If it is brief," said Kerish lying back again. "I don't think Tayeb means to let us go."

"I'll make him," said Forollkin, as if he was comforting a child.

Kerish smiled crookedly. "Forollkin the warrior will make him."

"The warrior ... do you know, Kerish, in that duel with Enecko I felt as if I were two people fighting." Forollkin looked down at his hands. "As if there was a shadow inside me, giving me strength, but forcing me to act against my will. I nearly broke that man's neck. It wasn't necessary but I wanted to kill him."

Kerish shrugged. "Tension, we break under it, more than we notice, and afterwards it's hard to put the pieces back together."

"Perhaps, and yet I felt as if something outside of me had got in and—"

"How could it?" snapped Kerish. "Do you know where they've taken our horses?"

"No I don't, but I intend to ..."

The tent flap was suddenly flung open and Tayeb entered.

"Kinsman, I have come to fetch you to your feast."

"Thank you," said Forollkin, "and Kerish ..."

The Chieftain shook his head. "This feast is only for men, for warriors. You will be brought food, sister-son, and if you are lonely my daughter will keep you company."

"I understand," said Kerish bleakly. He stroked Lilahnee and seemed absorbed in her presence.

"Come, Gift-bringer."

With an anxious glance at his impassive brother, Forollkin left with Tayeb for his triumphal feast.

Kerish did not seek out Gwerath. He lay quietly until a bowl of curds was brought for his supper. After he had eaten, he took up his zildar, tuned it and began to play.

It was only then that he remembered Gidjabolgo. He slipped out of the tent and called softly to the Forgite. Gidjabolgo had used the full length of his tether to crawl out of sight behind the tent. Now he limped towards the Prince.

"My gentle Master summons his slave?"

"I'm sorry, Gidjabolgo. I forgot about you," said Kerish honestly, "until my music reminded me."

120

For once Gidjabolgo seemed to have no sharp answer ready. "Your music reminded you of me?"

"Yes, come into the tent; at least you can sleep under cover and tomorrow I'll make Tayeb release you."

"And where is my other generous Master?"

"At his victory feast. He fought a duel and won it. He is now a warrior of the Sheyasa."

"So strength triumphs and thought is left to pine."

Kerish tossed a fur to the Forgite.

"You can sleep on that."

Gidjabolgo settled himself in reasonable comfort and finished Kerish's half-eaten supper.

"So you are now a priest of our melancholy sorceress," said Gidjabolgo, through the last mouthful of curds.

"By Imarko," murmured Kerish, "if you tell anyone here what you know about Sendaaka I will cut your tongue out."

"I'll say nothing. They'll learn their folly soon enough when their Goddess has abandoned them, and perhaps it will teach you to think about yours."

"I am sorry for you, Gidjabolgo," began Kerish.

"No, I don't think so," said the Forgite coolly, "just angry and slightly afraid of being pushed into thoughts you do not want."

Gidjabolgo scuttled back towards the tent flap.

"My prattling has displeased my courteous Master. I will leave you."

Kerish mastered his anger, pushed Lilahnee from his lap and picked up his zildar.

"Go or stay as you please."

He bent over the instrument and began to play a lament from Far Tryfarn. It told of a young man's obsession with the Ultimate Mountains and his sweetheart's vain attempts to stop him trying to reach them. He had never returned across the grasslands of Morolk and the song ended with the girl's curse on all distant beauty.

Next Kerish played a complex set of dance tunes and improvised variations. Gidjabolgo sat listening quietly and it was nearly an hour before he spoke: "Master, you are tired. The notes sing in your mind, but your fingers stumble. Let me play you to sleep."

Kerish hesitated.

"I promise you," said Gidjabolgo, "my words will be as meek as milk and can music be insolent?"

"Did you play for your Masters in Forgin?" asked Kerish.

"Lewd songs and spiteful, yes, but there is music in me that I do not sell."

"Show me." Kerish handed his beautiful zildar to the Forgite and lay back with his arms around the purring marsh cat.

Gidjabolgo plucked out a gentle tune and his voice added the pounding rhythms of the sea. He sang of ships reaching a safe harbour and the seabirds swooping like messengers of hope.

As the harmonies deepened Gidjabolgo watched the tensions in Kerish's body melt away. The Prince smiled dreamily and closed his eyes. When the Forgite was sure that Kerish was asleep he reverently set down the zildar and blew out the lamps.

When Kerish woke the next morning Gidjabolgo had already crept out of the tent and the first thing he saw was a woman's layered skirt and the ends of two braids of chestnut hair weighted with clips of horn.

Eamey was stooping over him. "Good morning, kinsman."

She set down two platters. "I have brought cheese and milk for you, and fresh meat for your beast."

Kerish sat up hastily. He had slept in his clothes but someone had spread a coverlet over him.

"Thank you . . . kinswoman."

"When you have eaten, go to Gwerath's tent. Your brother will meet you there, if he wakes before noon," said Eamey, smiling down at him. "Gwerath will show you our camp. When you have leisure, come to my tent and talk to me about Taana."

"I hardly knew her," answered Kerish stiffly, "I was very young when she died."

"But your father is still alive, and she loved him?"

"I think so."

"Then by telling me about him you will teach something about Taana."

Eamey paused and then said gently: "Kinsman, I think you are as afraid of me as I am of you."

"Afraid!"

"Taana was my dearest friend, closer than a sister."

Eamey knelt in a billow of blue and crimson leather.

"I can see nothing of her in you and yet you have the power to break the Taana who lives in my memory. Do you think I will take away the mother of your dreams? Perhaps you are right, but if we share our knowledge we can build a new image of her."

"I will come as soon as I can," said Kerish.

Eamey leaned forward and kissed him on the brow.

When Lilahnee had dragged each piece of meat off her platter, covered it with dust and slowly eaten it, and Kerish had finished his own breakfast, he changed back into his travelling clothes. The blue leather tunic and breeches were not unlike Erandachi dress—only his colouring would make him conspicuous.

The Prince called to Gidjabolgo but the Forgite was no longer tethered to his pole and was nowhere to be seen.

With Lilahnee at his heels Kerish strode over to his cousin's tent.

Inside, Gwerath and half a dozen women were sitting cross-legged in a circle with a green banner spread out between them. Gwerath dropped her bone needle and leapt up to meet them, ignoring the other girls' squawks of fear at the sight of the marsh cat.

"Welcome, kinsman. Look, we are sewing you into place."

"What?"

"In our circle."

She knelt and pushed a handful of the soft leather towards Kerish.

He also knelt to look at it and Lilahnee sat at his side, growling at the nervous girls.

The banner was embroidered with interlocking circles, each containing a colourful symbol.

"See, here is the crimson of the warrior, that's for your brother."

Gwerath's fingers were slim and well shaped but the nails

123

were ragged and grimy. She was dressed like a boy again and her hair was winning loose from its half-hearted braids.

"And this is the windflower in white and blue for a Torgu of the Goddess. At least, it should be, but I'm not very good at flowers."

"And is all your family embroidered here? You must be forever sewing and re-sewing."

Gwerath nodded.

"The unpicking is very tedious. I'm glad I only have to do our own circle."

"How many circles are there?" asked Kerish.

The other girls had taken up their needles again and were bent over the banner, looking at him through lowered lashes.

"Seventy," answered Gwerath with some pride, "though of course they are all linked. You can see on the banner."

"So people can marry outside their own circle?"

"Marry?"

The Zindaric word seemed to mean nothing to the Torga.

Kerish tried again. "Mate?"

"Oh yes, of course, but not outside the tribe, except during the Great Gathering. Sometimes though, women are carried off by raiders."

"As my mother was," murmured Kerish.

"Yes, but only the Geshaka would have sold her to slavers!"

"They are your enemies?"

"They are the strongest tribe whose circle overlaps with ours."

"Overlaps?"

"Yes." Gwerath sounded a little impatient at his ignorance. "We only share territory for two weeks but there are always battles. We shall overlap at the next move."

"Why not change territories then?"

Gwerath stared at him horrified and several of the girls stopped sewing.

"Leave our circle and become nameless wanderers! The Hunter drew the circles with his spear so there should be

124

room for all the tribes. He would strike us down if we broke our circle!"

"But must you always keep moving?"

"In summer, yes, or how would the herds graze and our warriors hunt? In the dark months we stay in one camp."

"So you will never leave your circle."

"Only at the Great Gathering," said Gwerath, "when we go to the Holy Mountain, one year in seven."

Kerish would have asked more questions but Forollkin walked into the tent with a face like bleached and crumpled linen.

Gwerath jumped up. "Good morning, kinsman."

Forollkin winced at the bright ring to her voice and the dazzle of her silver hair.

"Thank you," he murmured.

Kerish smiled sweetly. "Gwerath is going to show us all round the camp."

Forollkin, who would rather have been lying quietly in his tent, muttered something polite and trod on Lilahnee's tail. The marsh cat spat and raked him with her claws. Kerish's laughter jarred his tender head and Gwerath insisted on leading them out into the sunlight.

"Cousin," said Kerish, suddenly serious, "where is Gidjabolgo, my servant?"

"Oh, he is being fitted with a collar. Then everyone can see he's a slave and we can let him loose without fear of his escaping."

"You have many slaves?" asked Forollkin coldly.

"No, the last time we raided a camp very few captives were taken."

"You enslave all those you capture?"

"Yes," said Gwerath, "except for the warriors, of course."

"And the warriors, I suppose, you kill?"

"How could we insult them with slavery?" Gwerath sounded puzzled. "Cousins, have I offended you? Forgive me, I do not know your customs. Are there no slaves in your country?"

Forollkin broke the short silence. "We buy slaves."

"Buy them! We would never do that," exclaimed Gwerath. "Are your people very different from ours?"

"Perhaps not," murmured Forollkin.

They were walking through the area of the camp reserved for warriors, who lounged outside their scarlet tents, polishing spears, tossing bone quoits or braiding each other's hair.

"And what do your warriors do when they're not fighting or hunting?" asked Kerish.

"Each man takes his turn at guarding the camp and the herds, what else should he do?"

They passed beyond the scarlet tents through noisy crowded rows of green tents.

"The children live here," said Gwerath, "and women who are not sharing a man's tent. All except me, because I am the Torga of the Goddess."

Children ran shrieking from the marsh cat, who growled and swished her tail, enjoying the terror she inspired.

Young women stared placidly at the strangers, while the old women bent over their looms or the cooking fires of dried Irollga dung.

Gwerath led them on through the black tents of the half-men, warriors who were crippled or old, to the brown tents of the craftsmen, the tanners, the dyers, the bone-carvers; all those who bore no arms and had no voice in the councils of the tribe.

There they found Gidjabolgo, held down by two slaves, as he was fitted with a heavy bone collar. The collar-maker saluted Gwerath and Forollkin, but not Kerish; as yet he had no place in the tribe.

Gidjabolgo was released and pushed towards them. "And which of my Masters have I to thank for my fine new ornament?" demanded the Forgite.

"Come with us," said Kerish, not looking Gidjabolgo in the face. "They won't tether you again."

Gwerath took them round the boundaries of the camp, past a stream where women were washing clothes and gossiping and a group of young men were noisily bathing and splashing one another.

They paused beside a pen where three Irollga were being broken as riding beasts, but the presence of the marsh cat made the geldings nervous and the warrior in charge asked them to move on.

"We will go to the edge of the herd and find your Iroll-ga," said Gwerath.

The wind had unbraided her hair and coloured her cheeks and she was smiling at Forollkin.

"The warrior's portion, four cows in calf and a gelding, but perhaps you will prefer to ride your horse still?"

"And what am I supposed to do with them?" murmured Forollkin, as the Torga of the Goddess led them to the open grasslands.

Children tended the cows as they grazed, but on every hillock was a scarlet-cloaked warrior, his spear sharp against the horizon, an alarm horn slung across his shoulders.

Gwerath bounded ahead to speak to one of the sentries.

"As Tayeb said, the camp is well guarded," muttered Forollkin.

"You spoke to him last night?" asked Kerish quickly.

"I did. He refuses to let us go. We will be watched night and day and hunted down if we try to escape."

Gidjabolgo laughed. "So here we stick and not all the slaves are collared. Still, my Lord Forollkin should be happy here."

Gwerath returned before either brother could answer. "I have found your Irollga."

The four Irollga cows were heavily in calf but they lumbered to their feet as they sniffed the marsh cat. Gwerath soothed them, stroking their velvety muzzles, unafraid of their short, curled horns. She tried to teach Forollkin their names but he protested that they all looked alike to him.

She went on to tell him what colours their horns should now be painted and what ornaments he should give them.

"Ornaments?"

"And they will need re-blessing by the Torgu of the Hunter or they may sicken."

"I thought you would have nothing to do with the Hunter," said Forollkin.

Gwerath stared at him.

"The Hunter gave us the Irollga; he made them with his own blood."

"And did he make the Sheyasa too?" asked Forollkin, not quite suppressing the amusement in his voice.

127

"We are the music the north winds woke from the Harp of the Hunter," said Gwerath quietly; "we are the Children of the Wind."

A scarlet-cloaked warrior strode across the grass to relieve the nearest sentry and Gwerath murmured, "It is time for me to gather windflowers to dress the Tent of the Goddess. I will show you the rest of the camp later, perhaps, if you can come to me after the noon meal?"

She took them back to the centre of the camp before changing into her Torga's robes and hurrying away.

The three travellers did not enjoy the privacy of Kerish's tent for long. Forollkin had just begun to outline the possible schemes for escape when Tayeb entered.

"Greetings, kinsmen. Gift-bringer, you will eat with the warriors and then ride with me on a hunting party. There is a small herd of wild Irollga close to the camp; we must kill the bull and take the cows. Talvek, learn all you can from my daughter so you will be ready for the Testing."

The Galkians received their orders in angry silence and Forollkin departed with Tayeb. At least the ride outside camp would help him get his bearings.

An old woman brought food to Kerish's tent at noon and he shared it with Gidjabolgo. Afterwards the Forgite asked permission to check a string he thought needed changing on the Prince's zildar. Kerish left Gidjabolgo hunched over the instrument, and Lilahnee asleep on the pallet, and set off to find the Tent of the Goddess.

Enecko and another warrior, leaning on his spear, barred his way. Enecko smiled lazily. "Come out without your cat to claw a path for you? How bold!"

Kerish gave him the kind of look that would have petrified a Galkian and made to step round him. Enecko grasped the Prince's shoulders and the other warrior closed in behind, caught hold of Kerish's hair and jerked back his head.

Enecko set the point of his spear against Kerish's throat. "And without your brave brother too, or even our spitfire Torga to guard you . . ."

The spear grazed his skin and a few drops of blood trickled down Kerish's neck. He stopped struggling.

128

"Let me go, Enecko; you only attack me because you daren't face my brother again."

The Erandachi pressed the spear harder against Kerish's throat and smiled as the Prince flinched.

"Perhaps so. What do you think, my friend, should we waste our weapons on one who cannot even bear arms?"

"Let him be," said the other man. "A warrior does not kill women or children."

"Or half-breeds tainted with foreign blood."

Enecko took away the spear and his companion released Kerish's hair with a final tug.

"Run along, little one. You can tell the tale to your big brother when he returns."

He pushed Kerish to his knees and they sauntered away.

Struggling with his helpless anger, one hand at his bleeding throat, Kerish did not notice Gidjabolgo watching from the tent flap.

"They are right, Master, you should not walk out with no-one to defend you; think of your quest!"

"I can look after myself," snapped Kerish automatically and then winced. But the expected sarcasm never came.

Gidjabolgo delved into the folds of his dirty tunic and brought out a small bone dagger.

"I don't doubt that you can defend yourself, but you may need this to do it with." He held out the dagger.

"Where did you get it?"

"I stole it," said the Forgite calmly.

Kerish stared at the slim white dagger. "The Law of the Godborn forbids . . ." he began.

"These men do not live by the Law of the Godborn. Will you let them treat a Prince of Galkis like a slave?"

"No, but . . ."

"And must you always rely on your brother's protection? What about those keys at your waist, would you let such men take them and stand by helpless?"

"No."

Kerish took the dagger and hid it in the breast of his tunic.

"Thank you, Gidjabolgo."

# Chapter 8

The Book of the Emperors: *Hope*
*But he spoke to them earnestly saying: "I beg you, use the*
*senses which you are given. Look deeply into every*
*stranger's eyes until you find your own need mirrored there."*
*"What need?" they asked of him.*
*"You will know," he said, "when you see it in another."*

KERISH knew that the tents of the Hunter and the Goddess were pitched just beyond the northern boundary of the camp. Too proud to ask the exact way, the walk was longer than it need have been and his back prickled with the stares of everyone he passed. As he walked between the outermost circle of tents he noticed a sound that came to dominate the ordinary noises of the camp; a sound between a scream and a sigh, sometimes fierce, sometimes sad, sometimes discordant, sometimes harmonious, but always disturbing.

Kerish could not understand why none of the craftsmen working outside their brown tents seemed to notice it. Then he stepped on to the strip of grass that marked the boundary of the camp, and understood. Some way ahead of him was pitched the black-and-scarlet tent of the Hunter of Souls and to each of its corner-posts was fixed a harp of bone, played by the ceaseless winds of Erandachu.

"The Children of the Wind," murmured Kerish, and wondered how his mother had ever endured the stillness of the Golden City.

To his right stood the blue tent of the Mountain Goddess, patterned in white felt with stars and windflowers.

Kerish ducked through its flap and left behind the plaintive music of the wind-harps.

As his eyes adjusted to the semi-darkness he saw the Torga filling the hanging lamps with fresh oil. Kerish's feet sank into the soft furs that covered the floor as he moved forward to look at the tapestry that spread over one wall of the tent.

It was woven from the brightly dyed fur of young Irollga and showed a woman with pale hair, as tall as the mountains against which she stood.

It was not a good likeness of Sendaaka.

Gwerath walked towards her cousin, a taper in her hand brightening her hair to molten silver.

"I did not hear you come in," she whispered. "Our image of the Goddess is very ancient, and I'm sure no other tribe could have woven one so beautifully."

The tapestry was patched in places but the blue-green of the goddess' robe and the star in her lifted hand were still brilliant.

"Do all the tribes of Erandachu worship the Goddess and the Hunter?" asked Kerish.

"Some now honour only the Hunter, and in the old ways, from the Dark Time before the Goddess came down to bring us wisdom."

"And why do people turn to the old ways?"

Gwerath began re-lighting the lamps. "For many reasons; the winters grow harsher, the traders from the West come only rarely, but the slavers from the East more often. My father says that none of the tribes prosper as they did and men blame the new ways."

"Men like Enecko?"

Gwerath nodded. "He is a votary of the Hunter of Souls and longs to return to the Dark Time, when the Hunter never spared his quarry. I am not strong enough to make them fear the Goddess. I dream so rarely and I cannot untangle the dreams of others. I know the charms but there is no healing in my hands. That is why your coming is so important to my father. I have failed him, but you will show the tribe the power of the Goddess and make them believe."

"Gwerath . . ." Kerish stared helplessly at the tapestry; on the pale woven face of the Goddess he seemed to see Sendaaka's frozen tears.

"Gwerath, I do not have power from your Mountain Goddess. I cannot help you."

The Torga of the Goddess blew out her taper and knelt to re-arrange the windflowers heaped at the foot of the tapestry.

"Cousin, I know you have the power; even I can sense that, and She sent me a true dream about you."

Kerish turned away to look at one of the other tapestries. He tried to speak lightly: "Does the Goddess dwell on your Holy Mountain or further north?"

"She is in all high places," said the Torga. "She loves mountains because they are closer to the stars She came down from."

Kerish looked down at his cousin. Her hands were full of windflowers.

"Why did She come down from the stars?"

"To look for her lost daughter, her only daughter," answered Gwerath. "She has not found her. She grieves always and so understands our sorrows."

"How do you know?" demanded Kerish. "How can you know?"

"It is the Lore of the Tribe. The Chants have been given from Torga to Torga, since the end of the Dark Time. In the snow months, in our winter camp, I chant them to the people. That is a good time," said Gwerath wistfully. "In winter, the Hunter of the Souls is not so strong . . . but I promised to show you the rest of the camp. Where is your brother?"

"Tayeb ordered him to join a hunting party."

Gwerath stood up. "My father is glad to have so brave and skilled a warrior to fight for us. Are there many men so tall in your father's country?"

"Oh, Forollkin is quite exceptional," murmured Kerish.

"I thought it must be so," declared Gwerath. "Come, I will show you the Sheyasa."

Late that afternoon they went back to the Prince's tent and, in return for his tour of the camp, Kerish showed Gwerath his treasures. She was shocked at first by the zildar; it seemed like a harp, which only the fingers of the wind could play, but she revelled in his zeloka jewels. Holding up the great collar, Gwerath traced the golden outline of the wings.

132

"Are there really such birds in your country?"

"There were once. They were created by Zeldin, the god of my father's people, for Imarko, his lady. They flew between them carrying messages, but no-one has seen a living zeloka for many centuries."

Gwerath asked him about the stones and metals and Kerish told her a little of the countries from which they came.

"Oh cousin, you have seen so much of the huge world, and I so little," said Gwerath. "I know it is wrong to want to leave my circle, but I wish I could see a city, or a forest or the sea itself, anything new and strange."

"Perhaps you will, if you want it strongly enough."

Gwerath broke the short silence by setting down the collar and asking timidly, "What is this?"

"This? This is the Book of the Emperors, in which all the lore and wisdom and history of my people is written down."

"Written?"

She was puzzled and Kerish realized that the Erandachu must have no system of writing.

"Let me show you." He opened the book.

"Oh, but it's beautiful," exclaimed Gwerath, "and all those marks mean something?"

Kerish explained to her as simply as he could the principles of writing and Gwerath grasped them very quickly.

She pointed to a line on the vellum page.

"What does that say?"

"*Geterish-na ti rarak-un len metiya-na alkit-en.* That is High Galkian, the ancient language of my people. In Zindaric it would be: 'On the rock of our love we will build a nation'."

"And can you make marks like these?"

"Of course."

Gwerath looked ashamed of her question and Kerish said hastily: "Shall I teach you to read and write? I am sure you would learn easily."

"Would you? Oh cousin, how can I thank you?"

Kerish's hand went to the dagger in his tunic.

"Can a Torgu also be a warrior?"

"Why yes, if he can defeat a warrior in combat. But why do you ask, you do not carry weapons."

133

Kerish drew out the bone dagger. "I do. Gwerath, can you use that knife you wear?"

It was Gwerath's turn to be indignant. "Of course, better than most men."

"Then will you teach me to fight the way your warriors do?"

"If you wish it," said Gwerath doubtfully.

"And tell no-one."

"I swear by the Goddess; but why does your brother not teach you? He is a warrior."

Kerish closed the book in his lap.

"My brother must not know."

"But surely he is your elder, you are bound to obey him."

"I am not bound," said Kerish harshly; "we have no such custom. Gwerath, please . . ."

His smile melted her doubts.

"As you will, cousin. What shall we do first?"

"Write," said Kerish. "I will show you the letters of the Galkian script and see how many we can fit to the sounds you use."

Kerish had preserved two quills and a single cake of ink among his luggage and tucked into the Book of the Emperors were a few spare sheets of vellum. One of them was half-covered with a translation of an Ellerinionn poem.

Gwerath exclaimed in delight at the graceful calligraphy and exuberant borders of intertwining flowers and fabulous beasts.

"Oh lovely, are there many men in your country who can make such pictures?"

"Yes, but I drew these myself."

"You, cousin? How I envy you."

To his amazement Kerish saw tears in Gwerath's eyes.

"Don't cry, cousin, please, not just for a picture."

"You don't understand," said Gwerath. "I want so much to be able to make something beautiful but my hands are clumsy, and so is my tongue. I see marvellous things in my mind, but I can't show them to anyone else, and it hurts so much!"

For Kerish it was as if she had struck a sudden blow at a gate he had always kept barred, and he was forced to let her in.

"Don't cry." He took her hands into his. "You will find a way of giving the images in your mind to others. I'll help you. Look, I'll teach you writing and music and . . ."

Forollkin walked into the tent, his tunic spattered with blood, and Gwerath leapt up to greet him.

"Are you hurt, cousin?"

"No, it is Irollga blood, not mine."

He could not quite keep the satisfaction out of his voice. "I killed the wild bull."

How strange, thought Kerish, Forollkin must have been in danger, and I never felt it.

Gwerath was already asking about the hunt and the number of wild Irollga captured.

"Fifteen or twenty, I think," said Forollkin, smiling down at her, "but one of our party was injured, a man named Atheg."

"I must go to him then," said Gwerath.

She glanced back at Kerish, who was still holding the piece of vellum and a half-sharpened quill.

"I will come back later for my lesson."

"What lesson is this?" asked Forollkin when Gwerath had gone.

"I am teaching her to write," said Kerish, rolling up the vellum.

Forollkin laughed. "Well, why not? The Sheyasa are teaching me a thing or two. They use a poison on their hunting spears. It doesn't kill but it makes the animals drowsy and easy to capture."

"But you killed the bull."

"Someone had to." Forollkin rubbed at the stains on his tunic. "We couldn't have got near the cows otherwise. One good thing. They let me see exactly where the horses and our baggage ponies are tethered. It may not be impossible to get out of here. I can't stay, I've promised to give Tayeb another archery lesson. It will help to gain his trust. Do you want to come?"

Kerish shook his head. When his brother had left, he searched out Gidjabolgo, who had found a quiet, shadowy corner between tents, and sat with him until Gwerath returned.

135

Forollkin demonstrated archery to a group of picked men through most of the long light evening. He shot as well as he could ever remember at a variety of targets and afterwards discussed how best to make twenty sets of bows and arrows, from bone, gut, stiffened grasses and the Sheyasa's precious supply of wood. He could hardly have guessed that his brother's thoughts were also fixed on instruments of death.

In her spacious tent Gwerath taught her cousin the art of fighting with a dagger, while Gidjabolgo crouched as a sentinel in the tent flap. If Kerish had been surprised at the quickness of Gwerath's intellect, she was astonished at his agility and the speed of his reactions.

The next morning Kerish and Forollkin went with Gwerath to the pens to watch the Chieftain of the Sheyasa garland the Bull of the Tribe. Gwerath had woven the garland and Tayeb took it from her hands. He strode calmly into the pen and the great bull came forwards to meet him. Tayeb slid the old garland over the long horns then he spoke a few words in the language of the Erandachi and Igeshu bowed his head.

"I'll swear he wasn't that tame when I was in the pen with him," muttered Forollkin.

"He is not tame," said Gwerath sombrely, "but he knows the Chieftain of the Sheyasa. He also knows when leadership has gone from a man."

Tayeb eased the new garland over the massive head and then used it as a halter to lead the Bull of the Herd from his pen. It was the signal to break camp.

Every tent was folded and bound to the broad back of an Irollga cow. The patient beasts were then loaded with all the owner's possessions: rugs, furs, lamps, bowls, everything that could not be worn or tied to the saddle of a riding beast. The furnishings of the Tents of the Goddess and the Hunter, of the Chieftain and the Torgi, were carried in two ancient, cumbersome carts.

The tribe travelled northwards for three days. Children rode behind their mothers or noisily helped to drive the great herd. Since they were moving into the territory of the Geshaka a large body of warriors rode ahead of the tribe and scouts constantly circled the moving mass of men and animals.

Forollkin's hopes of escaping during the confusion were quickly dashed. The Galkians were never watched by less than half a dozen warriors, and firmly encouraged to ride in the centre of the tribe.

Forollkin treated his guards as if they were chance companions, talking cheerfully and persuading them to speak about past hunts and battles. Gwerath, riding astride like a boy, was usually close beside him and Gidjabolgo, struggling to lead all three pack ponies, listened with real or simulated interest.

Kerish, however, sought out Eamey.

He found her close to the lumbering carts riding a plump Irollga whose harness was hung with bone rattles and flowers of many-coloured felt. It shied at the scent of the marsh cat but Eamey kept her seat and soothed the Irollga by scratching its ears and whispering endearments.

Kerish reined in his horse to keep pace with Eamey's slow mount. She straightened, smiled and said: "What is your earliest memory of her?"

Kerish responded hesitantly at first. He was uncertain how much he should say of his royal birth and the life of the Inner Palace. But did it really matter?

What is the Emperor of the Godborn to the Sheyasa? thought Kerish. Just a name. I am Taana's son, Tayeb's nephew and I am not a warrior; that is all that matters here.

Even so, there was little he could tell Eamey. His recollections were too thickly covered by his father's extravagant grief.

"So your father loved her the best of all the women of his tent?"

"He loved only her," answered Kerish; "that is his nature."

"It was Taana's too," said Eamey; "she was worthy of being loved so deeply. I cannot praise her more but perhaps it is fortunate that she died young, before love faded."

"My father would have loved her always," insisted Kerish.

"But not as much as he loves her dead. You shake your head, kinsman. Well, your mother always said that I saw

137

the world too darkly. We were not alike, but that was the heart of our friendship."

She spoke for a time of her childhood with Taana until Kerish asked: "And my uncle, did he love her too?"

"Very much, though they were always quarrelling, for they were both strong-willed. They had great plans for the Sheyasa. Taana, I remember, wanted to journey to the northern mountains and seek out the Goddess herself. Tayeb thought that an impious wish. He was very devout as a young man and nothing horrified him more than the thought of breaking circle."

"Does he ever think of anything beyond the tribes' circle?" demanded Kerish, his fingers plaiting and unravelling his horse's mane. "He has never asked me about Galkis, or about our journey. I might as well not have existed before I entered Erandachu!"

"It is not only Tayeb who would feel so."

Eamey looked round at the slowly moving tribe: the warriors in the vanguard; the women and the old men riding side-saddle; children and slaves running beside the overladen pack beasts and, to either side, the great herd.

"Kinsman, you think of our circle as narrow, almost a prison. It is not so to us. It is a world. Each man has a circle of kin, interlocking with the circles of his tribe. The territory of each tribe joins with three others. They, each in turn, are joined to a different three. There is room for all in the circles drawn by the Hunter's spear, and all the Children of the Wind are linked. Each man knows that he is part of the great circle and there is comfort in that, Kerish-lo-Taan, under such empty skies."

The Prince looked up for a moment at the cloudless sky and the featureless horizon.

"And when my mother was wrenched from her circle, did Tayeb try to get her back?"

"He was newly made Chieftain then and the Geshaka asked a ransom in Irollga that would have beggared the tribe. He had only two days before our circles ceased to interlock," said Eamey. "He decided an attack was too dangerous. He would certainly have lost many men and still might not have saved her. I hated him for a while and refused to share his tent, so he was forced to choose another.

Gradually, I came to see how much he had been hurt by Taana's loss and I knew that he was right to think only of the Sheyasa."

"And his own power," murmured Kerish.

"He has been a good Chieftain, kinsman. I remember that when he grieves me. Do not think that because he uses you, he does not love you. He acts as he does for the sake of the tribe. I understand that. Gwerath's mother did not."

"She is dead?"

"Yes, she died nine years ago, in another man's tent. Tayeb has carried more than his load of sorrows."

"But he has you to share them, and Gwerath."

"He has me," agreed Eamey, "but not Gwerath. Tell me, kinsman, when you visited the tent of the Goddess, did Gwerath show you both the tapestries that hang there?"

"She praised one," said Kerish, a little puzzled, "that showed the Goddess and the mountains."

Eamey nodded. "The other shows the Goddess and the Hunter. Do you know the story of their meeting? He saw her when first she came down to the plains, and hunted her. She fled light-footed and the frost-stars that fell from her hair sprang up as windflowers. For all his long strides the Hunter of Souls could not catch up with her, until she slowed her steps, just as the Holy Mountain was in sight. The Hunter caught her by her silver hair and raised his spear to strike. She did not struggle but turned her face to him. Her eyes pierced him deeper than any spear and in submission was her victory. I have heard Gwerath chant the tale many times, but she does not understand it."

After three days on the move, the Sheyasa pitched camp again. The travellers found themselves almost the only people without a specific task and the encampment seemed to rise around them with incredible speed.

That night Gwerath sat with them in Kerish's tent and sang and interpreted the chants of the Goddess to them. Her voice was dry and small and to the Galkians the chants seemed monotonous and unmusical but they listened intently to her translations.

The next day was the Feast of the Spring Calving and Kerish's Testing.

"You must climb the Mountains of the Goddess," was all that Gwerath would say about the Testing.

Kerish's sleep was wracked by nightmares but he woke without remembering how Gidjabolgo had quietened them.

It was still very early when Tayeb entered the tent and ordered Gidjabolgo out. The Forgite crept into the cold greyness of morning but listened at the tent flap.

Tayeb watched his nephew dress in the robes of the Torgu. In his hands the Chieftain held a drinking horn and he murmured over it in the language of the Sheyasa. Beside the pallet Lilahnee arched her back and growled softly. Kerish leaned over to stroke her. When he straightened Tayeb was offering him the horn.

"Drink, sister-son, this will help you in the Testing."

Kerish stood up. "Not unless you give me your word that you will let us leave the tribe. Uncle, I have tried to tell you, we cannot stay with you. I am on a mission of the greatest importance to my people . . ."

"We are your people. You are my sister's only child."

"I am my father's son," said Kerish. "My duty is to him."

"That is not so," insisted Tayeb. "It is the uncle who cares for the child, not the sharers of his mother's tent."

"Not in my country—"

"But you are in *my* country now, and I claim your obedience if you will not give me your trust. You were sent here by the Mountain Goddess, do you deny it?" asked Tayeb. "She has heard my long lament. She knows that I have no heirs, no-one to help me fight the returning darkness." Tayeb gripped Kerish by the shoulder. "Can you help your father's people as surely or as much as you can help mine, you and your brother? I say again, the Goddess sent you. She has sent me Taana's son, with her smile, with just her trick of tossing back the hair from the brow . . . Drink, Talvek!"

Shaken, Kerish lifted the horn to his lips. It was filled with a liquid that looked like milk but smelled like blood. Tayeb knelt and stroked Lilahnee's green flanks.

"Sister-son, I cannot make you drink, but I beg you not to shame me before my tribe by refusing the Test."

140

Kerish drained the horn, though the contents almost made him retch.

Tayeb smiled at him. "Come, first we must visit the Tent of the Hunter. Your brother will be there, and Gwerath. This is a glad day for our circle and I know you will not fail."

Kerish wished his uncle would not speak so confidently. Almost instinctively his hand went to the Jewel of Zeldin, beneath his robe. As he touched it, he realized that the liquid in the horn reminded him of irandaan, the juice of starflowers, too strong for ordinary men and dangerous even for the Godborn.

"Come, sister-son."

Still smiling, Tayeb led his nephew from the tent and across the camp. Gidjabolgo followed, uninvited and unnoticed. The whole tribe seemed to be gathered round the black and scarlet tent of the Hunter and their chatter drowned the music of the windharps.

Forollkin was honoured by a place among the warriors inside the tent. From where he stood he had a clear view of the Torgu of the Hunter, masked like an Irollga with scarlet horns. Beside him was Gwerath, a wreath of windflowers crowning her silver hair.

Behind them, faintly seen in the flickering light, hung a tapestry. It showed a tall man, naked except for his scarlet cloak, and horned like an Irollga. In each hand he gripped a bloody spear.

The Hunter of Souls, thought Forollkin, and a merciless hunter by the expression on his face.

Then the chanting began, and beating of drums and the wailing of bone-flutes. Forollkin found himself beating time and, absorbed in the music, he hardly noticed Kerish and Tayeb enter and take their places beside Gwerath.

As the chanting rose to a climax, Forollkin heard the crowd outside shouting and crying, as if they were lamenting the beloved dead, or those about to die.

Three warriors entered the tent. The first carried an Irollga calf, no more than a few hours old. Enecko and a second man stood behind the first warrior with basins of bronze. The Torgu of the Hunter stepped forward, casting a grotesque shadow. The first warrior held the calf still; the

141

others knelt beside him. The Torgu turned to face the tapestry and, his cracked voice magnified by some trick of the mask, chanted the gratitude of the Sheyasa for the priceless gift of the Irollga.

The Warriors in the tent took up the chant and Enecko's voice soared above them, exalting in the fierce, ancient rhythms. The Torgu of the Hunter lifted the barbed spear in his left hand and thrust it into the calf's throat. He jerked it back, pulling out a lump of flesh, and blood gushed into the bronze basins as he stabbed the struggling calf again and again.

Its small body was a red mass of wounds. Then the Torgu thrust his bloody spear into the ground, where it quivered before the image of the Hunter of Souls.

He raised the spear in his right hand and Tayeb knelt before him. The Torgu scratched the Chieftain's hand with the point of the spear and a few drops of Tayeb's blood fell into one of the basins.

He dipped an already crimsoned hand into the basin and drew a circle on the Chieftain's forehead.

Next Gwerath came forward and she did not flinch as the spear cut her palm. Nor did Kerish. He had begun to feel strangely detached and did not protest when the bloody circle was smeared on his forehead.

Still singing, all the warriors in the tent gave their blood and joyfully received the mark of the Hunter. Then the basins were borne outside and the crowds jostled enthusiastically to reach the spear of the Torgu.

Kerish waited for what seemed like many hours, while children shrieked with excitement; laughing mothers held their babies to the Torgu and even slaves clamoured to be anointed. When the basin was nearly empty, the rest of the blood was thrown wildly on tents and clothes and grass, with shouts of praise to the Hunter.

Enecko knelt to drink the dregs, his face ecstatic.

Then Kerish was led to the Tent of the Goddess. The floor was thickly strewn with windflowers but Kerish crushed them indifferently underfoot. It suddenly seemed to him that everything that was happening was some vast and ludicrous trick, played to hide the truth.

Someone tied Kerish's hands behind his back with bright

cords. He moved because he knew he must but it was like walking through water, he couldn't feel the ground under his feet. He struggled against unseen pressures, surrounded by shadowy figures: Gwerath, Tayeb, Gidjabolgo; none of them seemed real, not even the man who spoke his name.

"Kerish!"

Whose name? Just another shadow. Suddenly frightened, Kerish tried to move towards the man who was speaking but other shadows thrust between them.

Kerish did not know he was falling but Tayeb caught him and laid him on a pile of furs beneath the image of the Goddess.

Now the tent was full of shadows, whispering, staring. With a great effort Kerish moved his head. The crowned woman staring down at him seemed more real than anything else in his suddenly contracted world. In a moment he would remember her name.

"Sendaaka!" He tried to say it. "Sendaaka, help me."

The star in the Goddess' hand pulsed with light.

She has lit her lamp to guide me home, thought Kerish, but it's so high, so far!

The mountains soared over him and he struggled to climb them, struggled to reach the light. Up and up, climbing away from touch and sound; climbing out of himself into the bright void, but a voice was calling, forcing him to look back.

Far below him Kerish saw the plains of Erandachu, infinitely far, painfully near. He saw the whole and every fragment of the whole at once. He saw from the mountains to the ocean and he saw each circle, each tribe, each man.

Tortured by the contradiction, Kerish fought to reach beyond sight, but the voice was forcing him further towards the limit. What limit? He could not remember, or even recognize the sensation of terror. He hung in the void, screaming "No", but the struggle was useless.

Kerish let go of the mountain and fell into the dark.

# Chapter 9

The Book of the Emperors: *Chronicles*
*But when they begged him to sing of Zeldin, Tor-Koldin*
*said: "I cannot, for I have lost simplicity and my complexity*
*is helpless before him. When life has given me new ears and*
*death a new tongue, then I will sing of Zeldin."*

WHEN Kerish woke he remembered nothing at all after the slaughter of the calf. Forollkin was bending anxiously over him, pressing a bowl to his lips. The Prince struggled feebly.

"Kerish, it's only a potion to give you strength."

"No!"

His brother's agonized whisper made Forollkin put down the cup and hold Kerish until he stopped trembling.

"A good slap might bring him to his senses."

It was Gidjabolgo's voice and a healthy anger stirred in Kerish. He turned his head to look at the Forgite and found the hideous face oddly comforting.

"Forollkin, I'm so tired."

"Gwerath said you'd need rest."

He carefully arranged the fur covelet around Kerish. "If she had warned me, I would never have allowed . . ."

Forollkin saw that his brother was already asleep and lapsed into angry silence.

When Kerish woke again, Gwerath was in the tent, sprinkling some scented powder in the lamps. A soft fragrance filled the air.

"Breathe deeply, cousin," she said, "you will be better soon. The first time is the worst."

"Your help is much appreciated. Now leave us," snapped Forollkin.

"I'm sorry. I didn't know you would be angry."

"You didn't know," repeated Forollkin incredulously.

144

"You half-killed him!"

"It is the Goddess—" began Gwerath.

"It is you. You and your father and your precious tribe. Now leave us alone!"

Gwerath fled from the tent.

"The tongue is mightier than the spear," murmured Gidjabolgo. "She'll bleed tears."

Kerish was trying to sit up but Forollkin pushed him back against the cushions.

"Forollkin, what happened? I drank from the horn that Tayeb gave me and began to feel strange. I remember the calf and the blood . . ."

"You were standing by the tapestry, looking three days dead," answered Forollkin. "When I tried to speak to you, Tayeb pushed me away. Then you collapsed and they laid you on a pile of furs. They were all crowding round you, but three warriors held me back and I couldn't get close. Tayeb began asking you questions about another tribe; the Geshaka. You answered, though it hardly sounded like your voice. You described their camp as if you could see it from above but your voice got fainter and Gwerath made them stop, I'll give her that. She spoke some prayer over you and they let me carry you back to your tent."

"What's happening now?" asked Kerish.

"The tribe are feasting and you are under Tayeb's orders to rest. Tomorrow we are summoned to his Council."

By the next morning Kerish was fully recovered and shortly before noon the Galkians were fetched to Tayeb's tent. Ten elders and ten warriors, Enecko among them, sat cross-legged on the furs. Gwerath, kneeling by her father's stool, looked anxiously at Forollkin but he did not meet her eyes.

"Welcome, kinsmen," said Tayeb, "to the Inner Council of the Sheyasa."

"And why should Gift-bringer be welcome, of all the warriors of our tribe?" demanded Enecko.

"Because of his name," said Tayeb placidly, "as you shall hear. Sit down, kinsmen."

When Kerish and Forollkin had taken their places Tayeb began: "Tribesmen, we are now in the territory of the

145

Geshaka. The Torgu of the Goddess has seen for us where they are camped and how they are guarded. Now the tribe must decide whether to cast the Spear of the Hunter, or keep the Peace of the Goddess."

Enecko sprang to his feet. "The Torgu of the Hunter is weary after the sacrifice and I stand in his place. I claim his right to speak first."

"It is your right," conceded Tayeb. "Speak, Enecko."

"Tribesmen, our Chieftain talks of the Peace of the Goddess. We have kept that peace and the Hunter scorns our cowardice and turns his back on the Sheyasa. Who can deny that our glory is diminished? In the dawn of time the Sheyasa were the firstborn Children of the Wind. Blood offerings to the Hunter were never stinted, and he gave us victory and our herds prospered. Our warriors lived for their brave deeds and went to the Hunter's spear with joy. Now we have turned to the new ways and our glories wither like windflowers in autumn.

"Now our warriors shrink from battle, our women and children are captured, our herds decline, and there are fewer slaves in our tents. The traders no longer come from the West and the grip of winter is harsher. All this since we followed the way of the Goddess! Tribesmen, I beg you, let us live and die once more as true warriors. Let us destroy our ancient enemies and honour the Hunter, so that he will raise the Sheyasa above all the Children of the Wind!"

"Enecko, the troubles you speak of have come to all the tribes," protested Gwerath. "Dead glories live only in the memory. Try to wake them from the grave and you will raise some horrible thing—"

"Peace, daughter. I will answer the tribesman who stands for the Torgu of the Hunter."

Tayeb's calm jarred on Kerish after the passion of Enecko's speech.

"Elders, warriors, it is not the Goddess who weakens the Sheyasa. She has sent us two gifts that will drive our enemies before our spears. She has sent us a new Torgu who has told us all we need to know of the Geshaka to plan an attack, and she has sent us Gift-bringer and his new weapon."

Tayeb paused and looked round the circle of tribesmen.

146

"I honour the Goddess, but I do not counsel peace. I say we should fight, and the Geshaka will be helpless before weapons that kill from far off. We shall attack their herds and bring back wealth to share between the tribe and dedicate to the Hunter and the Goddess at the Great Gathering."

After a few seconds' silence came an excited babble of agreement. Enecko's voice cut through.

"Well spoken, Chieftain, we shall shed blood together!"

Tayeb smiled and Forollkin finally realized what he had done in placing a new weapon in the hands of the Sheyasa.

"Tayeb, I taught you the bow to use in hunting; against animals, not men!"

"And do your father's people never kill men with their bows?"

"Yes, but it is not just to—"

"Just? Without strength there is no justice," said Tayeb, "and war makes a place for peace."

"That is not the way of the Goddess!" cried Gwerath.

"Silence, daughter!"

"I speak as the Torga of the Goddess," said Gwerath, with angry dignity. "She taught us that it was shameful to crimson our spears for plunder!"

"We fight to teach the Geshaka to respect us," answered Tayeb, "and for the tribe to come. Who will follow his Chieftain into battle?"

One by one, all the elders and warriors assented and Tayeb outlined his plans for the attack. There was a brief discussion and Enecko made several intelligent suggestions which Tayeb at once accepted. The Council dispersed and the Galkians were left alone with Tayeb and his daughter.

After a brief, hostile silence, the Chieftain spoke to Forollkin: "You will continue to teach my men how to shoot and you will ride with me on the raid, in the place of honour."

Forollkin got up to face him. "I will do neither. You will get no further help from me now that I know your purpose."

"You will help, and until you understand that I act for your own good and the good of the tribe, I will force you, if I must. You also, Gwerath."

147

"Father, I had to—"

"You can keep us prisoner," interrupted Forollkin, "but you can't force me to fight."

"I hold the power of life and death over my tribesmen and my kinsmen. Obey me, or I will make my sister-son suffer for your disobedience," said Tayeb coldly. "Do you understand me? Even a Torgu may be punished for endangering the tribe. Now go back to your tents."

Two days later, just after dawn, Tayeb rode through the camp with the best of his warriors, watched by a crowd of silent women and old men. Twenty of the warriors had been hastily trained to fight with the new weapons: crude bows, and arrows barbed with bone. The Torgu of the Hunter sang a war chant and touched each warrior with the spear in his right hand.

The Torga of the Goddess walked among the mounted warriors, offering star-shaped badges of horn. Wordless, she pinned one to her father's scarlet cloak and then turned to Forollkin who was checking his saddle girth close by.

"Cousin," she began timidly, "will you wear the token of the Goddess, to keep you safe in battle?"

"Thank you, no," said Forollkin, without looking up.

"Kinsman, I know you do not fear death," pleaded Gwerath, "but I could endure the waiting more easily if you would wear this."

He looked at her then. "A badge will not turn a spear, but if it soothes you ... Gwerath, I've spoken to you more harshly than I should. Will you forgive me before I ride out?"

Gwerath nodded mutely and pinned the badge to his cloak.

Beyond her stood Kerish and Gidjabolgo. Forollkin could think of nothing to say to his brother. He hugged him briefly and mounted the sole horse among the Irollga. Tayeb gave the order to move off and they cantered northwards. Kerish saw them out of sight and then walked back with Gwerath to her tent.

Watched by Gidjabolgo, Kerish gave his cousin another writing lesson. It was her fourth and she could already form a dozen letters neatly and recognize far more.

148

After an hour, the hand guiding Gwerath's suddenly clenched on her wrist. "They have begun," he said.

Gwerath took him to the Tent of the Goddess and they knelt together before the image of Sendaaka until the blackness left Kerish and he knew that the raiding party was returning.

Gwerath was frightened by the exhaustion in her cousin's face.

"You look as if you have fought the battle for them. Do you know if they are safe?"

"Forollkin is safe," said Kerish.

Two hours later they stood at the western edge of the encampment to greet the thunder of hooves. Kerish pushed his way to the front of the crowd that had gathered by the pens. He saw at once that the raid had been a success.

Some hundred Irollga, their horns striped with the colours of the Geshaka, were being herded into a pen. Nearby huddled a group of women and children roped together like animals.

All but five of the Sheyasa's Irollga had been led away to graze. The remaining beasts stood placidly, untroubled by the weight of their dead masters slung across their backs. A girl drew back the matted hair from one lolling head and screamed. A warrior ran past her to embrace another woman, eager to show her the ornaments he had stripped from the dead.

Kerish moved among the Sheyasa like a sleep-walker. When at last he found Forollkin, he didn't rush to greet him, as he had imagined he would. His half-brother stood beside Tayeb and the Chieftain's hand rested carelessly on his shoulder. Forollkin's cloak was torn and stained but he seemed unharmed.

Tayeb was speaking to one of the elders, laughing every few seconds; Forollkin was silent. Then Gwerath ran towards them and kissed her father, all quarrels for a moment forgotten. Tayeb returned her embrace.

"Well, here's one who is glad of our victory!"

Instantly her joy was shadowed.

"I'm glad at your safe return, father."

"Yes, our losses are very small and for that you must thank your kinsman."

She turned to Forollkin. "Thank you from all our tribe."

Forollkin said quietly: "I'm sure the losses on the enemy side were all you hoped for, Tayeb."

"So they were," agreed the Chieftain; "your arrows put the fear of the Hunter into the Geshaka. They killed a few but they terrified many. It was easy to spear them as they fled. And see, a whole herd of young bulls, fresh blood for our Irollga. Later, Gwerath, I'll show you what I've brought for you."

He would wash the blood off the necklace first.

"Thank you, father."

Tayeb smiled on his daughter and then noticed Kerish. "What, sister-son, have you no words to welcome us?"

"I am not sure what you want me to say."

He spoke only to Forollkin who answered with repellent brightness. "Why, praise our bravery, give thanks for our safety. Try, brother, it should come easily to such a golden tongue as yours."

"I'm sorry," said Kerish.

"Sorry? No, that's all wrong. Am I not a hero of the Sheyasa, Tayeb?"

"You are indeed, and tonight, when we divide the spoils you shall have the richest share."

"There, you see?" said Forollkin; "now I must change my cloak."

"I'll go with you."

Forollkin pushed through the crowd, ignoring his brother but answering the anxious questions of women and old men.

Kerish caught up with him and seized his arm. "Forollkin, please, what happened?"

Still smiling tightly Forollkin pushed him away. "Kerish, I don't want to talk, not now, can't you understand?"

The Prince let his half-brother walk away to the tents of the warriors.

For the rest of the day Kerish helped Gwerath and Eamey tend the wounded and in the evening, as an acknowledged Torgu, he was grudgingly allowed to join the victory feast.

150

The sentries round the camp were trebled but those who had fought in the raid sat at their ease on the grass, close to the Tent of the Hunter. Tender Irollga calves were roasting whole over the firepit and women hurried round the circle of warriors with bulging skins of fermented milk.

Kerish sat between Gwerath, robed as Torga and wearing a new bronze necklace, and Forollkin, who talked incessantly to Tayeb on his right. Kerish caught snatches of their conversation while ostensibly listening to Gwerath's account of the customs of the feast.

"And then my father carves the meat and gives the best portion to the warrior at his side, and the Votaries of the Hunter dance. Here, cousin."

Kerish accepted the heavy clay bowl of Irollga milk, drank deeply and passed it on.

"Then the plunder will be displayed and we shall have to take a share on behalf of the Goddess."

Kerish's attention drifted away from her again as he caught sight of Gidjabolgo, crouching in the shadow.

"Well, what news of our hero?" The Forgite had asked when Kerish returned to his tent.

"He is safe, unwounded."

"He has a gift for keeping a whole skin. I must congratulate him on his prudence."

"Forollkin is a hero of the Sheyasa!"

"No need for your temper to flare, Master. What deeds has the Lord Forollkin done?"

"I don't know," Kerish had said tersely. "He didn't want to talk to me."

"What? Will he not talk to you now about warriors' deeds? He treats you like a child, my Master. He should remember that you are his Prince, and you should command him to leave the Sheyasa, in spite of their adulation."

"Forollkin wants to escape just as much as I do."

"Just as much? Well, my Master knows his brother best, even if he no longer confides in you."

The meat was ready and the plumpest of the calves was carried to Tayeb to be carved. The first slice, spitted on the Chieftain's own dagger, was handed to Forollkin. Remembering the tangled emotions Kerish had sensed in his

151

brother during the battle, he wondered what Forollkin had done to deserve the honour.

Torches were lit and the bowls of fermented milk passed round again. Kerish drank and, after all the warriors were served, he and Gwerath received their portions of meat.

Tayeb spoke, promising another attack and the Votaries of the Hunter put on their black and scarlet robes. In the centre of the circle they danced to the beat of drums and the wailing of horns.

Neither of the Galkians really watched the dancers leaping and twisting to avoid the spears they carried. Gwerath gave up trying to talk to Kerish and sat with bowed head, the silver hair she had combed so carefully hiding her face.

The bowl of Irollga milk came round again and this time Forollkin noticed how much Kerish was drinking and spoke to him in Galkian.

"That's too much and you've hardly eaten; it will make you sick."

"It doesn't affect me, but what about you–you haven't devoured your hero's portion. Don't you think you deserve it?"

"Kerish,you wouldn't understand—"

"Wouldn't I? You think you can shut me out but you can't," whispered Kerish. "I don't know what you did in the battle, but I know how you felt. What made you hate yourself so much?"

"How do you know, Kerish?"

Even in the torchlight Forollkin was pale and he gripped the Prince's shoulder hard enough to hurt him. "How?"

"The powers of the Godborn, brother, the powers you scorn," said Kerish. "I felt what you felt and lent you my strength. You see I know you better than you could ever believe."

"I don't believe you at all. You're guessing, lying—"

"The first time was when you fought the or-gar-gee, and were so proud of your victory. You bungled the spear cast but I remembered the dagger."

"Kerish, you're lying, stop it."

"I am not lying. The second time you felt me with you, when you fought Enecko."

"When I nearly killed Enecko, dear Zeldin . . ."

152

Appalled, Forollkin released his half-brother, recoiling from the eyes of the Godborn that blazed with anger and excitement.

"Dear Zeldin, you have no right. No-one has such a right."

"The Godborn do, and may I not defend myself? Must I always be beholden to you? On the *Zeloka* you refused me weapons, you were afraid of what I might do, what I might become—"

"Afraid, yes . . ." said Forollkin, "afraid to trust a child with a sharp sword!"

"I am not a child," whispered Kerish, "and I will prove it to you, brother, even without the powers of the Godborn. Gwerath, when may a man be tested as a warrior?"

Gwerath had listened bewildered to the anger in her cousins' voices. Now, when Kerish switched to Zindaric, she answered hesitantly: "At any time when a third of the warriors, or more, are present and the Chieftain permits."

"Good." Kerish got up from his place and drew the white dagger from his tunic. "Tayeb!"

The Chieftain set down his skewer of meat and paused in his conversation with the Torgu of the Hunter.

"Kinsman, why do you disturb our feast?"

"Tayeb, I carry a weapon and claim the status of a warrior."

"A warrior . . ." Enecko's voice floated across the circle. "You are a Torgu."

"May a Torgu not also be a man?" demanded Kerish.

"Yes," said Tayeb reluctantly, "if he proves it in combat."

"Then let me fight."

"No," whispered Forollkin, alarm beginning to blunt his anger. "Tayeb, he is drunk."

"I am not drunk," said Kerish furiously. "I demand my right of combat!"

"He should have it," shouted Enecko, casting off his black and scarlet robes and drawing his dagger. "I will gladly fight you, Torgu."

"Kerish, no!" Forollkin bruised his brother's arms again. "Sit down at once. I absolutely forbid it."

153

"Kinsman, do you challenge Enecko?" asked Tayeb calmly.

"No," said Kerish, "I challenge Gift-bringer."

Gwerath gasped. Gidjabolgo scuttled forward to the edge of the torchlight and Tayeb's calm was broken.

"Kinsman, you cannot challenge your own brother!"

"Half-brother," said Kerish cruelly. "Is it against the lore of the tribe?"

"It is not," murmured the Torgu of the Hunter. "Let them fight."

Forollkin's hands had dropped to his sides.

"And if I refuse the challenge?"

"Then I will fight Enecko," answered Kerish, "dagger to dagger."

Forollkin closed his eyes. Angry as he was, the thought of his brother at Enecko's mercy was intolerable.

"Imarko," he prayed, "give me the skill to disarm Kerish without hurting him." Aloud he said, "I accept the challenge."

"Oh no, kinsmen, no!"

Gwerath would have run between them but Tayeb held her back.

"The challenge is accepted; make a circle for them."

Forollkin drew the High Priest's dagger from its sheath at his belt and tossed it on to the grass.

"I cannot use this against a kinsman. Tayeb, lend me yours."

"Gladly, Gift-bringer," said the Chieftain and handed across his bronze weapon. A circle was marked out with torches and the Galkians stepped into it.

Kerish saw Forollkin's shadow, but he would not look up at his face.

He is sure he can defeat me, thought the Prince, but not this time.

"Begin," said Tayeb softly.

There was a long ridiculous moment while neither moved and then Forollkin lunged, intent on disarming his brother as quickly as possible. He aimed to kick Kerish in the shins and bring the flat of his hand down hard on his brother's wrist; but Kerish moved more swiftly and effectively than Forollkin anticipated.

154

He parried Forollkin's blow, side-stepped the kick and danced back. Forollkin tried a feint at his brother's face and only just escaped a slash on the arm as Kerish seemed to read his thoughts.

Doggedly, Forollkin attacked again, only to be parried by a dagger hand of surprising strength. For several minutes they circled each other, falling into a pattern of grim attack and lively defence.

Kerish made no mistakes; he moved more swiftly than his brother and obviously planned to tire him, before he made his own attack.

Dangerous as it was, Forollkin realized he must get in close and overpower Kerish by sheer strength. He rushed at his brother and their daggers clashed in mid-air. Forollkin tried to twist the dagger from Kerish's hand and while his brother concentrated on that threat, Forollkin seized his left arm and dragged him into a fierce embrace.

Kerish kicked out but Forollkin had anticipated that. Taking the kick with a grunt he twisted his right leg around Kerish's and they fell together, Forollkin uppermost.

With the breath half-knocked out of him Kerish bit into Forollkin's hand. Startled by the pain, Forollkin's grip on his dagger relaxed just long enough for Kerish to knock it from his grasp. But by then his own dagger hand was paralyzed, trapped beneath Forollkin's weight. Kerish twisted his body and bringing up his left hand scratched viciously at Forollkin's cheek.

Forollkin still gripped Kerish's dagger hand but with his own free hand half-lifted the Prince and slammed him down again with his left arm pinioned beneath him. Kerish thought at first that his arm was broken, the pain was so bad, but then Forollkin relaxed the pressure a little to concentrate on forcing the dagger from the Prince's right hand. Forollkin squeezed his brother's wrist until he thought he would hear the bones crack.

Kerish felt beneath his back the hard shape of Forollkin's discarded dagger. If he could lift his body just an inch and free his trapped arm . . . Kerish knew he only had the strength to resist his brother for a few seconds.

He cried out as if the pain were unbearable. His right hand jerked open and the dagger fell on to the grass. Then with all his strength Kerish arched his back and thrust his body upwards. Sure of his victory, Forollkin reacted just a second too slowly. Even as a strong embrace pushed him back, Kerish had freed his left arm. His groping hand found the dagger and faster than thought, he plunged it in his brother's side. The warm gush of blood seemed to wake Kerish from a vicious trance. He pulled himself from under Forollkin, rolled over and lay gasping, his bloody hands marking his face.

Forollkin, who had never thought he was fighting for his life, sighed and began to crawl towards his brother. Kerish shrank back. Forollkin's body shuddered and lay still.

Gwerath ran to him while Tayeb pulled Kerish to his feet. "Are you hurt?"

Kerish shook his head as he watched Gwerath open Forollkin's tunic to get at the wound.

"Kinsman," said Tayeb, "you are welcome to our tribe as a warrior."

Kerish stood impassively as a scarlet cloak and fillet were fetched and bound on him by the Torgu of the Hunter.

Tayeb spoke to his daughter, "Will he live?"

"I do not know," said Gwerath; "let me take him to Eamey."

"First you must welcome your kinsman as a warrior," ordered Tayeb.

"Welcome, kinsman," said the Torga of the Goddess bitterly. "You have learned your lessons well."

# Chapter 10

The Book of the Emperors: *Sorrows*
*Though to all men his action seemed strange, each day of his*
*life had brought him closer to it. Each day he could have*
*turned aside from the path that led to sorrow, but none*
*showed him the direction of his steps.*

K ERISH crouched in his tent and Lilahnee came to him
and began to lick the blood from his hands. Violently,
he pushed her away, buried his face in the cushions and
sobbed.

"What, crying like a child, when you have proved yourself a man?"

Kerish sat up, trying to control the shuddering of his
body. Gidjabolgo stood over him.

"I have brought you some water to wash in. That bright
face should not be marred by blood." Gidjabolgo smiled
down at the Prince. "You are not so handsome now as
when I saw you first."

Kerish could not stop the dry sobs.

"Go away, Gidjabolgo!"

"No, not so handsome."

He set down the bowl of water by the pallet. "They say,
of course, that beauty springs from the soul. How pure and
bright I thought your soul must be when I first saw your
face. Well at least learning the truth about you has kept me
amused on our journey together."

"Stop it, stop it!"

Merciless, the Forgite watched Kerish's sobbing and
when the first paroxysm was exhausted, knelt beside him.

"I will cleanse you."

Ignoring Kerish's protests, he scrubbed the blood from
the Prince's hands and face.

"Now, do you remember who you are and the reason for your journey?"

Kerish nodded.

"Then go to your brother," said Gidjabolgo.

"I can't!"

"Are you so afraid to look at what you've done? It was a brave fight. Get up!" ordered the Forgite. "Would you have Forollkin die among strangers without his beloved brother to comfort him?"

"Why are you so cruel?" Kerish's face was still hidden by his hand. "I don't understand you."

"Is the truth cruel? What will you do if he dies?"

"Kill myself."

"Oh, a coward and a fool," said Gidjabolgo. "And what of your splendid quest? Will it never be completed?"

"Yes. No. I can't do it without Forollkin."

"So more than your brother suffered with that stroke. Will you still not look at what you've done?"

"Oh Zeldin," whispered Kerish, "yes, I will go to him."

Forollkin was still unconscious. Eamey had washed and bandaged the wound. He lay very still under the fur coverlet, paler even than Kerish.

The Prince came into the tent so quietly that neither of the women noticed him until he spoke.

"How is he? May I stay with him?"

"No!" Gwerath spread out her arms to shield Forollkin. "Go away, he mustn't see *you* when he wakes."

Kerish backed away from her but Eamey came quickly round the bed and took his hands.

"Of course he must. Sit here by his head and try not to get in our way."

"But he hates Forollkin," protested Gwerath, "he—"

"What do you know about hate and love?" asked Eamey sharply. "Go and sleep and at midnight you can take my place."

"I will pray and watch here all night."

"Gwerath, you're exhausted," said Eamey, more gently. "If you won't leave, sleep on the pallet there for a while."

"I won't sleep while he's here!" Gwerath had begun to cry but Kerish did not seem to see or hear the two women.

He looked perfectly composed, kneeling beside his brother. Eamey moved round the tent, re-filling the lamps, and allowed Gwerath to cry out her angry misery.

A little before morning Gwerath did sleep where she was, on the end of Forollkin's bed. Eamey leant over the Galkian's still figure; a fresh stain had appeared on the bandages. Her deft fingers paused for a moment when Kerish spoke. She had almost forgotten his presence.

"Will he die?"

"It is possible," she answered gravely, "but I have seen men survive worse wounds."

"Thank you," whispered Kerish.

At dawn Forollkin grew more restless. Once he was almost conscious and whispered Kerish's name but the Prince moved back as far as he could from the bed.

Eamey woke Gwerath and they boiled milk and herbs to make a drink that might calm the wounded man. Unless he kept quite still Forollkin would lose more blood and he had already lost too much.

"Dear Zeldin," repeated Kerish silently. "Zeldin, Imarko, don't let him die! Take my life, not his."

Agonizingly he remembered those who had trusted him. Izeldon, the Emperor, Elmandis, Sendaaka . . . he had failed them all.

"If he lives," swore Kerish, "I will give all my strength to our quest. I promise to complete it, even if it costs me my life, but let Forollkin live."

They tried to make Forollkin drink the potion, but with little success. An ominous flush had replaced his pallor. He began to toss and moan. Gwerath obeyed Eamey's orders neatly and swiftly, the tears sliding unnoticed down her cheeks.

Kerish had crept closer again and when Forollkin turned over and flung out a hand, he caught it and held it to his heart. He remembered how easily Elmandis had cured Forollkin's wounded leg but there was no sorcerer to help them now.

"A healer's hands," Elmandis had said.

Kerish leaned over his brother and placed his right hand on the wound.

"What are you doing? Eamey, stop him!"

"Please, let me," whispered Kerish.

"It is your right," said Eamey and stifled Gwerath's protests.

For six hours Kerish stayed in his cramped position, one hand on the wound, the other holding Forollkin's, while his brother lay quiet.

Just after noon Forollkin opened his eyes.

"Kerish," his voice was the barest whisper, "I've had such bad dreams."

"Yes, but it's over now and you must sleep."

Forollkin sighed and murmured something. His limp hand slipped from Kerish's grasp.

Eamey knelt to feel Forollkin's forehead. "He is cooler now; the fever is dying already."

"Then surely he will live!" said Gwerath.

Eamey was watching Kerish. "Kinsman, you should rest; we will need you again soon."

Kerish let himself be led to the pallet. He slept through a visit from Tayeb, about to lead his warriors in a second attack on the Geshaka, and when he woke it was evening and Forollkin was conscious.

Gwerath had just fed him some broth. Kerish approached the bed like a man walking on to a sword.

"Are you in pain, Forollkin?"

"A little. Kerish, what happened?"

The Prince's composure broke. "Forollkin, I wish I'd died first. How can you ever forgive me?"

"Forgive you what? I can't remember. There was the raid. I didn't think I'd been hurt, the blood wasn't mine . . ."

Kerish saw his brother's face change as memory returned, and waited. Forollkin thought over what had happened until Kerish, unable to bear the continuing silence, stumbled back, ready to run, to hide where he need never see his brother again.

"Kerish, come back!" Feebly Forollkin tried to get up but Gwerath sprang forward to push him back. He ignored her.

"Kerish!"

The Prince turned to face him.

"Kerish, I can't understand, not yet, but please don't look like that."

Kerish threw himself down by Forollkin.

"I swear I'll be better. I swear I'll never lose my temper again. I'll do whatever you tell me . . ."

At that Forollkin even managed a smile. "Not you, Kerish, not ever."

"I will!"

"It doesn't matter now," said Forollkin wearily. "It doesn't matter."

Neither of them noticed Gwerath leave the tent.

Though the wound healed cleanly Forollkin was slow to recover his strength.

During the next move, after being jolted all day in a litter, the wound re-opened and Forollkin lost more blood.

Eamey nursed him with gentle firmness but Gwerath no longer came near the Galkians.

Now it was clear that Forollkin would recover, Tayeb was not displeased with Kerish and pressed him to join a third raid on the Geshaka, the last before their circles ceased to interlock.

It was Eamey who answered for him and Tayeb did not argue with her.

Each day Kerish sat at the end of Forollkin's bed, with a bored Lilahnee sprawled across his knees. Often Gidjabolgo was with them crouched in the tent flap, watching the life of the camp.

As if by mutual consent, the brothers talked only of the distant past. In the privacy of High Galkian, they recovered together forgotten events and feelings from the placid pools of memory.

"Do you remember," said Kerish, one blustery morning two weeks after their combat, "when we went to Hildimarn? You wanted to meet that pretty musician after the temple gates were shut."

"And you waited up till three in the morning to help me climb back in through the Dawn Window."

"And the guard came along and I had to pretend I was studying the stars for an astronomy lesson, though the sky was thick with clouds."

"I remember. Kerish, I have been thinking. In Lan-Pin-Fria, I feigned sickness to help us escape. Surely we can do the same again. Tayeb can't still be guarding us."

161

Kerish winced at the comparison but said quietly, "No, he is not; he thinks there is no danger while you're so weak."

"Good, then I shall go on letting him think me weak."

"My uncle is a hard man to deceive," warned Kerish.

"We have to do something!" said Forollkin. "We have to get away from Sheyasa."

"Do you hate them so much?" Kerish fiddled with the coverlet. "I thought you liked it here."

"There is a part of me that could be happy here," answered Forollkin, "the worst part. I should have told you about the raid, but I couldn't. You would have understood. I always knew that but I felt if once I had to describe it, I'd never forget it . . . . I hadn't thought I could feel like this about a battle. Zeldin knows I've killed before but . . . . They were guarding their herds, Kerish, when they saw us. They ran and galloped closer to get within spear's distance. The men I'd trained were shooting them before they could cast a spear. They were so stupidly surprised about it. We speared the survivors. They say I killed more than anybody. It was better than sitting there watching the expression on their faces as the arrows struck. Then there were the children—"

"Forollkin, you don't have to tell me."

"Kerish, I killed one of the children. He snatched up a dagger and tried to stab me in the leg. I put a spear right through him. I couldn't bear to pull it out again. Tayeb did that. He said the boy was the Chieftain's son and I'd avenged your mother. I didn't want you to know."

"Did you think I would condemn you?" asked Kerish.

"No, but I would have seen the revulsion in your face."

"I wouldn't have cared; you mean more to me than a dead child."

"You would have cared, Kerish; you see things more clearly than I do, you see things whole. We won't talk about it again, or what happened afterwards. We must concentrate on getting to Seld."

Shaken as he was, Kerish related some useful information.

"In two days' time the tribe starts its journey to the Great Gathering. They'll join with other tribes on the route. I'm

162

sure we can escape in the confusion and Tayeb can't follow us very far without breaking circle. Rest, Forollkin, we'll need your strength."

On the day of the Great Move, Tayeb visited Forollkin and found him still unable to ride. Eamey confirmed that Gift-bringer was not recovering as quickly as she had hoped.

Tayeb leaned over the bed: "Well, kinsman, you must heal yourself soon; you have the esteem of the tribe to win back. In the meantime, my daughter shall keep you company on the Move. If you like a woman who talks, she talks well."

Forollkin's litter was slung between the two horses. Gidjabolgo led them and Kerish rode one of the pack ponies.

In the middle of the morning, Gwerath joined them at the centre of the moving mass of the Sheyasa.

It was a noisy progress but above the beat of hooves, the braying of Irollga, the creaking of carts and the shouts of the herdsmen, Gwerath described the Great Gathering. She spoke only to Forollkin.

"I was only ten years old at the last Gathering but I remember it well. I was not a full Torga then but since I was marked for the Goddess I went with the Torgi, high up into the Mountain. We looked down on the plains and sang a blessing over all the Sheyasa. I walked on the snows which never melt. I saw my footprints on the Holy Mountain and I wished I could always stay in the High Places, where the Goddess is close."

"How long does the Gathering last?" Gwerath would not look at Kerish but she did answer him.

"The tribes camp on the lower slopes till the eldest Torgu of the Sheyasa casts down his spear from the summit of the Mountain. Then each tribe returns to its circle and the peace of the Great Gathering is over."

"You are at peace during the journey?" asked Forollkin. "Even with the Geshaka?"

Gwerath nodded.

"A good custom," continued Forollkin; "you have told us a great deal about the Erandachi, perhaps you would like to hear about the Galkis."

163

"Yes please, cousin, tell me."

Forollkin shifted among the cushions, trying to make himself more comfortable.

"Oh, Kerish can do it better than me. Tell Gwerath about the nine cities."

"Gladly, if . . ." began the Prince but Gwerath broke in, "I do not have time now, I must look after the Tent of the Goddess."

She pulled round her Irollga's head, rather too sharply, and rode off.

"There's one lady not beguiled by our Prince's charm," murmured Gidjabolgo.

"I don't understand her," said Forollkin blankly. "Kerish, the scab's itching again – do you have any of Eamey's ointment with you?"

They stopped to rest and eat at noon. Sitting cross-legged beside Forollkin's litter, scraping out a bowl of curds, Kerish suddenly heard the raised voices of Tayeb and his daughter.

After a few moments Gwerath came towards them, past the groups of seated women and restless pack animals.

"I'm sorry," she said. She was looking at Gidjabolgo as if she'd never seen him before. "I've tried but my father will not listen. The Torgu of the Hunter is coming for your servant."

Forollkin raised himself on one elbow.

"Coming? Why?"

"My father says the Votaries of the Hunter must be pacified and that this will do it at little cost."

"What will do it?" said Forollkin impatiently. "Tell us!"

The shadow of the Torgu fell across the litter. Beside the old man were two warriors with ropes of hide in their hands. The Torgu of the Hunter touched Gidjabolgo with the spear in his left hand.

"Bind him."

The Forgite tried to run but the warriors seized him and dragged his arms behind his back for binding.

"Stop!" said Kerish; "how dare you touch my servant!"

"It was agreed," said the Torgu of the Hunter calmly, "on the day you entered the tribe. He belongs to the Hunter

164

and I shall keep him safe, till we reach the foot of the mountain."

"He belongs to no-one," protested Forollkin.

The Torgu turned to his warriors: "Take the slave to the Tent of the Hunter."

"I forbid you to take him," shouted Kerish.

"It was agreed by the tribe, Torgu of the Goddess, and ordered by the Chieftain. Save your anger for him."

"By Zeldin I will."

Kerish found his uncle among the calf herders, settling an argument.

"I must speak to you. The Torgu of the Hunter has—"

"Not here." Tayeb took Kerish's arm and led him amongst a group of tethered Irollga, where they could not be overheard.

"Now, sister-son, I know you are angry and I will not say that it is a slight thing to let your slave die on the spear of the Hunter, but try to understand that I act for the good of the tribe."

"Your tribe!"

"No, ours."

Tayeb seized the Prince's hands, awkwardly, as if touch was not natural to him.

"Ours. All my life I have dreaded the day when my strength will weaken and I may die on the horns of the Bull of the Tribe, while others choose my successor. Now the Goddess has sent me back my sister's child and it is not unknown for a warrior Torgu to take a chieftainship."

Kerish could not bring himself to wrench away his hands but he said coldly: "That is deep in the future, but Gidjabolgo . . ."

"Talvek, for twenty years I have struggled against the return of the old ways but the followers of the Hunter have loud voices in the councils of the Sheyasa. I cannot always defy them or in fighting every battle I may lose the war. Can you not believe that I serve the Goddess?"

Kerish stared past his uncle at the russet flanks of the Irollga, placidly cropping the grass.

"I think, I believe, that you meant to serve her but this cannot be right."

"Would you rather I gave the Hunter a woman or a child?"

"What will they do to him?"

Tayeb's hands dropped. "I have never attended their rites. I do not know, Talvek, but it is only one death in seven years. In the dark times, the spear of the Hunter was never dry."

"And you are setting the tribe back on that path, if you permit this murder," said Kerish harshly. "Your guilt will be as great as theirs."

"They are not murderers, Talvek; they only seek to honour the Hunter. Enecko loves the Sheyasa as much as I do. We struggle to serve the tribe in different ways."

"But you are giving up the struggle!" protested Kerish.

The hem of Tayeb's cloak was a pool of scarlet among the trampled windflowers. He stared down at it as he spoke.

"Sister-son, men are not perfect, as you would make them. All of us must yield part of our dreams or die of the world's harshness. My daughter will not understand this and wounds me with every word she speaks. Surely you can see that much must be painfully sacrificed to achieve a little."

"Painfully? You sacrifice lives on the altar of your power, but I have never seen you weep," said Kerish. "What of the children of the Geshaka . . .?"

"That is war, a different thing."

"It is not different to those who die! Their blood—"

"Blood? Are your hands so clean that you can condemn me? At least I have never tried to kill a kinsman."

Kerish stepped back as if he were evading a blow.

"Is that different, Talvek?" demanded Tayeb.

"No."

At the sight of Kerish's stricken face, Tayeb seemed to soften.

"You are young, you speak as Taana used to do, but you have a man's courage."

He took something white from the breast of his tunic.

"Here is your dagger; wear it like a warrior. Don't flinch, sister-son. Wear it," said Tayeb ruthlessly, "as a reminder of the blood you have shed, till you draw it in a better cause."

166

"You are just." Kerish took the dagger and tucked it in his belt. Through the thin leather his fingers felt the golden chain at his waist.

"I can do nothing for your slave," continued Tayeb. "I am sorry that one whose life cannot have been happy should die so cruelly, but the Hunter will take him into his own circle and the tribe will keep his name alive. Be brave, sister-son."

Tayeb kissed Kerish on the forehead and quickly walked away.

That afternoon another tribe was sighted on the horizon. Within an hour it was possible to make out the symbols on the banner carried by the first riders. Tayeb gathered an escort and rode out to greet the Chieftain of the Besh-goreen.

A peace was sworn, gifts were exchanged and the tribes made a temporary camp, side by side. They would travel together to the Holy Mountain. To escape the confusion and excitement Kerish slipped away to the hastily erected Tent of the Goddess, leaving Eamey to make Forollkin comfortable.

Only one of the tapestries had been unrolled, the rest of the furnishings were still in their cart, and the Torga of the Goddess sat sobbing on the ground, her lap full of wind-flowers. After a moment she sensed that someone was watching her and looked up.

"Cousin, should I leave, or can you share your grief?"

"Why did you come here?" Gwerath scrubbed the tears from her eyes and tossed back her hair.

"To think," answered Kerish simply.

"What did my father say about your slave?"

"A great deal," Kerish came a little closer, "but the kernel of it was that Gidjabolgo must die."

"He will never listen to me, never. I hate him."

"Gwerath, you can't hate someone who loves you."

"I hate him." She was sobbing again.

Kerish knelt beside her but he dared not touch her.

"He doesn't love me," said Gwerath. "I am no use to him. I cannot be a Chieftain and I cannot make men fear the Goddess."

"Your father loves you as a daughter, not a Torga."

"He didn't love my mother." Gwerath tore the petals from a windflower. "She died because he didn't love her and he never even speaks of it."

"Silence often covers grief," said Kerish. "Cousin, thank you for caring about Gidjabolgo."

"Of course I care! You think the Sheyasa are barbarous, don't you? Perhaps we are. I hate the tribe too, I shall never feel part of it."

"The Sheyasa are afraid of the dark. So am I," admitted Kerish. "It is only wrong to try to appease it."

Gwerath attempted to stop crying. "What will you do about your servant?"

Kerish risked the truth. "We will try to rescue him and then escape together. We have to get to Seld."

"But Forollkin can't ride yet!"

"He is stronger than he looks. Gwerath, you won't tell your father ?"

"I would never betray Forollkin!"

Kerish was abruptly reminded that his cousin had not forgiven him. He got to his feet. The windflowers spilled from Gwerath's lap as she followed him across the tent.

"How do you mean to rescue your servant?"

"I'm not sure yet. I'm going to the Tent of the Hunter to try and find out how he's guarded."

"They won't let you near him. I'll discover what you want to know. Then I'll come to Forollkin and we can plan."

"Gwerath, this is our trouble, not yours. If your father found out—"

"I am the Torga of the Goddess," said Gwerath, "and you are my cousins. The trouble is mine. As for my father, he thinks I only have words to use against him. He thinks I am helpless, but I am not!"

"No, indeed, cousin," answered Kerish carefully, "and it is true, we need your help."

She almost smiled at him.

Kerish walked back through the camp, the smoke of the cooking fires drifting across his path. Only a handful of tents and windscreens had been erected but Forollkin had one of them.

Eamey had just brought him one of her potions. Forollkin sniffed the horn of liquid approvingly. "Your potions are the tastiest thing I've had among the Sheyasa. This will never encourage me to get well."

"But I see you drink it anyway," said Eamey dryly.

She turned to Kerish: "You have been to the Tent of the Hunter?"

The Prince hesitated.

"Perhaps you should not tell me." Eamey looked at him gravely. "Tonight, Tayeb will feast the Chieftain of the Beshgoreen, where the two camps meet. I will be with him. May the Goddess be with you."

She took the empty horn from Forollkin's hand and left the tent.

Lilahnee was butting at Kerish's legs, demanding attention. He knelt to stroke her and related his conversation with the Torga. When he had finished Forollkin raged at his brother for allowing Gwerath to help them, but waited for her return as anxiously as Kerish.

It was not long before she was with them, sinking down on a pile of cushions to recover her breath.

"Do you remember the Tent of the Hunter?" she asked. "It is made into three parts with tapestries. They have set up a stake in the third part and tied your servant to it. The tapestry is drawn back, so a guard beneath the image of the Hunter can always see him. The Torgu is there too and another warrior walking round the tent."

Forollkin grimaced. "Worse than I thought. Still, if I . . ."

"No, listen, I have thought of a way."

It was a good plan. Forollkin admitted that before he turned it down.

"Why?" demanded Gwerath.

"You cannot possibly help us openly," said Forollkin. "Your father—"

"My father may beat me," answered Gwerath, "but he cannot really harm the Torga of the Goddess. Besides, you will need me to lead you round the camp and through the herds. I know where every sentry will be; you don't."

"Forollkin," said Kerish softly, "we have no choice. We must go on."

Reluctantly Forollkin nodded. Gwerath looked at him eagerly and he took her hands.

"Cousin, we can never repay the gift of your courage."

Her smile was ecstatic. "It is a good plan, kinsman, it will work!"

Later that evening the Galkians left their tent. They placed cushions under the fur coverlets to deceive the casual eye, and, cloaked and hooded, with Gwerath at their side and Lilahnee at their heels, they slipped through the camp.

Stopping in a pool of shadow they looked at the Tent of the Hunter. Through its flap they could see a dim light but they could hear nothing but the windharps. Hopefully no warrior had come to make offerings. They had not watched for more than half a minute before a tall, scarlet-cloaked figure paced round the front of the tent. He carried a spear and there was a dagger at his belt.

"Kerish," hissed his brother, "are you sure you can . . ."

Kerish nodded and gestured for them to go on. Beneath the folds of his thick cloak, Forollkin drew his dagger, left-handed. He placed his right hand on Gwerath's shoulder and seemed to lean heavily against her. With dragging steps they approached the entrance and were challenged by the guard.

Gwerath answered him. "The Gift-bringer comes for healing as I told the Torgu."

The warrior nodded and lowered his spear. They passed through the flap. Unnoticed, Kerish had slipped round the back of the tent. As close to the sentries' path as he dared, Kerish knelt and put his arms around Lilahnee. All through their walk to the tent he had pictured to the marsh cat what he wanted her to do. As footsteps approached he repeated the image and released her.

As the guard came round the corner of the tent Lilahnee padded across the damp grass. The man started and lowered his spear but Lilahnee looked at him with guileless gold eyes and mewed softly. It was a reassuring and slightly ridiculous sound to come from so formidable a creature.

The sentry relaxed. He had seen the new Torgu pet the beast and it seemed friendly. He let her twine round his legs and even stooped to stroke her. Kerish came silently up behind him and struck him across the head with the rock in

170

his hand. It was a heavy blow and the man dropped without a sound.

To the Prince's relief the man was not dead. Kerish took a hide rope from his sleeve. Praying his clumsy knots would hold he bound the warrior's hands and feet, stuffed a kerchief in his mouth and dragged him into the long grass.

Inside the tent, a second guard was frowning at Gwerath and Forollkin. Behind him, in the unlit portion of the tent, they could see Gidjabolgo tethered to a stake, his slave-collar replaced by the scarlet garland of the victims of the Hunter. The frail figure of the Torgu of the Hunter stood, leaning on a staff, beneath the image of his god.

"You are welcome, Gift-bringer," the old man murmured. "The Torga has told me of your need for healing. Come closer."

As if every step was painful, Forollkin came slowly forward and Gwerath helped him to kneel. He heard the rasp of boots on grass as the other guard walked past the tent-flap. They must give Kerish enough time to act.

"Teach me what offerings are acceptable to the Hunter," said Forollkin. "My wound will not heal."

"You must offer your soul to be skewered on the spear of the Hunter," answered the Torgu. "You must be caught in his snare, trapped in his net."

Ignorant of what the Torgu had shrewdly read in Gwerath's face, Forollkin wondered fleetingly why the old man had accepted her story so readily.

"I promise to fight for the Hunter; tell me . . . ." Forollkin swayed as if he were about to faint. The Torgu grasped his shoulders to support him but with startling speed Forollkin rose to his feet dragging the old man with him. The guard shouted for his comrade as he ran forward. There was no response.

"Make another sound and I'll cut his throat," said Forollkin, his dagger already pressed against the old man's neck.

The guard hesitated. His spear was poised but the Galkian was shielded by the Torgu's body and Gwerath stood behind them.

"Drop your dagger and your spear," ordered Forollkin, "and kneel with your hands behind your back."

Blood speckled the wrinkled skin as the dagger pricked the Torgu's throat.

"Do as he says," gasped the old man, "and leave them to the Hunter." The guard obeyed. Gwerath bound him and collected his weapons and then dealt the same way with the Torgu while Forollkin held him. Together they pushed the two prisoners behind a hanging and left them lying there.

Forollkin's hand flew to his dagger again as a man entered the tent.

It was Kerish.

Half-overcome by relief and exhaustion and the very real pain in his side, Forollkin sank down on to a pile of furs.

"Cousin, are you all right?"

"Don't fuss me," said Forollkin testily. "The sentry?"

"Bound and gagged," answered Kerish, "where no-one should stumble over him."

"Remarkable. I congratulate my Masters on their unexpected talents. Deceit and violence."

Gwerath turned on the Forgite. "How can you speak so when—" but Kerish was laughing as he cut Gidjabolgo free.

He handed the Forgite a spear and a scarlet cloak taken from the first guard.

"Tayeb—" began Gidjabolgo.

"He no longer guards us or the horses," interrupted Forollkin, "so tonight we leave the Sheyasa."

"What, the lady too?" inquired Gidjabolgo.

He was looking at Kerish but it was Forollkin who answered: "She is merely guiding us through the herds, but you owe Gwerath your life."

"When we're safe away I'll thank her," said Gidjabolgo.

The three travellers, the girl and the marsh cat left the black and scarlet tent, hoping its prisoners would not be discovered till morning. Most of the Sheyasa were mingling with the Beshgoreen where the camps met and they could faintly hear shouting and laughter.

The south side of the camp was dark and still. Few fires were still alight and only women and children slept around them. Nevertheless the travellers were cautious as they skirted the camp, slipping from shadow to shadow, to reach the place where the horses were tethered.

172

Once they nearly walked into a laughing couple looking for an empty tent, but the young lovers hardly glanced at them. Once they stood holding their breaths while a group of half-men walked within a few feet of them discussing the best horn for carving belt-buckles.

Silently they approached the makeshift pens. The moon was hidden and the night was very dark. Among the black shapes of seated Irollga, Forollkin could just make out the glimmering white of their horses. They edged their way towards them but the Irollga soon sensed Lilahnee's presence. A few stumbled snorting to their feet and Forollkin was afraid that their uneasiness would soon bring a sentry to investigate.

"Kerish, take Lilahnee and wait for us by the stream."

The Prince obeyed and he and the marsh cat were soon lost to sight in the gloom. Kerish stood quietly, trying to blend with the darkness and wishing Lilahnee would not purr so loudly.

He didn't see Gwerath walk boldly up to a sentry and Forollkin strike him from behind, but he soon heard the jingling of harness. Forollkin was leading both the horses and the pack ponies followed obediently, re-loaded with the luggage that had been dumped where they were tethered.

The Galkians mounted and Gidjabolgo scrambled on to one of the ponies who whickered in annoyance at the familiar clutch of his hands in her mane. Gwerath was also to ride a pony, since her own Irollga might bray at the scent of Lilahnee and raise the alarm.

She mounted nimbly and an experimental kick brought her alongside Forollkin's tall steed.

"If we ride to the left of the second herd, we should avoid the sentries."

Forollkin silently reproached himself for letting her help them but it was Kerish who said, "Cousin, are you sure this is what you want?"

"We must hurry," answered the Torga of the Goddess.

Hoping to avoid the sentries guarding the herds from night marauders, Gwerath led them a crooked course through dangerous moonlight and welcome darkness. Afraid of making too much noise, they began at walking pace. Every time the moon came out from behind the clouds Kerish longed to break into a gallop. Even from a distance the silhouette of a horse could not be mistaken for that of an Irollga.

About half an hour after they had left the camp, as they were trotting up a slight incline, Forollkin said: "We should be clear of the sentries now surely. How long before we are out of the tribe's circle?"

"An hour's ride south, no more," answered Gwerath.

Forollkin leaned down to take her hand. "You have guided us well, cousin. I wish I could be sure that no harm will come to you through this."

"It won't," said Gwerath boldly, "if you take me with you."

Before Forollkin could answer, the moon came out again and Gidjabolgo yelped a warning as three spear-men rode over the ridge.

Forollkin reached for the bow at his saddle but it was already too late.

"Move, Gift-bringer, and I will spear you," said Enecko.

# Chapter 11

The Book of the Emperors: *Chronicles*
*But the Emperor said to his son: "However good the cause, I beseech you not to depart. There are wrongs enough here for you to strive against. You may break free but you will wound those bound to you. Therefore, my dearest son, be sure the prize is worthy of their pain as well as your own."*

FROZEN by Enecko's words, Forollkin thought furiously. They were four against three but Gidjabolgo was useless and Kerish . . . well nearly so, and would the marsh cat help them?

"How dare you threaten the kinsman of the Chieftain?" Gwerath rode towards the unwavering spears.

"He attends the Torgi, on the business of the Goddess."

"And the slave?"

"The Torgu of the Hunter has agreed to release him."

"You lie," said Enecko calmly, "the slave is marked as the hunted one and the chase ends only in death."

"You cannot threaten us," repeated Gwerath but her hand was moving towards the dagger at her belt.

"I serve the Hunter," answered Enecko, "and may pursue his slave. True, if I kill Torgi it will bring my own death, but there is nothing to stop me spearing Gift-bringer. My brother warriors will witness that he was helping the slave to escape. I will do it, if you do not throw down your weapons and ride back with me."

"Enecko," called Kerish, "if you take us back you will return a victim to the Hunter, but you will be making a far greater gift to the Goddess and to Tayeb. The Chieftain will rejoice at the return of his daughter and his nephews and he looks on me, not only as a Torgu, but as his heir. Understand that if we cannot escape I will accept my captivity with grace and strive to rule the Sheyasa!"

In the watery moonlight Kerish could not judge the expression on Enecko's face. Perhaps he was only driving the Votary of the Hunter to thoughts of murdering them all. Would Enecko's companions agree to that? They already looked uncomfortable levelling their spears at Gwerath.

Kerish went on cautiously: "Consider the Goddess—she has a Torga and a Torgu now. I have shown a little of my power in her already and I can win new followers to her worship. But if you let us go, Tayeb will be made a fool. He will have lost his heir and the Goddess her Torgu. All this you can accomplish by riding by us in the darkness."

The two other warriors began to talk at once but Enecko hunched in his saddle, stroking the butt of his spear, and murmured a prayer to the Hunter.

The marsh cat was beside Kerish, her head level with his stirrups. As a silence lengthened, he began to prepare her with images of attack.

Then Enecko spoke. "You speak well, Torgu, and there is much I would ride past to show our people the folly of honouring a Goddess who sucks the blood from the men of the Sheyasa. Our Chieftain has no heart to break but there is much I would give to see his pride crushed. I agree: I will let you go, even the slave, for there are other victims and the Hunter will spear him in his own time. But there is one condition. The Torga of the Goddess rides with you."

"She should return," said Kerish.

Forollkin would have added his protest to Kerish's but Gwerath whispered: "Agree. I can slip back to the camp later."

While he hesitated, she called out: "We accept your condition."

"Good, then we shall ride with you to the edge of our circle. Ride in front of us and slowly," said Enecko. "Try to escape and I will spear Gift-bringer through the back."

As they were ordered, the travellers rode slowly south, with Enecko and his companions always a few paces behind them. After a silent hour they reached a shallow stream, sparkling fitfully in the moonlight, and Enecko rubbed his forehead and murmured: "The circle tightens—can you not feel it, daughter of Tayeb?"

"I feel it." She was very pale.

"Cross!" ordered Enecko.

The marsh cat splashed over first, the horses followed.

Gwerath came last so the others did not see her face as she urged her pony into the cold, swift water.

"Farewell, Torga of the Goddess," called Enecko, "look your last on the Children of the Wind. Your circle is broken."

"I will not turn back," said Gwerath.

Enecko raised his spear in mocking salute and shouted to his companions.

They wheeled round and galloped back towards the camp.

"What does he mean?" demanded Forollkin.

Gwerath was staring after Enecko. "I cannot go back. They would witness that I have broken my circle and the Bull of the Herd would know it was true. I would die on his horns."

"But Tayeb ..." Forollkin noted furiously that Kerish did not look surprised and Gidjabolgo gave a throaty chuckle.

"Well, here's a useful companion on your quest. What sorcerer can stand against you now?"

"Be quiet," snapped Forollkin. "If I'd known, Gwerath, I'd never have let you help us, never!"

"There is nowhere I can go in Erandachu now," said Gwerath in a small voice. "The other tribes would know me for a circle breaker."

Forollkin took a deep breath. "Well, cousin, you must come with us and we'll try to find a place where you can be happy."

"Wouldn't I be happy in your Galkis?"

"We are not going to Galkis," said Forollkin grimly.

It was a subdued group of travellers who rode south-westwards towards the forest of Everlorn and the Gap of Lamoth, and Kerish was not the only one whose thoughts rested with Tayeb. He would know soon just how much he had lost.

"Forgive me, uncle," Kerish prayed, "but at least you have Eamey's love. Forgive me if all I can offer you is guilt."

177

At midday they shared some of the food that Gwerath had hidden in the saddlebags and rode on, fast and silently. Towards evening they saw a mass of green humps in the distance. They proved to be a large group of low turf huts, apparently deserted.

"This must be the winter camp of the Beshgoreen," said Gwerath.

"We'll shelter here for the night," ordered Forollkin.

Leaving the horses to graze untethered, they chose one of the nearest huts and crawled through its low entrance into a dank room.

"Well, at least it's out of the wind," said Forollkin, wondering how the Erandachu endured the winter months huddled in such huts.

"Worms live out of the wind," said Gidjabolgo sourly, "but I don't envy them."

Gwerath showed the Galkians how to build a turf fire and soon the hut was filled with light and warmth and smoke. Forollkin went out to shoot something for supper. Coughing and complaining, Gidjabolgo curled up in a corner and pretended to sleep.

Gwerath knelt, feeding the fire, and Kerish watched her. She was dressed in boy's clothes and a borrowed scarlet cloak. The clothes and her knife were all she had brought with her from the Sheyasa.

When the fire was burning steadily, Gwerath sat back, wiping the soil and grass from her hands.

"If you are not going back to Galkis, where are we going?" she asked.

"To the Queendom of Seld and the citadel of the sorcerer Saroc."

"A sorcerer?"

"You look horrified, Gwerath," said Kerish, risking a smile; "do you have no sorcerers among the Children of the Wind?"

"It is forbidden," answered Gwerath. "The Hunter would be angry and the Goddess too. Why must you visit this sorcerer?"

"Gwerath, do you remember my telling you about the great Chieftain of Galkis and his golden city? Well, I am his

178

son, the Third Prince. Taana was his Queen, his Chieftainess."

"His son? And Forollkin too?"

"Yes, but . . ." Kerish knew that the Sheyasa made no distinction between wives and concubines, so Forollkin's position was difficult to explain. "Yes, though not by a queen. Our family has ruled in Galkis for a thousand years, but now our power wanes and we are threatened on many sides."

Kerish told his cousin all he could about the darkness encroaching on Galkis and their search for the promised Saviour and he drew out the golden keys.

Gwerath gazed at them longingly. "Oh cousin, how fortunate you are. I should always be happy if I had something so important to live for!"

Kerish hooked the keys back on their chain.

"Gwerath, I'm afraid Forollkin is right and we should never have let you leave the Sheyasa, but perhaps this quest was meant to be shared by you."

"Do you truly think so?"

"The Goddess herself sent us to the Sheyasa. There must have been a reason."

"Then you don't think the Goddess will be angry with me?"

Kerish's answer was lost in the noise of Forollkin crawling through the entrance carrying a plump bird. He tossed it to Gwerath.

"Here we are. A nice fat bird to prepare."

Gwerath looked at it haughtily. "A Torga of the Goddess does not do the work of ordinary women."

"I might have guessed that you and Kerish would make a pair," groaned Forollkin. "Well, I'm too tired to pluck it. Wake up Gidjabolgo."

After they had eaten, the travellers rolled themselves up in their cloaks and slept. Even Kerish was now inured to sleeping on the bare ground but Gwerath seemed to find it hard. She lay awake, trying to shut out memories of Tayeb and Eamey.

Kerish and Gidjabolgo heard the smothered sobs and both, for different reasons, pretended to be asleep. Finally, Lilahnee padded over and settled down by Gwerath, purring softly. The girl buried her face in the marsh cat's glossy fur and soon fell asleep with one arm around Lilahnee.

The next day they journeyed south, faster than before. Forollkin made no concessions to his own injuries, nor to Gwerath's presence, and she demanded none. He even agreed to teach her how to shoot, and on the tenth evening of their journey she managed to bring down a large flightless bird. Jubilant, Gwerath dragged it to their camp fire and tossed it to Gidjabolgo.

"A curse on all feathered things and the fluke that killed this one," muttered the Forgite.

"You are always ungrateful," said Gwerath. "You never even thanked my cousins for saving you from the Hunter."

"They did it for fear of a sorcerer's curse."

"It was our duty," began Forollkin.

"Then I'll thank duty," snapped Gidjabolgo.

"Oh here, let me help you with that," said Kerish and pulled the bird on to his lap.

"But a Prince should not do the tasks of a slave!" protested Gwerath.

"I've told you before," said Kerish patiently; "Gidjabolgo is our travelling companion, not a slave."

His deft fingers began plucking out the brindled feathers and Forollkin sat down by the fire.

"We should reach the edge of the forest tomorrow."

"And then?" asked the Forgite.

"We travel along the edge to the Gap of Lamoth. Once in Seld we have to find the Red Waste and the citadel of Tir-Tonar."

All through the next day the forest of Everlorn drew closer, till they could distinguish the shapes and colours of the great trees that bordered the plain. The travellers spurred their mounts to a gallop to reach the shadow of the forest.

Gwerath slipped from her pony and ran to the nearest tree, caressing the rough bark. The wonder in her face was faintly mirrored in all her companions.

Gwerath tried to embrace the trunk and reached up to the lowest branch and ran her fingers through the glossy leaves. Lilahnee rubbed against the bark, purring loudly.

"What trees are they?" asked Gidjabolgo.

"I have seen them in the Emperor's garden," answered Kerish. "They are watch trees."

"Think of these trees standing against the wind for many lifetimes," said Gwerath, "watching the plains, guarding the forest!"

Her words made Forollkin curiously uneasy. He wanted to ride back across the windy plains, away from the sombre ranks of ancient trees and the ordered darkness they created.

"We are not to enter the forest, Gwerath, not even by a few steps. Now mount up and we can get in another hour's riding."

They travelled along the edge of the forest until sunset. Throughout their ride Kerish noticed no signs of life in the forest. No birds sang in the branches, no animals scurried among the leaf-mould. The wind which haunted the plains had dropped away. Nothing stirred the branches of the watch trees or trembled the smallest leaf.

They made a camp by a stream that ran into the forest, the rush of its waters oddly muted as it reached the trees. After a supper of cold fowl, the travellers lay down to sleep.

Kerish could never remember clearly all the dreams of that first night but he knew that he and his companions were running, through a darkness filled with shifting terrors, towards a shining archway of trees. He saw Forollkin reach them but suddenly the branches swept down to bar his way and the Galkian turned back as if he neither noticed nor cared. Then Gwerath came, and for her too, the way was barred. She turned away, weeping, and was lost in the darkness. Yet when Gidjabolgo appeared the boughs lifted and he passed through the living archway and out of sight.

In his dream Kerish approached the trees fearfully but the branches seemed to dip in salute and then drew back to let him pass. He ran joyfully down a golden tunnel of trees, forgetting his companions left in the darkness. He came to a shining glade and there he first heard the music. He could never afterwards reproduce a note of it, but he knew it was the sweetest that he had ever heard.

Kerish caught up with Gidjabolgo and found himself running effortlessly beside a golden stream and past clusters of tall flowers with petals of darkest purple, streaked with silver. Their scent was overpowering, the music swelled;

Kerish knew he had nearly reached the heart of the forest. Soon he would understand everything but just as he caught sight of dancing shadows among the trees, he woke to the brittle cold of midnight.

A full moon shone on the forest and the music was gone but Kerish was certain that it had lasted just a moment longer than his dream.

Now he could hear bird-song and the rustling of leaves. The Prince sat up and saw that Gidjabolgo was also awake. He was staring at the stream that now rushed noisily into the forest as if swelled by some new spate.

"What is it, Gidjabolgo?"

"I heard music, but it was only in my head."

Kerish suddenly remembered another night and another kind of music in the foothills of the Ultimate Mountains. At the same moment they both noticed a single purple flower, bowed over the stream, just where it vanished among the dark trees.

Gidjabolgo tugged at Kerish's arm. "We must follow the stream!"

"I can't," whispered Kerish, "I can't leave them."

"Then stay in the dark," hissed Gidjabolgo.

The Forgite got up and walked towards the trees.

"If you go now, you'll never come back!" Kerish did not know why he was so certain. "Your quest will never be completed."

Gidjabolgo hesitated.

"Stay with us."

He caught at the Forgite's cloak and Forollkin suddenly turned over, grunted, and opened his eyes.

The bird-song stopped and the babble of the stream sank to a murmur.

"What's the matter?" asked Forollkin sleepily.

"Nothing," said Kerish, "there's nothing to see now."

In the morning it was only Gwerath who spoke of her dreams. "I saw her," she said. "I saw the Goddess, but she was walking away from me, back to the Mountains."

Gwerath did not dream again but every night that they camped beside the trees, the forest called to Kerish. He woke haggard and tinged with grief, feeling he had refused some priceless gift.

Gwerath noticed his pallor and offered to sing a sleep charm over him. She put one hand across the Prince's forehead and began to chant.

After a few words she faltered and her hand dropped. "It is gone," she said, "the words are empty."

Even Forollkin saw the desolation in her face.

"Cousin, what is it?" He put an arm round her shoulders.

"I am no longer her Torga," whispered Gwerath; "the Goddess has gone."

Ten days' journey along the edge of the forest brought them to the Gap of Lamoth. On one side of a broad, grassy track were watch trees but on the other the red-leaved crown trees of Seld. There was good hunting on the edge of the woodland and they ate well.

For two days they met no-one on the Lamoth road, though the track was pitted with hoof-prints and cart tracks.

On the second night Kerish had a different dream. When the boughs lifted he found himself in the Emperor's garden and his father stood before him. The white sarcophagus lay at his feet, but Kerish knew that it was empty. The Emperor of Galkis smiled, kissed his son and vanished into the shadows.

At noon a week later, the travellers heard horns among the crown trees and distant shouting and laughter. Hoof-beats were coming in their direction and suddenly a dainty, silver-horned creature broke from the wood. It shied away from the travellers, bounded across the track and disappeared into the silence of Everlorn.

A few seconds later three riders galloped out of the crown trees and reined in their horses as they realized they had lost their quarry. Then they noticed the travellers.

Two of the riders were young men, fantastically dressed in brilliant silks and gauzes; the third was a woman. She wore a simple green robe and a plain golden circlet, eclipsed by the richness of her copper hair.

"You!"

One of the men pointed his dainty, ivory-handled whip at Forollkin. "Did you see the greshel pass?"

183

"If you mean the beast you were hunting, it fled into the forest."

The woman clapped her hands together: "Djezaney, I fear we have lost our morning's sport."

Djezaney was frowning at the travellers: "Are you barbarians, that you stay mounted before the Queen?"

"They may not know . . ." began the second man but the travellers were already dismounting and Kerish and Forollkin made courtly bows.

The Queen of Seld acknowledged them with a slight inclination of her head and stared at Kerish: "Where do you come from, strangers?"

Forollkin looked up into eyes that were startlingly green.

"From Galkis, your Majesty."

"Liar," called out Lord Djezaney, "no-one comes overland from Galkis."

"Yet we do." Kerish pulled an emerald ring from his finger. "Your Majesty, here is your sister's ring, as a token that we come from the court of the Emperor."

Queen Pellameera took the ring and held it up to the light to read the inscription.

"It is hers," she affirmed, "the very ring I gave her when she sailed for Galkis. Why should Kelinda entrust it to you? Ah, I know." The Queen's slow smile was dazzling. "You are the lost Prince."

"What has your Majesty heard of such a Prince?" asked Kerish.

"That the Third Son of the Emperor has left his father's court," answered Pellameera, "that he travels through Zindar on some unknown quest. His name is Kerish-lo-Taan, and I recognize you from Kelinda's letters."

"I am Kerish-lo-Taan," the Prince admitted. "Your sister asked me to tell you that you were right, and if she had her life again she would not leave the temple of Trykis."

"Kelinda was always innocent of the ways of Zindar," said Pellameera, "as the Queen's sister should be. She expected love and that is foolish. But tell me, Prince, who are your companions?"

"May I present my half-brother, the Lord Forollkin?"

Pellameera smiled at him but her eyes were on the silver-haired girl who stood by his side.

184

"And this is my cousin, Gwerath, a . . . Princess of the Sheyasa."

"Cousin? Ah, welcome . . . Princess."

Gwerath stared at the Queen, saying nothing.

"And this," continued Kerish hastily, "is our travelling companion, Gidjabolgo of Forgin."

The Queen broke into peals of pretty laughter. "Look, Djan, what a splendid grotesque! He could be the model for one of those dwarfs in the frieze above your bed."

"And this," cut in Kerish, "is Lilahnee, a Frian marsh cat."

"Such fur! Why, Djezaney, I'm sure *you* never gave me so charming a pet. But she should have a jewelled collar. I shall find her one."

Before Kerish could explain that Lilahnee would not wear a collar, however jewelled, a group of the Queen's attendants cantered through the trees.

"Now, Prince, you must come back with me to Lamoth," ordered Pellameera, "and you shall tell me the history of your wanderings."

"I thank your Majesty for your kindness," answered Kerish, "but our quest is urgent. We must find the citadel of Saroc."

"Of Saroc? Do you hear, Djan? Djezaney? The Prince dares an adventure that all the gallants of my court have shrunk from!"

"All but one, Madam," said Djan, very softly.

Pellameera looked for a moment as if she might strike him, but she said sweetly: "Thank you for reminding me, Djan. Prince, journey south with me. When you are rested I shall help you prepare for your quest. I will even have you escorted to the edge of the Red Waste."

Kerish bowed. "Thank you again, your Majesty. We gladly accept your hospitality."

"Then ride by me." Pellameera gave the Prince her hand to kiss.

He mounted his white horse and rode beside her. The Queen's Lords and attendants fell in behind. Forollkin, Gwerath and Gidjabolgo followed silently as they rode towards the royal lodge of Lamoth.

# Chapter 12

The Book of the Emperors: *Love*
*And they asked Jezreen-lo-Kaash why he wept for the
lovers, and he answered them saying: "There are some that
love others only for their virtues. Often they seek all the days
of their life for one who seems worthy of their love. The
object of such love is always to be pitied, for they dare not be
less than perfect. There are some who love the faults of others
and use them to feed their own strength. The object of this
love is also to be pitied, for they dare not outgrow their
weaknesses." Then the youngest Prince asked: "Should we
then renounce love?" and he answered: "Never, my dear
son, but the lesser love cannot lead to the greater unless the
spirit is undiminished by yielding its mysteries to the
beloved."*

GIDJABOLGO squatted in the shadow of a crown tree
watching the Galkians through a screen of leaves.
Behind them stood one of the famous wooden castles of
Seld, recklessly delicate, with every surface covered in
glazed tiles of green and gold and amber.

All around the Royal Lodge stretched a tamed forest and
lawns scattered with white and crimson flowers. Amongst
the trees the noblemen of Seld were playing with a ball of
silver filigree, as roughly and noisily as children.

Kerish-lo-Taan stroked the marsh cat at his feet as she
growled at passing strangers. Forollkin was frowning
intensely while he watched the Queen of Seld approach.

Like all her ladies, Pellameera was sombrely dressed in a
clinging robe of silvery grey. A single green jewel em-
phasized the whiteness of her brow and the lustre of her
copper hair.

Kerish tried for a moment to define the Queen's extraor-
dinary grace as she glided across the grass. Then his attention
was caught by another figure and a different kind of grace.

186

Beside the Queen was Gwerath, nervously clutching at the pale silk of her dress and trying, unsuccessfully, to hide the wonder in her grey eyes.

"Dear Prince," Pellameera gave him one of her melting smiles. "My nobles beg me to attend their game and a good Queen must not deny her subjects. Come and sit by me and you shall tell me what you think of Seld."

She gave the Prince her hand to lead her to a porcelain throne beneath a crown tree. One of the other chairs was offered to Gwerath. For a moment Kerish thought she would refuse and squat on the ground in her usual fashion. Then Gwerath sat down, very cautiously, as if she was afraid the frail chair would collapse under her.

"We have a saying in Seld," murmured Pellameera. "The man uses his body, the woman her mind. And so our tasks are divided."

"In Galkis we might consider such a division unprofitable."

"In Galkis, you keep female slaves," answered Pellameera sharply.

An area of grass had been marked off with ribbons and the court gathered round it. The Queen's favourites, Lord Djan, in feathered cloak and silver lace, and Lord Djezaney, even more splendid in gold-spangled apricot silk, bowed before her.

"Must you always be playing against one another?" asked Pellameera.

"One of us must be proved the worthier in your Majesty's eyes," declared Djezaney, the crooked hand he chose to accentuate with glittering rings held to his heart.

The Queen sighed deeply. "Men are such quarrelsome creatures, but I cannot change your natures. Lord Forollkin . . ."

Uncomfortably conscious of the plainness of his travelling clothes beside the brilliant nobility of Seld, Forollkin knelt before the Queen.

"The Prince has told me something of your deeds. Will you show us a little of your strength and skill and join our simple game?"

"Most gladly, your Majesty, if it pleases you."

"I'm sure it will please all who watch. You may join the followers of Lord Djan."

The game was simple indeed. It consisted only of tossing the silver ball from man to man until it passed the ribbons at either end of the lawn. Each team tried to hinder the other and Forollkin rapidly found that the courtiers played with vicious determination.

The sound of tearing silk and grunts at unmannerly blows soon mingled with laughter and applause from the watching ladies.

No trace of the Prince's distaste appeared in his face but Pellameera watched the game with a smile, half of indulgence and half of contempt.

Neither side succeeded in keeping the ball for more than a minute until it was thrown to the tall Galkian. Forollkin side-stepped an opponent and tossed the ball to Djan. The young nobleman dived nimbly past two attackers, kicked Lord Djezaney out of the way with one spurred foot and flung the silver ball across the ribbon.

The Queen rose and summoned Djan, while Djezaney searched for a lost earring in the trampled grass. Silently assessing the cost of replacing his muddied finery, Djan knelt before the Queen. Pellameera wiped a smear of eye paint from his cheek and tied the victor's ribbon round his blond curls.

"Today, Djan, you are the worthiest. But now, my Lords, I must leave you to your amusements. Prince, I must attend my council but tonight I have planned an entertainment for you."

She stopped to stroke Lilahnee.

"Do not forget to bring your pet, and of course, your fellow travellers."

The Prince bowed and murmured his thanks. The Queen and her ladies went back into the castle but Gwerath did not go with them.

Forollkin joined Kerish, rubbing a bruised arm. "You're a judge of beautiful things, Kerish—don't you think she's lovely?"

"To me, she is not as beautiful as her sister."

"Kelinda? Why she only has a shadow of the Queen's beauty!"

"Kelinda's beauty is the reality," said Kerish gravely, "and Pellameera's the shadow."

"Forollkin is right," Gwerath's nervous fingers unravelled her braided hair. "No-one could be more beautiful than the Queen."

"Still, cousin," said Forollkin cheerfully, "you must meet Kelinda; she is a poet and you would like her."

Kerish smiled. "Do you remember her poem about the crown trees of Seld?"

"I remember you singing it," answered Forollkin. "And they are fine trees. The Emperor would enjoy this garden."

"What is a garden?" asked Gwerath.

They were disturbed by a sudden burst of laughter. Djezaney had dragged Gidjabolgo from his hiding place and was displaying him to his companions.

"Come, Forgite, you've made us laugh with your looks; now sing or dance and I'll give you this jewel to hang round your neck."

That caused more laughter among the noblemen.

"Surely, my Lord," protested one, "you'll not waste so pretty a treasure on such as him!"

"The blacker the setting, the brighter the jewel will shine. Yes, the contrast is exquisitely pleasing."

He swung the jewel in front of Gidjabolgo's face.

"What will you give for it, my splendid ugliness?"

"I do not sing for painted dolls," rasped Gidjabolgo and Djezaney struck him across the cheek with the sharp-edged jewel.

"You will sing till your throat is as parched as the Red Waste. You will dance till you sweat yourself slender—"

Forollkin's strong hands descended on Djezaney's shoulders and the Prince spoke with quiet authority.

"Her Majesty would be gravely displeased if she knew that one of her guests had been insulted. I suggest that you apologize to Master Gidjabolgo."

Furiously, the Seldian muttered something to Gidjabolgo and walked away. Awkwardly, his companions hastened after him.

"Gidjabolgo, must you always provoke people into hurting you?" asked Kerish.

"I thought that I was the one provoked." Gidjabolgo

189

rubbed his bleeding cheek and continued unexpectedly, "Nevertheless, I thank you."

Later, in their opulent quarters, Kerish and Forollkin dressed for the Queen's entertainment. The Prince wore his zeloka jewels and the best of the clothes Sendaaka had given them.

Forollkin had accepted a gift of full Seldian dress from the Queen. He explained at unnecessary length that it was sensible to adopt the customs of their hosts, and put on the emerald and umber silks. Kerish found the clothes disturbing but loyally said that Forollkin looked magnificent.

With Gidjabolgo tagging behind they went to Gwerath's apartments. They found her sitting on the floor staring at the elaborate furniture. Forollkin pulled her up and dusted down her dress.

"It rustles when I move," said Gwerath faintly.

"You look like a Princess. Shall we go down now, Gwerath?" asked Forollkin.

She clung to his arm and they went down the gilded staircase.

Throughout the long summer night Queen Pellameera entertained her guests beneath silken canopies, on the greensward. Musicians were hidden among the trees and there was to be dancing after the singers of Lamoth had presented their offerings.

Kerish was seated in the place of honour, on Pellameera's right, with Forollkin by his side and Lilahnee at his feet. Gwerath sat, stiff-backed, on the Queen's left, next to the High Stewardess.

Gidjabolgo was incongruously placed among the gaudy, scented ranks of Seldian nobles, who lounged in a circle on embroidered cushions. Their dyed curls, feathered cloaks and vivid silks were in violent contrast to the pastel shades of the women's simple robes.

Goblets of wine were offered to the Galkians and the noblemen but not to the Queen and her ladies. To eat or drink in public was below the dignity of a Seldian lady.

The Châtelaine of Lamoth brought forward a solemn-faced child with hair brighter than the Queen's. The child curtsied carefully to Pellameera, and after some prompting, to Kerish.

190

"I did not know your Majesty was blessed with a daughter," said Kerish.

"I have two," answered the Queen lightly, "but the younger is being reared on Trykis."

"As your sister was?"

"As all sisters of a Queen must be," said Pellameera. "They leave it only to marry or to die. You should see our royal tombs, Prince. Only for the dead do we build in stone, for life is brief and death is everlasting. I will show you my tomb if you come to Mel-Kellin; it is not completed yet but it will be very fine. Now, if you have finished your wine, let us begin."

Pellameera clapped her hands and a tall grey-haired woman tuned her harp and began a traditional song in praise of the Queen, lauding her beauty, wisdom and clemency in elaborate verse. When it was over Pellameera turned to the Galkians and asked their opinion.

"No song could do your Majesty justice." Forollkin stumbled over the trite compliment.

Pellameera's limpid green eyes met the Prince's cool gaze and her smile was of self-mockery: "No indeed."

The next performer sang an ancient ballad that Kerish had once studied with Kelinda. The memory of their quiet hours together made him suddenly intensely homesick. Then the singer announced the Lay of Pergon of Lamoth.

"An old story," said Pellameera, "but one that should interest you, Prince," and she, herself, translated the Seldian into Zindaric for them.

"It is said that Saroc was a kinsman of the first Queen of Seld. He studied deeply in the arts of sorcery, for men were capable of learning in those times. Some secret source of immortal power he must have discovered. He has dwelt in Tir-Tonar for many centuries, dividing the Queendom of Seld, for no-one crosses the wasteland between the White hills and the Red mountains.

"And yet," said Pellameera softly, "the Red Waste was once a garden and Tir-Tonar a peaceful citadel. Over the centuries the power of Saroc has darkened, the garden has shrivelled and Tir-Tonar has become a place of fear."

"They say," called out Lord Djezaney, "that the Citadel

of Saroc is guarded by fearsome beasts, that hover above the Red Waste."

"It is true," said the Châtelaine of Lamoth, "I have seen their shadows on the red sand and I did not dare set foot on the wasteland."

"Nor would any of my lords, except Theligarn. Alas, Prince, he did not return to us but he died for the glory of his Queen and lives on in my daughters."

Her voice was perfectly calm but Kerish didn't know what to reply and Forollkin stared into his empty goblet.

"Only Pergon has ever returned from the Red Waste," said the Châtelaine of Lamoth.

"Pergon of Lamoth," Pellameera took up the story again. "All Seld knew that the Saroc held captive a young and lovely girl. Pergon swore to rescue her from Tir-Tonar. He crossed the Red Waste, slaying the monstrous guards with the strength of his sword. He breached the Citadel, defied the sorcerer and found the captive maiden in an enchanted garden. They fled together, facing many terrors and at the edge of the Wasteland Pergon cried out in triumph. He swept the maiden into his arms, kissed her lips and set her down on the green grass of Seld. Before his eyes she aged, died, crumbled to dust. Saroc had his revenge."

Saroc, her father, thought Kerish numbly and understood a little of Sendaaka's agony.

"Are you still determined to reach Tir-Tonar, Prince?" asked Pellameera.

"We must," answered Kerish.

"How grim you look, and Lord Forollkin too." The Queen laughed. "Tomorrow I will try to dissuade you again; tonight we will forget Tir-Tonar. Princess, I hope you will delight us with some song or story of your own people? The Prince has told me of your learning."

Gwerath shook her head and, at a scowl from Forollkin, said: "They would not be fitting here."

Pellameera's fingers played with the winking jewel at her throat. "Why not, Princess?"

The question seemed serious, but Gwerath noticed the ripple of amusement among the courtiers.

"Because you would not understand the ways of the

Sheyasa," she answered, "and our songs are made in praise of the Goddess and the Hunter of Souls."

"A Hunter of Souls! When he catches souls, what does he do with them?"

"Our songs tell us that he hangs them as trophies in his tent, but that is a way of saying—"

"Why what a dangerous huntsman!" exclaimed the Queen; "how fortunate we are in Seld to have no souls."

The courtiers laughed but Gwerath looked bewildered. "Everyone has a soul."

"Do they, Princess? Then where is mine?" The Queen tilted back her head and spread out her lovely arms. "Can you see it?"

"No," said Gwerath fiercely, "I see no soul in you."

For a moment Pellameera ceased to laugh and her green eyes seemed drained of life. Then the familiar smile appeared again."I am glad you have been so swiftly converted to the ways of Seld. Here you will soon forget your gods and goddesses."

"Never," said Gwerath, but she spoke now like a sulky child and Kerish intervened: "Your Majesty, allow me to divert you, in place of my cousin."

"Most gladly," answered Pellameera. "It will be curious for us to hear a man skilled in the higher arts."

Kerish's zildar was fetched from his quarters and swiftly tuned. After a moment's thought, the Prince began the song of the Poet Emperor and his cat. The voice that reminded Gidjabolgo of the crystal wind chimes of Forgin filled the hushed summer's night.

Kerish told of the pair of golden cats brought to Galkis by Imarko herself and of their descendants, cherished in the temples of Hildimarn until only one remained—Reshad, the beloved companion of the Poet Emperor. When he sickened, the Emperor of Galkis despaired of his life but one night in the Emperor's garden a servant tending the yilg trees, whose ashen blossoms open only in moonlight, saw a cat; a cat that seemed to leap down a stair of moonbeams to hunt among the shadows.

Night after night the Emperor tried to catch the moon cat and failed. Finally he carried Reshad into the gardens and sat with the sick cat in his lap, in the heart of the yilg grove.

193

When the moon rose, a second cat climbed on to his lap and licked Reshad from his dry nose to his limp tail. The Emperor sat patiently until dawn and at the first ray of sunlight the moon cat's silver fur turned gold and Reshad sprang up and chased his tail. The Emperor named the moon cat Lilahnee and her kittens filled the temples of Galkis with beauty and mischief.

In spite of the sincere applause for his song, Kerish refused to sing a second time and returned to his place to stroke his own Lilahnee. The Queen clapped her hands and a page brought forward an ivory box, containing a golden collar set with green gems, and a silken leash.

"A pretty story, Prince, and here is the collar I promised for your pet."

"Your Majesty is kind, but I cannot accept your gift. A cat should not be collared. Gold and silk mean nothing to her; she would believe I had betrayed her."

"But think how beautiful it would look, set against her green fur!"

"She needs no ornament to be beautiful," said Kerish firmly. "I cannot accept your gift.

The nobles were murmuring at his discourtesy but the Queen said slowly: "You are the first man who has ever refused a gift from me."

She turned to the page. "Take the collar away."

There was a nervous silence but Pellameera smiled at the Prince: "Will you also refuse to dance with me?"

"Never, if your Majesty will teach me your Seldian steps."

"Gladly, Prince Kerish-lo-Taan."

The musicians hidden among the trees struck up a stately tune and the ladies of the court chose their partners. The High Stewardess asked Forollkin to dance but Gwerath was too shy to choose from among the dazzling courtiers. Her eyes followed the graceful figures of the slender white-robed Queen and the Prince of Galkis.

Forollkin was clumsier, looking beyond his partner and treading on the hem of her gown. The music stopped and with a rustle of white silk, the Queen curtsied to her partner.

"We dance well together, Prince." Pellameera called to the musicians: "Play 'The Weeping Queens'."

"Does your Majesty prefer a melancholy tune?"

"I do, though men say I am never sad," murmured Pellameera.

"Men in Seld are not renowned for their wisdom," countered Kerish.

The music began again.

"I see your cousin is not dancing."

"She may only dance with a kinsman," lied Kerish; "it is a custom of the Sheyasa."

"Then you must be her partner," declared the Queen, "and I will teach your brother to dance." She gave Forollkin her exquisite hand.

Gwerath at first refused to dance but Kerish persuaded her. He led his cousin to the centre of the greensward. With solemn concentration, Gwerath copied the Prince's steps, never looking up into his face.

Nor did Forollkin dare to gaze at his partner. She talked incessantly but afterwards he couldn't remember a single word she had said, or whether he had replied.

Neither of the brothers noticed a royal messenger cross the lawn and wait beneath the silken canopy for the dance to end.

The music faltered. Laughing, the Queen called for another tune but one of the court ladies hurried to her side and whispered something.

"Prince," said Pellameera, "here is an envoy from your father's court, seeking an immediate audience."

Kerish saw the white cloak of the messenger and his hand tightened round Gwerath's wrist.

The Galkian envoy, who had been staring at Kerish, bowed to the Queen and handed her a scroll of purple vellum. She scanned it frowning.

"The Emperor of Galkis announces his death. When did you leave his court?"

"I sailed from Ephaan two months ago, Madam."

"Then by now he is dead."

Kerish finally understood his dream in the Gap of Lamoth, and Pellameera said: "So my sister is now Queen of Galkis."

195

And Rimoka is Empress, thought Forollkin numbly, and rules the nine cities.

Pellameera finished reading the scroll. "The Emperor asks that we celebrate his death with the customary festival. Tomorrow will be a day of rejoicing."

"Your Majesty honours the memory of my father," murmured Kerish.

Forollkin came anxiously to his brother's side and Gidjabolgo had risen from his place among the courtiers, but the Prince did not need their help.

"If your Majesty had known my father," said Kerish, "you would see that a festival is fitting. For him death was the only gateway to joy."

"He was fortunate to believe so," answered Pellameera. "In Seld it is the gateway to extinction. More music! Shall we dance again?"

Kerish bowed. "I will dance, but we must leave soon for the Red Waste."

"Are you so anxious to rush into danger? Djezaney shall guide you then. You have not told me what you seek in Saroc's citadel."

"No, your Majesty."

Kerish offered his arm and they led off the dance. Gwerath timidly approached Forollkin. "Why did your father welcome death instead of fleeing from the Hunter and struggling on his spear? Was his life so sad?"

"He thought so."

"I'm sorry." Gwerath was trying to read Forollkin's face. "It must hurt you."

He shook his head.

"I hardly knew him. I had no part in his life, I can have none in his death."

Kerish and Pellameera danced in the gathering dusk and three days later the four travellers took the road to the Red Waste and Tir-Tonar.

*By Geraldine Harris*

# MAP OF ZINDAR IN